COLD
PRESSED

JJ MARSH

TRISKELE BOOKS

Cover design: JD Smith

Published by Prewett Publishing.
All enquiries to admin@beatrice-stubbs.com

First printing, 2014

978-3-9524258-2-4

For Julie Lewis and Tracy Austin,
whose glasses are always half full

Chapter 1

That's funny.

Eva's guiding hand on the front door usually resulted in a gentle click, but tonight it slammed shut with far more force than she'd intended. A draught caught the back of her neck as she put down the carrier bag with a reassuring clink of bottles.

She locked the door behind her and stopped to listen. Rain beat on the roof, like fingers on drumskins, and a hollow dripping echoed from the guttering outside. The occasional hiss of wet tyres on tarmac. The hushed rush of the gas fire and the tink-tink of its ceramic surround from the living room. Her antique clock on the hall table echoing its woody tock with the regularity of a dripping tap. *Maybe I just don't know my own strength.*

Coat on the hook, boots off and slippers back on, she shuffled through to the kitchen, then remembered the carrier bag and shuffled back. The plastic was still wet. *I had an umbrella when I left, I know I did. Must have left it in the shop.* A foul night into which only a fool would venture. But when only a quarter of a bottle remains, it calls for desperate measures. She laughed out loud. *Desperate measures!*

Eva hummed to herself as she put two slices in the toaster and got the butter out to warm. A fresh highball from the cabinet, some ice cubes from the freezer compartment and a healthy slug, a good third of the glass, topped up with tonic. A slice of lemon would be nice, but she only had a couple of oranges and one of them had a covering of blue fur. A cold breeze brushed the back of her neck and she put down her glass with a slam. All the windows were closed. The draught came from the back door. Ajar by no more than an inch, with its peeling paint and rusted lock, the garden door allowed cool evening air and the smell of soggy grass to creep into her warm, cosy kitchen.

With a dismissive tut, she struggled with the ancient lock, but finally secured it. Very important, safety, for a woman living alone. She took a long sip of her drink, half-attempting to recall the last time she'd been out the garden door, but found she couldn't care less. Her memory wasn't the best, and anyway it was a peaceful neighbourhood.

Peaceful. Only the tiny chinking of ice cubes as she replaced her glass on the pine table disturbed the thick silence of the evening. Time to put the telly on; she was beginning to get the willies. The toaster ejected its contents with a jack-in-the-box metallic clatter, making Eva jump. She looked out at the darkness and made herself a promise, not for the first time, to get some curtains for the kitchen windows. The vodka was just beginning to work. Her cheeks warmed, her head lightened and a tune danced through her head.

She opened the fridge for the butter and remembered it was already on the table. The overhead fluorescent flattened everything but the light from the fridge door glinted on the lino. Water.

That's funny.

Two patches of water. No, four, five. Footprints. She stared at the pattern reaching from the back door to the hallway and laughed at herself. Spooked by her own wellies! She looked down at her feet, in dry sheepskin slippers. Her wellies were still in the hallway. She'd put them on to go up the shop and took them off when she came back. She hadn't made those prints.

Her head was muddled. That toast was going cold, so she closed the fridge and rubbed her arms against the chill. Time for a top up and her Saturday night entertainment. She scraped butter across the cooling toast and grabbed a quick slurp of Prussian magic. A slice of lemon would be nice.

A song. A singer. Tonight she'd try to vote, and fingers crossed she'd get through this time. She hummed to herself as she fetched a tray and ripped a piece of kitchen roll as a substitute for a doily. A movement in the hallway. She squinted into the dimness, wondering if she'd left the front door open as well. Darkness expanded and blocked out the hall light.

A man stepped into the kitchen doorway. Eva dropped her glass onto her toast and gasped so hard her bottom lip caught on her teeth. She tasted blood.

He entered the room, the light behind him, his face in shadow. Leather jacket, sunglasses, big chunky boots, black gloves and slick wet hair. He looked like the Terminator. She shrank backwards and his lips split into a grin, showing his teeth. Vodka and tonic trickled across the table and dripped onto the floor.

"Hello Eva," he said.

He didn't sound like Schwarzenegger. Strange accent. She swallowed some bitter saliva and tried to focus her thoughts.

"Who are you?" she asked, her voice trying for authoritative but missing it by a country mile.

He showed his teeth again. "That's what I've come to find out. I have a few questions for you."

She shook her head. "How did you get in here? I'm not answering questions from a total stranger. You come back tomorrow and we'll see."

"Sorry, Eva. Tomorrow's no good. You're not going to be here tomorrow." He took off his dark glasses. "So in the words of the King, it's now or never."

Eva's jaw slackened and her mouth gaped. She recognised those eyes.

Chapter 2

"I said to you, I distinctly remember, not to forget a screw of salt. I told you they wouldn't think of it."

"It's not the end of the world, Maggie. Eat your egg and stop fussing. Enjoy the view and the silence."

Maggie stared out at the Aegean Sea, an expanse of peacock shades, punctuated by white sails and wakes, the cliffs stretching away to their right and the harbour barely visible to their left. Distant misty calderas lay on the horizon like hump-backed whales. Sunlight sparkled from every angle, an omnipresent sprite banishing ill-will. Vast sky, endless sea and more shades of blue than she knew words for.

"It's a beautiful spot, I'll give you that. Just hidden away enough so we won't cross paths with any tourists. But I have never in my life eaten a hard-boiled egg without salt, Rose Mason, and have no plans to start now."

Rose selected a stick of celery and scooped up some hummus. "Just as I have always said, you're inflexible to the point of fossilisation. Have another look in the picnic basket. I'm sure I asked for salt."

Maggie adjusted her sunhat and returned to the hamper, placed in the shade of the chunky little moped. She pushed aside the empty wrappers and found something that looked like a pencil sharpener. In one end she could see ground black pepper, in the other...

"Salt!"

"What did I tell you? Now, is there anything else you want to grumble about, or can we enjoy our first civilised meal in a week?"

Clutching her condiments, Maggie arranged herself on the blanket and tucked her skirt under her knees. She inhaled and closed her eyes, savouring the warm citrus and herbal notes wafting from the hillside. A butterfly, freckled and rust-coloured, flitted from shrub to shrub on its own balletic mission. Rose poured two glasses of iced tea and handed one to Maggie.

"Thank you. I'll have my boiled egg now, if you'd be so kind. And to say this is the first civilised meal in a week is a wee bit harsh. I won't deny the conversation has bordered on the tedious at times, but I've no complaints about the food."

They gazed out at the beauty of the sea, its constantly shifting contours, accented by the graceful arcs of gulls.

"The food, I grant you, has been of superior quality." Rose sipped her tea and Maggie peeled her egg, bracing herself. She knew Rose was building up for an almighty moan. "But the deadly boring company gives me indigestion. I resent being told with whom and when I must eat. It feels like boarding school all over again. There is no reason on earth why we can't dine alone at a table for two and enjoy our meals rather than suffer more tales of unfortunate operations, dead or divorced husbands and overachieving offspring. Oh God, would you listen to me? We came up here to escape all that and what do I do? Bring it with us. Ignore me. Are you going to have some taramasalata?"

Maggie eyed the pinkish gloopy substance, the consistency of tapioca. "I might when I've finished my egg. Not all the other passengers are that bad. Mr and Mrs Emerson are pleasant enough. And that language fella, when he pokes his head out of his shell, can be entertaining on occasion."

She bit into her egg and absorbed the panorama, assessing photographic compositions with professional enthusiasm and an amateur eye. Rose's cornflower-print dress seemed to complement the colours, but looked incongruous amongst the scrubby flora of a Greek hillside. Her straw hat shaded her eyes and the 1950s sunglasses hid her expression. But Maggie could tell perfectly well Rose's eyes were smiling.

"Mrs Make-The-Best-Of-It is at it again." Despite her best efforts, Rose couldn't quite manage to make her voice sound stern. "You and I both know that a cruise is not our sort of holiday. We're trapped on a tub with people we'd actively avoid in everyday circumstances, fed at regular intervals and provided with something laughably called entertainment. On reaching dry land, we're dragged around a historic site in an air-conditioned coach, often sitting directly behind an incontinent nonagenarian and only let out for a three-minute photo opportunity. Maggie, I'm not being ungrateful and I'm happy to try anything once, but can we agree that despite our advancing years, we are still women of independent minds?"

Maggie wiped her fingers and picked up the camera as she considered her response. She caught several shots of the bay, zoomed in on a yacht then turned to her left to see what compositions the harbour might yield. Low white houses tumbled in Lego formation towards the sea, but the ridge hid all the port activity from view. In the distance, impossible to overlook, lay the *Empress Louise*, docked at the distant ferry port. She shook her head at the breathtaking scale of the thing. How something so vast could float around the world, operating with unfailing efficiency, still awed her.

She rounded on Rose with more theatre than passion. "How many years have we been holidaying together? Don't answer that, I can't remember either. How many of those holidays would have been anywhere but Brittany, Cornwall and Ireland, had it been left to you?"

Rose sniffed. "I have one word to say to you – Tenerife."

"Agreed." Maggie swallowed some iced tea. "A mistake you'll never let me forget. Neither will I let you forget the time we sailed along the Dalmatian Coast. Or the whales we saw in the

Azores. Or that funny little place at the top of Capri."

"Yes, yes, I can see what you're doing. Sea, boats, adventures and some exceptional memories. This is not the same. In Croatia, we went off the beaten track. We made our own discoveries. Took our own stupid risks. A cruise ship offers no opportunity for... well, no opportunity for individuality. Yes, I admit I'm too old for camel-trekking, but holidays are supposed to make me feel younger than I am. This cruise makes me feel decrepit."

"You're being a snob, Rose. I'm sorry, but you are. As soon as I mentioned the C-word, you got all superior and made your mind up you would hate it. Well, I'm enjoying myself. I find the other passengers a curiosity and the only thing spoiling my fun is your moaning. So stick that in your pipe and smoke it."

Rose made a point of swivelling her entire torso towards Maggie. A hard stare, no doubt. Maggie kept her eye glued to the lens. She retracted the zoom from the ship to the sliver of bay visible below.

"And you're not being precisely the opposite? Dazzled by a 1920s mirage of charming bejewelled society folk doing the Charleston in the ballroom. Whereas the reality is bingo, aquarobics, whatever they are, dubious tribute bands and a desperate crowd of blue-rinsers colluding in the myth that... what are you looking at?"

Maggie didn't answer, twisting the magnification so she could pick out more detail in the middle distance. The vantage point, halfway up the cliff and beloved of coach parties, was empty. All the tourists had left, heading for the town's many restaurants for lunch. But one had come adrift.

An elderly lady wandered along the cliff path towards the car park. Her movements were irregular and she seemed disorientated or suffering from the heat. Maggie sat up straighter. They could scramble down there in minutes and help the poor old dear.

"Maggie? What is it? You look like a meerkat. Maggie Campbell, I'm talking to you!"

"There's someone down there. An old lady. I can't be sure at this distance, but it looks like one of the Hirondelles."

"I doubt it. Their coach passed us on our way up, so by now they've been herded into a local taverna to be force-fed moussaka. Why do you say it's one of them?"

"Same outfit. Blue blazer, white skirt, you know. Whoever it is, she looks distressed. We should help."

"Let me see. Where are the binoculars?"

Below, a second figure appeared and strode across the car park, heading towards the pensioner. He wore the classic white and blue-trimmed uniform of the ship's crew and reached out a hand to the woman.

"It's all right. One of the crew has found her. You'd think they'd do a head count before driving off. She shouldn't be wandering around alone at her age. He needs to get her out of the sun."

The pair were walking slowly back in the direction of the car park.

"Are you done, Maggie? Only I'll cover this lot up, I think."

Maggie took her attention from the camera to see Rose wave a hand at the abandoned tomato salad, shooing away flies which immediately resettled elsewhere on the picnic.

"Yes, best had." Maggie returned her attention to the couple in the distance, who had stopped to look out over the cliff.

The man was pointing along the coast, in the direction of the *Empress Louise*. While the little woman faced the ocean, he turned, apparently scanning the path in both directions.

"He should take her back and stop messing about; you can see she's had too much sun. Very irresponsible."

"Enough of your rubber-necking and help me put this lot away. Then I suggest a ten-minute snooze to aid the digestion." Plastic lids snapped and greaseproof paper rustled, but Maggie's gaze was fixed on the brilliantly white path and the mismatched pair facing the sea. As she watched, the man lifted the woman, scooping one arm under her knees and bringing the other up to catch her shoulders. A gesture almost playful in its gallantry. He stood that way for several seconds, holding her in his arms as he glanced behind him once again. Then he swung her backwards and with all his force forwards, releasing her frail form out over the cliff.

The woman fell in silence, with a few jerky movements like a puppet. The man remained at the cliff edge. Then, as if hearing some inaudible starter gun, he ran towards the car park and disappeared from sight.

Maggie sat frozen, her mind an uncomprehending loop. *I just saw... I couldn't have seen... he didn't... he did...* A sound like a chainsaw ripped through the silence and broke her petrifaction. Too late, she pressed the shutter and burst into tears.

Chapter 3

Nikos Stephanakis had wet trousers. The police speedboat had made a sharp turn as they approached the port of Athinos, hitting a wave broadside and spraying the solitary passenger down his left leg. Nikos gritted his teeth and pulled out his handkerchief. The irony was that if he'd still been in uniform, it wouldn't have shown. Wet black trousers look the same as dry black trousers. But his casual chinos were now beige on one leg and brown on the other. Could have been worse. At least it wasn't his crotch.

He got to his feet, hoping the sun and wind would hasten the drying process, but the boat had already begun to slow as they entered the harbour. And there, dwarfing every other vessel, loomed the *Empress Louise*. His eyes ranged across the expanse of white, drawn up and up towards the bridge. He squinted into the brightness, despite his police sunglasses. The speedboat drew closer and Nikos couldn't help but be impressed by the scale of the thing. A floating skyscraper. As the police boat nosed up to the quay, the liner's shadow fell over them. Nikos couldn't even see the top deck without craning his neck back as far as it would go.

In all the time he'd been with the Hellenic Police, he'd never actually set foot on one of these. He saw them every day, moored out in the bay, or like this one, a leviathan docked at the quayside. Like everyone else, he disguised his curiosity as contempt. Now, for his first assignment, he was entitled to board this sparkling, bustling world and ask all the questions he'd ever wanted.

A uniformed crew member checked his ID and motioned him up the gangway, with the assurance that someone would meet him at the top. A group of older women passed him on his way up. Some smiled, some greeted him with a quavering 'Good morning'. He responded in kind and for the first time, his enthusiasm for the case and his new role faltered. English. Ninety percent of the passengers were from the UK, and with an international crew the lingua franca could only be English. After two years living with a native speaker, his English was fluent and comfortable in the bar or when advising victims of petty crime. But at murder enquiry level? He sent a quick prayer to the Virgin – please let none of them be from Scotland.

When he and his guide arrived at the bridge after a long and confusing journey through the ship, the captain was on the phone. The huge room, which resembled an air traffic control centre, hummed with activity. Like a small boy, Nikos gazed around him, itching to ask questions about the consoles, screens and various items of equipment. The captain finished his phone call and swivelled his chair to face them.

"Captain Jensson, this is Inspector Stephanakis from the Hellenic Police, Cretan Region."

Nikos held out his hand to the huge Swede as he rose to his feet. The man was easily two metres tall, and to Nikos's surprise, wore no uniform cap or traditional captain's beard.

"Good morning, Inspector, and thank you for coming. I'm sorry to drag you all the way from Heraklion, but under the circumstances, I had no choice. Please, come through and I can bring you up to date."

Nikos smiled. So far, the captain's slow, clear English posed no problems. Maybe the language was nothing to worry about after all. He followed the man into an inner office with a desk, leather chairs and an old-fashioned globe. Sunken spotlights cast pools of warm light around the room and vast windows afforded a panoramic view out to sea. A delicate scent emanated from a vase of lilies standing on a column by the door.

"Rough trip?" asked the captain, with a glance at Nikos's trousers. "Would you like some tea?"

"Bad driver. Yes, please. No milk." The small talk came automatically, but details of sudden death were a different matter.

Nikos opened his briefcase and withdrew the file as Jensson spoke into the intercom to order refreshments. Behind the captain's head hung a beautiful antique map, showing the two hemispheres surrounded by angels and exotic birds, with golden lettering in Latin. He soaked it all in, recalling his own grey office, with its strip lighting and plastic chairs, perfumed by coffee breath and sweaty shirts.

"So Inspector Stephanakis, how should we begin?"

"Can we start with the deceased? What can you tell me?"

"Esther Crawford, from Shaftesbury in Wiltshire, England. She was eighty years old. I don't know all our guests' ages with such precision, but she celebrated her birthday on our first day at sea. Part of a group called the Hirondelles, who apparently holiday together every year. She seemed very pleasant, and certainly active for her age."

"And the fall?"

"The ladies joined a tour of the island this morning. We offer a variety of excursions and they opted, as a group, for the pottery and sightseeing. It seems Ms Crawford became separated from the others and either fell, or according to one witness, was thrown from a cliff."

A knock at the door signalled a crisply dressed steward, who placed a tea tray on the desk, complete with an assortment of biscuits. Jensson waited until he had left before continuing.

"Your job will be to establish which of those it was." He rotated the teapot and poured the honey-coloured liquid into the first cup.

"Of course. Can I ask your opinion? Do you think it possible that someone threw her?"

Jensson stopped pouring and looked directly at Nikos. "No. I think it was a sad accident. The ladies who claim they saw a murder are a little over-imaginative. Not to influence your investigation at all, but I think it unlikely they can be sure of what happened. The distance, their age... to be honest, Inspector, I think we're wasting your time. But I am forced to take them seriously and report their statement. It's unfortunate, as I say. But having captained twelve of these cruises – this is my thirteenth – I notice old people have a tendency to die. Few as spectacularly as Mrs Crawford, thankfully."

Nikos took the tea from the captain. An unusual perfume wafted from the cup, but the taste was delicate. He took the opportunity of a pause to formulate his next question.

"Your thirteenth cruise? So you are not superstitious?"

Jensson shook his head. "Like most modern sailors, I believe there's no room for superstition at sea. Having said that, many of our passengers and certain elements of the crew feel differently. So it's a piece of information I have not made public. To all intents and purposes, this is my twelfth. For the second time."

"I understand. This morning's excursion – were there any men on the trip?"

"Yes. Several. Andros Metaxas, who was the tour guide, along with five male passengers, two off-duty staff members, but no crew. I have prepared a full list for you."

"There's a difference between staff and crew?"

"Most definitely. In the crudest possible terms, the staff interact with the passengers, front-of-house, as it were. The crew are operations. They run the ship."

"I see. Thank you for the list. I would like to talk to these people and the ladies who were travelling with the deceased. I also will need to visit the location. First priority is to meet the two ladies who think they saw a crime."

Jensson gave him a long look. His eyes, the pale green of shallow water, appeared to grow warmer. Nikos sensed his relief. Responsibility transferred, the death and allegation were someone else's problem now.

"All that can be arranged. I suggest you use the casino for your enquiries as it is closed during the day. One of the witnesses is still under sedation in the infirmary. When she's able to talk, you might want to interview them both together. The lady who says she saw something unusual is quite difficult to understand. She has a strong Scottish accent."

Nikos nodded. Of course she did.

"I appreciate your help, Captain. One more question, what was that tea?"

Jensson turned the label dangling out of the pot. "Earl Grey. Was it not to your taste?"

"It was delicious. I must remember the name."

Nikos took his mobile from his ear to look at the screen in exasperation. It didn't help. Chief Inspector Voulakis continued to talk, without pause for breath. Today he was in one of his moods. No matter what Nikos said, Voulakis would misunderstand. He placed the mobile back to his ear and looked around at the casino. Only the bar area was illuminated, low lights glinting off bottles and chrome. Thick carpet muffled all sound and the room smelt of furniture polish and air freshener. The voice in his ear was silent for a second, then repeated the question.

"No sir, that wasn't what I said. I can handle this case alone, I assure you. Another inspector is unnecessary. All I need is someone experienced with older British people. A native English speaker, ideally. I just need a bit of help with the language side of things."

He willed Voulakis to come to the obvious conclusion. If Nikos could get his girlfriend assigned as language support, life would be about as sweet as it could get. He closed his eyes as Voulakis embarked on another long recital of the burdens he bore and the impossible demands made of him. His eyes snapped open again as his senior officer swerved off on a different tangent.

"No, no sir. That wouldn't solve the problem at all. You don't need to bring someone from Britain. This can be managed locally. I was thinking more like a language consultant. In fact, I know at least one person..."

He may as well not have spoken. Voulakis rattled on with great enthusiasm while Nikos stared at the gleaming optics behind the bar.

"Sir, can I just..." but Voulakis had a call on the other line and promised to call back. Nikos hung up and swore. He didn't want a British detective treading on his toes and taking over. It was his case and he wanted to manage it alone. Maybe Voulakis would forget. Maybe the Brits wouldn't loan them anyone. Or maybe he should just achieve as much as he could in the next few hours and solve this problem on his own. He sat at a small table and picked up his briefcase. At least he'd remembered to download the dictionary app. He was looking up 'dementia' when there was a sharp rap at the door.

Before he could respond, the door opened and a tall man strode towards him with a scowl on his face.

"This is a waste of time. Yours and mine. I don't know what Jensson's playing at, calling in the police on the say-so of a pair of dotty old hens. I've already talked to the coroner and the local pathologist. It's clear that she fell. Sad, but nothing nefarious. My name's Fraser, by the way, Doctor Lucas Fraser."

Nikos shook the doctor's hand, trying to assemble some kind of meaning from the rapid-fire string of words. *Time, Jensson, police, sad...*

"Inspector Nikos Stephanakis. Pleased to meet you. Where are you from?"

"Fort William. Do you know Scotland at all?"

Nikos shook his head and wondered how soon Voulakis could arrange a British detective.

Chapter 4

The walk through the forest provoked a peculiar nostalgia in Beatrice as she kicked up piles of spice-coloured leaves. She stopped to admire sunlit dewdrops on a spider's web. Strands of mist still hung over the meadows and the low sun painted the landscape with an almost painful vivacity. A wood pigeon repeated its advice to sheep rustlers, '*Take TWO ewes, you fool,*' and a pair of magpies clattered off towards the village. Berries against the sky amid bare branches and a chilly breeze blowing parchment leaves across the path all combined to make her think of a phrase she'd not considered for decades. *Back to school.*

Matthew, his yellow woollen scarf wound twice around his neck, added to the dampness in the air by continuing to drone on about planning for the future. Beatrice changed the subject.

"Yes, well, as I've only just returned to work, retirement – early or otherwise – seems rather premature. What time did you book the table for tonight?"

"Eight o'clock. I know it seems premature now, but I'm talking longer term. One has to be prepared financially to give oneself the greatest range of opportunities."

"Eight? Isn't that a little late for Luke? I thought his bedtime was no later than seven."

An odd expression crossed Matthew's brow. "Luke won't be there. I told the girls that much as I adore them both, and of course, my grandson, I would prefer to spend the evening alone with you. Though I have invited them for Sunday lunch."

Beatrice stopped to look at him. His face was flushed with cold, and his hair blew around his head, giving him a boyish appearance, despite his insistence on talking about pensions.

"How very romantic of you! It's rather nice that after all these years we can still enjoy dinner *à deux*." She linked her arm in his and they trudged on. "I hope they've got that rabbit and prune pie on the menu tonight."

"They'll have some sort of game. Roger is a great believer in seasonal cooking. Isn't that your phone?"

Beatrice registered the sound and pulled off her gloves to reach into her pocket. Her heart sank as she saw her Chief Inspector's name on the screen.

"Oh God, it's Hamilton."

Matthew rolled his eyes and walked on. Beatrice answered the call.

"Good morning, sir. What can I do for you?"

"*Where are you, Stubbs?*"

"In Devon, sir. In a forest."

"*Damn and hell blast.*"

Beatrice followed in Matthew's wake, pressing the phone to her ear while she waited for Hamilton to continue. Distant muttering and computer noises were all she could make out. Hamilton's voice returned.

"*No, it's not going to work. Stubbs, you there?*"

"Yes sir?"

"*Listen here, apologies for the short notice etcetera, but how soon could you get on a plane to Greece?*"

Matthew held the gate open for her as they left the woodland for a sunny field. A few sheep glanced in their direction and went back to cropping grass.

"Greece? Monday, I suppose. I'm back in London Sunday night, so could be ready to travel first thing Monday morning."

"*Hmm. Bit more urgent than that. Suspicious demise of an octogenarian on a cruise ship. Any chance you could get back* tonight? Fly tomorrow? I would consider this a personal favour."

Beatrice squeezed her eyelids together. "That's rather difficult, sir."

"No doubt it is. But I need a trusted pair of hands. Nothing complex, only take you forty-eight hours or so. Should be able to compensate with time in lieu. And after all, two days on a Greek island in an advisory role is hardly six months in Siberia."

The cottage came into view as they descended the slope, smoke weaving from the chimney. She'd have to forego dinner tonight and Sunday lunch with Matthew's daughters and the always entertaining little Luke. But if she accepted the job, she could take three extra days next week to make up for it. What with next weekend, that made five full days of crosswords, forest walks, pub lunches and circular arguments about her future.

"Very well, sir. I'll catch a train back this afternoon. Could someone book me a flight for first thing tomorrow? And if you email the case details now, I'll study them on the journey back."

"Tip top. Will do. All info to be sent soonest. Good show, Stubbs. Appreciate it." He rang off.

Matthew's head appeared to revolve as slowly as an owl's.

"You're going back to London." His intonation was as flat and hard as his eyes.

"I have no choice. Hamilton wants me to go to Greece for forty-eight hours. But I'll get time off in lieu, so I could be back by Wednesday. I'll cook dinners for us, we can spend time with the girls, teach Luke some new songs, visit the garden centre... oh Matthew, please don't be difficult. It's work, surely you can see that?"

He strode ahead, leaving Beatrice to hurry after him. She caught up as they reached the gate to the cottage and they trudged up the path in silence. Matthew unlocked the front door and sat on the bench to remove his boots. Beatrice stood in the doorway, determined to make him see the rationale behind her decision.

"Look, I know it's disappointing, but if I give a little now, I gain a lot more next week."

"Indeed. One must defer one's gratification. And it's not like I have any say in the matter, after all. Come on, pack your things and let's see if we can make the 12.23. What's happening in Greece?"

"No idea. Hamilton, cryptic as ever, said something about a suspicious death on a cruise ship."

"How awfully Agatha Christie!" Matthew's voice had a forced jollity, and as his head was bent to lace his shoes, she couldn't judge his expression. But she knew how precious their time together was to both of them.

"I am sorry, Matthew. I hate spoiling your weekend."

"It's not spoilt. I shall merely postpone my plans for a week. Now would you get your skates on? It'll take us a good half hour to get to the station."

She pecked him on the cheek and kicked off her wellingtons, her curiosity already piqued about exactly what her advisory role might be in Greece.

An extra five minutes spent looking for her hairbrush meant she missed the first train and had to wait half an hour till the next. Matthew bought her a baguette for the journey and stood at the ticket barrier to wave her off. She apologised once again for the interruption to their peaceful weekend routine.

"I'm used to it. Nothing involving you ever goes to plan," he said. "Now you'd better go. The quiet carriage is Coach C. And let me know when you're home."

She boarded the train, found a seat at an empty table in Coach C, unpacked her laptop and baguette and settled down to read Hamilton's email. He'd included flight details and information on her accommodation. She was flying to Heraklion, the capital of Crete, then travelling by boat to Santorini, where the liner was currently docked. An Inspector Stephanakis would meet her at the airport. It all sounded exotic and a world away from damp Devon mornings. She had no idea of distance or proximity of these places but their names alone set off all sorts of ideas. A quiver of anticipation ran through her as she imagined herself standing on a deck, watching the sunset, wearing a chiffon scarf and drinking a gin sling. She trained her attention on the case.

The situation at first glance appeared really rather simple. An old lady took an unfortunate tumble while on holiday with friends, and one of them seemed convinced it was no accident. Not the first time an excess of Sunday night television had affected perceptions in those with failing faculties. In the final year of her life, Beatrice's own mother had often ascribed incidents from *Downton Abbey* or *Coronation Street* to her neighbours, resulting in some awkward misunderstandings.

In such a non-starter of a case, Hamilton's request for her assistance struck her as an over-reaction. Nevertheless, she would follow orders. If he considered it a personal favour, it probably meant politics were involved.

Her phone rang and she checked the screen. It was Marianne, Matthew's eldest daughter. Instantly, images of a white-faced Matthew in an ambulance flashed through her mind. Ridiculous, she'd only left him ten minutes ago.

"Marianne, hello. Is everything all right?"

Against a background of pop music, she heard Marianne's laugh.

"I was calling to ask you the same question. Dad just phoned to ask if I'd like to join him at The Toad tonight because you had to go back to London. There's nothing wrong, is there?"

"Not at all." She dropped her voice for fear of disturbing the other passengers. "My boss needs me to go to Greece to assist with an investigation, so I have to fly out tomorrow. Didn't your father tell you that?"

"Yes, that's what he said. I just wanted to check he hadn't, you know, upset you or anything."

"Far from it. To be honest, I think it's the other way around. My dashing off has put his nose out of sorts. But he's being decent and has accepted it with typical grumpy grace."

"He would. And there's always next weekend to put his plans into action. OK, so long as everything is fine between you two, I'll call Tanya to rearrange next Sunday. I'm so looking forward to this! Good luck in Greece and see you soon!"

Beatrice ended the call and watched the fields flicker by, glowing as if irradiated in autumnal sunshine. Marianne's words suffused her with a sense of belonging, of acceptance and a depth of almost maternal affection she'd never expected to experience. Her phone beeped again. A text message.

Sorry to miss the big lunch! But can't wait for next weekend. Love, Tanya and Luke xoxo

So much spontaneous warmth made her smile and hug herself. That feeling took a long time to fade.

Until she started thinking.

A delay between Reading and Paddington meant she eventually got back to Boot Street at half past four. The City cast long shadows across the East End as shops and stalls began the process of giving way to the alternative landscape of the night. Impatient to discuss her theories, Beatrice was irritated to get no response from her neighbour's bell. On a Saturday afternoon, with a new boyfriend in tow, Adrian could be anywhere. Probably on the South Bank, dallying in a second-hand bookshop, pottering about in a craft market or enjoying good food by the river. The fact that she could have been doing the same things in a Devon village only made it worse. She stomped upstairs and started repacking her weekend bag. Greece, in November. What to wear? Which essential medicinal products to take?

She yanked out an article on wine she'd intended to share with Matthew and her conscience pricked. However, the conviction she'd arrived at on the train precluded a call. She sent a brief, upbeat text message assuring him of her safe arrival and opened the bathroom cabinet to find the Imodium.

Chapter 5

Unable to settle to television, book or case file, Beatrice opted for the Internet. Ostensibly research, but actually distraction. Images of Greek islands proved rather alluring. So much so that the doorbell gave her a real start. She picked up the intercom.

"Hello?"

"Oh, Beatrice, it is you. That's a relief. We saw the light and assumed the worst. Why are you back so soon?"

"Hello, Adrian. I have to work, unfortunately. What are you two up to tonight?"

"Clubbing, I think, but not till later. Now we're having cheese, crackers, a rich Bordeaux and *Strictly Come Dancing*. Want to join us?"

Beatrice weighed her loathing of reality TV against her urge to talk.

"I'll have a look in the cupboards to see what I can contribute. Then I'll be down in two shakes of a ham's tail. Are you sure I'm not intruding?"

"Don't be silly. Hurry up. I want to show you my new hair."

Holger opened the door and stooped to kiss Beatrice on both cheeks. He wore a tight lilac T-shirt with a tea-towel flopped over his shoulder and smelt of a crisp sea-breeze shower gel. He unbent to his full height and pointed with a frown at her carrier bag.

"You didn't need to bring anything. We have more than enough. Are you fine, Beatrice?"

She nodded. "Yes. I'm only back here because I have to fly to Greece in the morning. Did you have a lovely day exploring the capital?"

Holger gestured for her to follow him inside. "Perfect. The weather is good for photographs and I love to spend time in markets and art galleries."

"Me too. Did you go to Camden?"

"No, Adrian said it was too touristy. We went to Borough and Spitalfields."

His muscular bulk blocked out the light as they entered the living-room.

"Our guest is here!" called Holger, offering to take her bag.

"Hello, Beatrice! Come in and let me pour you a glass." Adrian, wearing a paisley-print shirt and jeans, stood at the kitchen island, uncorking a bottle of wine. His dark hair was spiked up into a mini-quiff reminding her of a young Tony Curtis.

"Hello you. Nice haircut. You look rather rockabilly."

"Do you like it? Couldn't do the whole James Dean thing but I fancied going a bit 'collar up' for a while. What's in the bag?"

"I brought oatcakes, Twiglets, some Godminster and one of Matthew's recommendations. It's a *Nuit Saint Georges*."

"You didn't need to bring anything, but seeing as you did, I'm glad it's something divine. Now sit down and tell me what happened. You haven't fallen out with Matthew, I hope?"

"No, no. Quite the opposite. Hamilton summoned me back so that I can be in Greece by tomorrow. A death on a cruise ship needs investigating. Looks straightforward enough so should only take a couple of days."

Adrian handed her a glass and pecked her on both cheeks. "Let's toast! To a glorious Sunday, whether in the East End, a Devon village or a Greek beach. Cheers!"

They repeated the toast, clinked glasses and drank. The wine was earthy and rich, and strangely soothing.

Holger gestured towards the living-room with his glass. "You two go and sit down. I'll add Beatrice's things and bring the tray in."

They did as they were told.

Adrian sat beside her on the sofa and dropped his voice. "I am utterly besotted. If I'd been given *carte blanche* to design my perfect man, I'd have never thought of some of those details. He's almost too good to be true."

"I must say, every time I see him, he gets better looking. When is he going back to Hamburg?"

"Monday. But two weeks later, he'll be back to stay for three months. He's got a job with an instrument-making shop in... where's that place again, Holger?"

Holger entered the room and placed a heavily laden tray on the coffee table in front of them. "South Thames College. I'm teaching advanced guitar-making. In Morden."

"Morden? Bit of a trek. Still, at least it's only one Tube line from here."

A look passed between the two men. "Um, Holger's not moving in, Beatrice. He has a place all lined up near Angel. But yes, it's still only one Tube line."

A blush crept up Beatrice's neck. "Sorry, I didn't mean to make assumptions. You're absolutely right to take things slowly. I mean, who knows what might happen in the next..."

Adrian laughed. "I think you'd better stop there before you dig yourself a deeper hole." He looked at Holger. "She means what she says about taking it slowly. How long have you and Matthew been together? Twenty years and they still haven't made the leap to cohabitation."

Beatrice forced a laugh to join in with Holger, despite a feeling of looming dread. Her observant neighbour picked up on her mood.

"Come on, let's eat. *Strictly's* on in ten minutes. Beatrice, you said earlier, when I asked if you two had fallen out, you said it was quite the opposite. Are you going to elaborate? Has he popped the question?"

This time it was impossible to fake a laugh. It took a second for Adrian to notice her frozen posture and locked jaw, as he was helping himself to a slice of Godminster and an oatcake.

"Oh my God! Beatrice? He has!"

She shook her head. "No, he hasn't. Not yet. But he's going to, I know it. If I hadn't got the call from work, he'd be doing it now, across the table at The Toad. As it is, he'll find the right moment next weekend. What the hell am I going to do?"

Holger stared at her and Adrian put down his plate. "This is serious. Holger, top up the wine. I'll set the TV to record. Now, DI Stubbs, kindly start at the beginning."

It took some time to explain: Matthew's recent obsession with planning the future, the 'just the two of us' dinner plans, Marianne's call, Tanya's text message and the sudden realisation that every expectation was pinned on an imminent wedding. She finally stopped talking and Holger handed her a plate. Dear man, he'd already prepared a variety of cheeses, slices of fruit and selection of crackers. Sharing her concerns left her lighter, so she tucked into Brie on a water biscuit with a couple of grapes.

Adrian swirled the contents of his glass. He seemed lost in the deep colours. Beatrice and Holger both waited for him to speak. He looked up and nodded.

"I have to agree. It definitely sounds as if that is what he's planning. Your detective work is flawless, as always. The question now must be, what next? Holger, what do you say?"

Holger examined a Twiglet and replaced it on his plate. "For me, there is only one question. Beatrice, do you love Matthew?"

She nodded, her mouth full.

"So what is the difficulty here? Go to Greece, do what you need to do quickly and return to him. Wait for his question and answer from your heart. If you love him, if your relationship has already lasted twenty years, why not marry the man?"

Beatrice swallowed. That was the trouble with Germans.

Always so logical. His argument made perfect sense and only someone wilfully perverse could disagree. She took a swig of wine and attempted to explain.

"You're absolutely right. The problem is that I can't help but see marriage as an end, rather than a beginning. I've spent over fifty years as an independent woman, and to give up now..." Her voice cracked and tears clouded her vision. Two bodies bundled close and draped arms around her back. She sniffed and yanked a tissue from her sleeve.

"Sorry, sorry. I know this is a problem of my own making. But I really don't know why things have to change. We've been happy like this for ages, so why rock the boat? I don't want to be a Devon housewife, tending courgettes and making jam and joining the Women's Institute. The very thought makes me hyperventilate. What the hell is the matter with the man? I don't know why he would propose now."

No one spoke for a few seconds. Beatrice thought back to one of her mother's favourite sayings, 'Old age don't come alone'.

Holger cleared his throat. "Are you sure you don't know why?"

She shook her head. "No, I do."

Adrian raised his eyebrows. "I think you'll find the generally accepted expression is just 'I do'. Might come in handy one of these days."

Beatrice gave a profound sigh. "Two little words that could change everything."

Adrian leaned forward to catch Holger's eye. "And you call me a drama queen?"

Taxi booked, online check-in complete, case packed and alarm set, Beatrice began preparing herself for bed. She was brushing her teeth when the phone rang.

"Hello?"

"Stubbs, Hamilton here. All set for tomorrow?"

"Yes sir. It doesn't seem especially complex. Is this more an exercise in cooperation?"

"*Yes and no. The fellow at the helm is new to the game and his grasp of the lingo is not the best. You're there as mentor. Play second fiddle, guide him in the right direction and only step in if he looks liable to bugger it up. And do it quickly, Stubbs. I need you back here.*"

"I'll do my best, sir. Is there another case on the agenda?"

"*Not exactly. Plan is, assign you to Operation Horseshoe, learn the ropes and take over from Rangarajan.*"

"Take over? But sir, Ranga's doing a great job! I don't understand why you would want to replace him now. Putting a white woman on the case instead of a senior Asian male seems counter-intuitive."

"*Of course you don't understand. Because as per bloody usual, Stubbs, you don't have the full picture. Rangarajan is taking early retirement at the end of this year. Horseshoe is an extraordinarily complicated operation, which requires a sensitive touch and a thorough understanding of cultural mores. When Ranga retires, I need a safe pair of hands on the tiller.*"

"Oh, I see. I had no idea he was thinking of early retirement as well."

There was an extended silence at the other end of the line. Beatrice winced. Another two little words.

"*I beg your pardon? Did you just say 'as well'?*"

"Sorry, sir. Nothing decided yet. Just an idea I've been considering."

"*Have you now? Well, you can damn well unconsider it. Do you have any idea whatsoever of the efforts I have made to keep you in your post? Of the political persuasion I've brought to bear in order to retain a person viewed by many as perilously close to being a loose bloody cannon? No, you don't. I refused to accept your resignation earlier this year because I believe in you. Sometimes, I wonder why. At your best, you are an asset to my team. At worst, you are a stubborn old coot who is a bigger pain than an infected wisdom tooth. On top of this, I am not prepared to lose two of my best senior detectives in one year. So please put all thoughts of premature retirement out of your mind and concentrate on the job in hand. Sort yourself out, Stubbs. Good night."*

The disconnection tone beeped in her ear and she replaced the receiver. She sat in the window seat, looking out over Boot Street. Thirty years she'd lived in this flat. Twenty four years she'd been with Matthew. Coming up fifteen years she'd worked with Hamilton. In five years, she could officially retire. And then? Time trickled through her fingers and she could no more hold onto it than water.

With a shake, she pulled herself back from such unhealthy introspection. She checked her bags again, took her medication and she focused on what tomorrow held in store, while applying face cream. As she switched off the light, a thought occurred. Even if some of her colleagues did see her as a 'stubborn old coot', a cruise ship full of octogenarians would see her as a mere spring chicken.

Chapter 6

Her documents obviously marked her as an official to be respected, so her passage through Heraklion's airport was effortless. In the Arrivals area, she spotted a good-looking young man in shirtsleeves and chinos waiting beside a uniformed officer who held a sign saying STUBS. Beatrice raised a hand and offered a smile. The detective came towards her.

"Pleased to meet you, Detective Inspector Stubs. How do you do?"

She shook his hand. "Very well, thank you. You must be Inspector Stephanakis."

"Correct. Welcome to Greece. How was your flight?" He relieved her of her bag, which he passed to the driver.

"Lovely. From London to Athens, I had the good fortune to sit next to the most fascinating lady. A sculptress who has lived there for over ten years. She gave me some very helpful cultural advice. For the first time I can recall, a flight went almost too quickly."

They followed the driver to the exit, where a police car was parked outside the door. The heat surprised her. London, when she left, had been a shivery five degrees.

Stephanakis opened the rear door. After checking she was comfortable, he went round the other side and joined her in the back. He shot some instructions at the driver in Greek and glanced at his phone. His chivalrous manner and clean-shaven face appealed to Beatrice. Very proper. He fixed his attention on her with a nervous smile.

"DI Stubbs, I am very pleased to meet you. I just got promoted to the role of inspector, and it is very exciting for me to work with someone with such a track record. But I must apologise in advance. This is my first investigation and although it is not really complex, my boss thought my enquiries would benefit from an experienced officer, so..." He looked down at his phone once more.

Beatrice smiled, well used to preparing speeches before joining a new team.

"... I will need your patience. I know this area and police procedure very well and I hope I can contribute much."

"Don't worry, Inspector. I understand this is your first case. But they wouldn't have promoted you if you weren't competent. I trust you entirely to lead this case to its conclusion, and I want to stress, I'm assisting you. You're the boss."

He nodded, his uncertain smile and restless eyes expressing both gratitude and trepidation.

Beatrice smiled back and looked out of the window. This would be just the tonic she needed. A mini-break disguised as work, with sunshine, delightful scenery and an open-and-shut case. She'd think about Matthew when she got back.

The driver dropped her at the hotel to settle in and Stephanakis promised to return in time to take her to lunch. She dumped her bags and as always on arriving at a hotel room, checked the bathroom for cleanliness. Perfectly satisfactory. Even the end of the toilet paper had been folded into a neat triangle. She bounced on the bed, explored the mini-bar and took a bottle of water out onto the balcony. A sense of foreignness overcame her and gave her a sudden thrill of anticipation. The building opposite was cracked and crumbling, large chunks of plaster revealing the bricks beneath. Faded green shutters framed the windows and a cluster of mopeds were strewn rather than parked under the shade of a palm tree. Electric cables hung above the narrow street like necklaces in a costume jewellery store and a blue sign announced the name of the street in Greek. In a gap between dusty apartment blocks, beyond decorative balconies with plants in terracotta pots, past roof terraces with rattan furniture and pergolas, lay the sea.

Beatrice beamed and took a deep breath. Yes, in amongst the scent of petrol rising from the street and stale chemicals wafting from the air-conditioner unit, she could detect ozone. Closer to land the water was paler, the colour of cornflowers, deepening to an intense azure as it met the sky, which seemed bigger and bluer than it could ever be in London.

The telephone rang. Stephanakis was waiting to take her to lunch.

"It's nothing special, but a place I use a lot," he said, as he guided her along the pedestrianised street. "I thought you might be hungry."

Beatrice was admiring the sandy colours and the mosaic kaleidoscope created by the sea-blue shutters, white umbrellas, wrought-iron benches and lamps lining the avenue between the trees. Echoes of beach everywhere, as if it had crawled up the street and into the consciousness. She realised the young inspector was waiting for a reply.

"Hungry? I could eat a horse."

He gave her a look of mock alarm.

"Horse might be a problem, but I could arrange a goat."

"So long as it's dead and comes with chips, I'll eat anything. I am entirely in your hands."

Noisy and crowded, the taverna smelt delicious. Several people greeted Stephanakis and shot curious glances at her. Without warning, a cheery sort with a once-white apron shouted something incomprehensible at Stephanakis and grabbed Beatrice to kiss her on both cheeks. Stephanakis muttered a brief explanation and the man laughed from the belly.

"Detective Inspector Stubbs, this is Dinos. He owns this restaurant and cooks the food himself."

"God Save the Queen! *Kalimera!*"

"*Kalimera!*" she replied, grateful for the crash course from the sculptress on the plane.

Dinos found them a tiny table and Stephanakis checked the blackboard.

"Would you like me to translate the menu?"

"I eat everything and I am very hungry. So let's order the dish of the day, lots of bread, a jug of wine and get cracking."

Stephanakis stared at her for a second. Then he broke into a grin and relayed their order to Dinos, who evidently approved. He clapped his hands together, gripped her shoulder and said "Very good!" With a shake and a wink, he barrelled off towards the kitchen.

"Well, if the food is as hearty as the welcome, we're in for a treat. Good choice, Inspector."

"Dinos is a minor local celebrity and he's obsessed with your royal family. You should have seen how he decorated this place for that wedding. But he's mostly famous for his food. So don't worry, your meal will be delicious."

"I can't wait. And that is no idle platitude. Now, can we talk about the case? From what I've read, an elderly lady's tragic fall has been rather blown out of proportion by some of her companions. They suspect a deliberate attempt to harm her. Do you see any evidence of that?"

Stephanakis furrowed his brow. "That's not quite right. The ladies who saw the fall are not of the same party. We will interview the witnesses as soon as the doctor gives permission. But their story seems unlikely. The deceased was eighty years old; the witnesses are both retired and saw the incident through a camera. It's very hard to get a clear account of what happened. That's why I requested a specialist, someone accustomed to interviewing in English. So I'm happy you are here. My language skills aren't bad but I have real problems communicating with some of these older ladies or people with a strong accent. Your help is really appreciated."

As he spoke, Beatrice studied the young man. A smooth olive complexion, with cappuccino-coloured lips, shiny black hair and mahogany eyes added up to a very pleasing overall effect. Nascent wrinkles at the corners of his eyes added a feathery effect to his lashes. His polite manner and respectful attitude had already impressed her and now he had passed the first test. With careful diplomacy, he'd corrected her inaccurate assessment of the case, topping it off with a sprinkling of humility.

"I'm happy to be here," she said, and meant it. "Can you tell me anything else?"

"Esther Crawford was travelling with a group of friends from England. Every year, they take a cruise together. Seven women, all in their seventies or eighties, who call themselves 'The Hirondelles'. The woman who claims she witnessed a murder is from Scotland and in her sixties. As far as I know, they had no contact with each other."

"Who else have you spoken to?"

"The captain, one of the ship's doctors, two of the deceased's companions and the Santorini police who recovered the body."

"So what is your plan?"

"Should we visit the site first?"

Beatrice cocked her head on one side.

He took the hint. "OK. First, we should visit the site and check the facts. Next, we interview the witnesses. If there is reasonable doubt, we conduct an investigation. I'm sure this can be resolved in a couple of days."

"Sounds like you have it all under control, Inspector. So should I act as interviewer while you take notes? Mind now, here's the food."

Dinos placed the plates on the table with a flourish. "*Stifado!*"

A rich-looking meat stew with jewels of oil floating on the surface, some roast potatoes decorated with cloves of garlic and sprigs of rosemary, a platter of bread and a generous terracotta jug of wine. The time to talk shop was over. She gave Dinos an approving smile and picked up her fork.

"How do you say *bon appétit* in Greek?"

"*Kali sas órexi.*"

"And the same to you."

The speedboat bounced over the waves and the island of Santorini grew larger on the horizon. Beatrice admitted relief. After the first half hour of sea spray, Mediterranean blue water, glittering sunshine and wind on her cheeks, exhilaration gave way to discomfort. Bless Adrian for insisting she tucked the Hermès headscarf he'd given her into her handbag. Without that, factor 50 sunscreen and her dark glasses, things could have been a lot worse. Stephanakis had stopped checking her every couple of minutes after it was clear she would not be regurgitating her lunch and now kept his eyes on the island ahead. She followed suit.

At first sight, the island did not live up to the pictures she had seen during her research. Stark, forbidding cliffs rose from the sea, while cruise vessels and ferries filled the busy harbour. A switchback road scored a zigzag up the cliffs like a lightning strike. Not at all the kind of environment to host terraces of blue rooftops, pots of geraniums or ginger cats.

The police boat slowed and all the signs of a busy commercial port emerged. Filthy water, slicked with oil. Massive rusting chains upon which noisy seabirds perched, adding their own form of decoration. The fresh whiff of the sea was overpowered by diesel and exhaust fumes, and the sound of ferries, coaches, and larger boats drowned out the now-familiar buzz of their own engine.

Stephanakis left his post beside the driver and sat next to her. He raised his voice above the noise.

"This is Athinos, the ferry port. Most cruise ships use the Old Port, in Thira. But the only way up to the town of Thira is donkey or cable car. For the ladies of the *Empress Louise*, that was not an option. They travelled by coach to Fira, the main city, which is where everyone goes. The classic Santorini of the postcards. So we follow the same route. The pathologist will meet us at the dock."

"The island has its own pathologist?"

Stephanakis watched as the boat nosed a path towards a berth. "No, he is based in Heraklion, but he always takes the SeaCat. He has problems with small boats."

Not only small boats, it seemed. The hue and tone of Konstakis Apostolou's expression reminded Beatrice of a morgue wall. He exchanged pleasantries in English, a strong scent of peppermint on his breath, before climbing into the police car with less enthusiasm for life than of one of the local donkeys. Stephanakis, in the front, conversed with the local officer; Apostolou, beside Beatrice, rested his head against the window while she gazed out at the sea and the distant calderas. The switchback road provided a constantly shifting perspective, climbing higher and higher; each new turn giving more spectacular views. Something inside her seemed to lift; not her heart, and certainly not her stomach, but in her solar plexus; this place, this endless landscape, this miracle of geography filled her with a joy which threatened to boil up and explode.

The road levelled out and the driver trundled along the coast. Beatrice decided Apostolou needed a distraction. Normally, discussing a corpse with a queasy sort would be inappropriate, but in this instance, it was practically home from home.

"What a wonderful view, Mr Apostolou! But I'm sure you're used to it by now and bored by a tourist's chatter. Could we make the most of our time? Would you mind if I asked a few questions regarding your initial examination?"

His head swivelled in her direction. The cold black eyes and skin the colour of uncooked pastry made her think of a gecko.

"Yes. No. I don't mind."

"On initial examination and after the full autopsy, did you

find any evidence to make you suspect anything other than accidental death?"

He wound down the window a few centimetres and breathed. His goatee beard was a masterpiece of precision.

"No, nothing at all. She obviously overbalanced, lost her footing and fell over the edge. No one could survive such a fall. At eighty years old, she probably had a heart attack before hitting the ground."

Beatrice gazed out at the bay, maintaining her smile.

"You say 'probably'. In all my experience of pathology, that's a word rarely used in physiological terms. When hazarding a guess as to circumstances or perpetrators, perhaps. But as to the definitive state of a corpse? Do you believe Esther Crawford had a heart attack? Before or after she fell?"

He tilted his head to the incoming breeze. Colour, if only a faint peach, returned to his cheeks.

"My investigation is not complete. I can tell you only that an elderly woman fell to her death from a cliff. A post-mortem on such a body will take time, especially with the complications of her being a tourist. And a two-hundred-metre drop makes any examination problematic. Regardless of what we find, one old woman's delusions will not reanimate the deceased."

Stephanakis leaned around to face them. "We stop at the site of the incident now, and then proceed to Fira, which is where the coach party stopped for lunch. We follow their route. But this is the place where Mrs Esther Crawford died."

The driver pulled into a parking area, an ideal spot for tourists to take photographs.

"You said Fira is the main tourist town?" Beatrice asked.

Apostolou answered. "The main tourist town is Oia."

"Here? But this is a car park."

"No," Stephanakis smiled. "He's talking about the town of Oia. It's pronounced 'ee-ya'. Famous for the sunset views and very popular with tourists, especially honeymooners. Many people come to Santorini to get married. It is a perfect location for a wedding."

Wedding locations were not a subject that interested Beatrice in the slightest. Several large coaches were lined up against the cliffs; huge protruding wing mirrors gave them the appearance of enormous soldier ants. Their passengers spread along the viewpoint, posing, snapping and pointing while their drivers smoked in the shade of the vehicles. Apostolou got out of the car and rested against the bonnet for several seconds while Stephanakis and Beatrice made for the edge.

"I'm puzzled, Inspector. There's a safety barrier all along the front. So how on earth did she manage to fall? And if she was pushed, how would you get an eighty-year-old over that without being seen?"

"It wasn't here. The incident happened further along the path. The barrier is only at the beginning. Mrs Crawford fell from the unprotected section."

"I see. Still, there are so many people hanging about, surely such an incident could never go unnoticed. I imagine this place has a constant stream of visitors throughout the day."

"Yes, it does, but between twelve and two is always a quiet time. It's the same with most scenic sites. The islands operate on a tourist timetable. Coach companies work with the restaurants to deliver all their passengers in shifts. So places like this are usually empty over lunch. Mrs Crawford died at quarter past midday."

"So what was she doing here? Why was she up here alone?"

Apostolou joined them. "Her party failed to realise she had been left behind. No one noticed until a head count was taken at the restaurant. She probably got lost and missed the departure time. I presume I'm using the word 'probably' in an acceptable way this time?"

Beatrice shot him a look, but his eyes crinkled as he smiled. Apparently recovered, he had a dapper, genial air with an observant expression.

"Yes, that is acceptable," she replied. "Time of death is 12.15? That's awfully precise considering your post-mortem is unfinished."

"Inspector Stephanakis can be more precise than I. There were witnesses."

Stephanakis nodded slowly. "Not the ladies up on the ridge, who claim she was thrown." He pointed above the coaches. "Although one of them took a photograph just after the incident. Nothing to see, of course, but the time was 12.16. But down in the bay, a couple of... what is the name for diving without the oxygen tank? Just with breath?"

"Free diving. There were free divers at the bottom of the cliff?" Beatrice asked.

"On a boat. These cliffs are the walls of a volcano. They go down a further 400 metres. The free divers were preparing to jump when they saw, and heard, someone hit the ground. They raised the alarm."

"That was at 12.20," added Apostolou. "The local police retrieved the body an hour or so later and I attended the mortuary at 17.00. Mrs Crawford had all the injuries consistent with a long fall. Broken neck, severe abrasions, various fractures and almost complete destruction of her internal organs. It's not the first time I've seen this sort of thing."

The party walked single file down the path until Stephanakis indicated they had arrived at the spot. The two men flanked Beatrice as they gazed down at the sheer volcanic rock, waves crashing spume into the base. Out of the corner of her eye, she saw Stephanakis cross himself, with a quick and practised gesture.

"Now," she said, "let's have a look at the witnesses' picnic spot and see what kind of a view they had."

Stephanakis looked at her feet.

"What?" she demanded.

"Nothing. It's very good. You are a detective. Of course you wear the right kind of shoes."

They clambered up the cliff path, Beatrice wondering why such a description of her footwear made her nose throb.

Chapter 7

It was hard to comprehend the proportions of the *Empress Louise*. Standing on the quayside, eleven floors were visible and there must have been more below the waterline. It was as tall as a cathedral and ten blocks long – a skyscraper on its side. The pristine whiteness and uniform patterns suggested a vast hotel complex, which was probably close to reality.

Beatrice looked at Stephanakis. "Big, isn't it?" she said.

"Big is one word for her. She carries just over two thousand passengers and another thousand people in terms of crew and staff. Fifteen decks, eighty metres high and two hundred and eighty metres long. She has eleven restaurants, four pools, three theatres, four bars, a nightclub, two cinemas, a casino, a place of worship and a shopping mall. The *Empress Louise* specialises in 'seniors', so she has a substantial medical centre, plenty of wheelchair accessible cabins and a morgue."

"Been doing your research, Inspector?"

"I'm fascinated by the scale of the thing. You know, this ship is bigger than the village where I grew up."

"Same here. Let's hope we don't get lost. Shall we make a start on these interviews?"

Greek speakers to Stephanakis and English speakers divided between them. The casino was easily large enough to accommodate two interview areas. Stephanakis took occupied a table near the bar, close to the door. Beatrice walked further back, past the serried lines of slot machines, the roulette wheel and the various card tables before she found what she was looking for. An elevated relaxation platform with comfortable banquettes and two highly polished tables that would serve as both work station and rather sophisticated interview room. The distance and the amount of wood and carpet between her and Stephanakis would ensure no conversations could be overheard. She unpacked her briefcase and gazed around the darkened space, curious as to how different it would seem with all the flashing lights, glamorous people, champagne, laughter, cheers and noise. She decided she could probably live without the experience.

Her first interviewee was Captain Jensson. Tall and blond in his impressive uniform, with Nordic blue eyes, yet disappointingly without a proper captain's beard. Nevertheless, he was clearly a professional. He had come prepared. Printouts of the itinerary, the passenger list from the excursion highlighted by gender, a file on the deceased including medical records and a photograph of the dead woman. He'd thought of everything.

Next up, Dr Fraser. Belligerent, impatient and judging by the difficulty of their exchange, possibly hard of hearing. He brought nothing but attitude, adding very little to what she already knew of Esther Crawford. His one revealing remark was his dismissal of the witness as senile. Beatrice pressed him as to the medical accuracy of such a statement, which he brushed off as a joke.

The Hirondelles followed, Esther Crawford's travelling companions. In their late seventies to mid-eighties, they were all visibly distressed by the death of their friend. Talking to a police officer alarmed them still further. Beatrice tried interviewing them in pairs, hoping they might feel less intimidated, but the effect was an echo chamber of cliché and emotion. After talking to four out of the six, the only useful piece of information they'd given was that Esther Crawford had been a bird-watcher and often wandered off during excursions.

Once they'd left, she wrote up her notes, the beginnings of

a headache thumping behind her eyes. The darkness, at first so calming and discreet, now felt oppressive and cloistered. Beatrice needed some air. She waited till her colleague's interviewee had departed, then suggested a break and comparison of notes so far. A bright young man, he welcomed the idea immediately. It served her less selfish agenda as well. She could ensure Stephanakis needed no additional support while getting an essential boost of sugar and caffeine. Her role as mentor was to lead by example, after all.

It was a strange experience to emerge from the ship's casino into brilliant sunshine. They chose to sit outside at The Boardwalk, one of the smaller restaurant-cafés on an upper deck, and share their findings. The sea breeze eased her headache before she'd even ordered coffee, plus something honey-soaked to boost her sugar levels. She dug out her sunglasses, settled opposite Stephanakis and absorbed the view, allowing herself to relax.

"What an afternoon! I feel like I've had the same conversation with four different people. I'm not sure I learnt anything more than what a sweet person Esther Crawford was. What about you? How were your interviews with the crew?"

"I didn't learn much either. Some of the staff and crew had gone ashore, but not to the tourist areas. No one saw anything and none of them seemed very interested. I have the feeling all the passengers are just one big faceless group to them."

"Not surprising, I suppose." The waiter brought their order: *baklava* and cappuccino for her, an Earl Grey tea for him.

Beatrice lifted her face to the sun while Stephanakis flicked through his notebook. Back home, she'd be donning her wellies to walk through the rain with Matthew. She changed thought tracks and focused her mind on the present.

"That doctor I spoke to. I don't think much of his bedside manner, do you?"

Stephanakis smiled. "Dr Fraser? He seems in a bad temper all of the time, if that's what you mean. But I can't be sure because I only understand about one word in ten."

"Yes, he has an accent all right. And a tendency to shout. Perhaps that's from talking to so many people with hearing problems. I believe he might have one himself. I'm sure a constant stream of old folks' ailments can be tedious, but if you work on a ship like this, what can you expect?"

"Did he tell you he never actually treated Mrs Crawford? She saw Dr Weinberg once about her low blood pressure, who prescribed iron tablets. But the nurse..." he opened his notepad and checked. "Sister Bannerjee said that she came back two days later because the tablets made her sick."

"Low blood pressure can cause fainting. I must ask her colleagues if she suffered from dizziness at all. Although even if she did, I can't see why she was wandering about alone or how she could fall over the edge of the cliff." She picked up her fork and tucked into her sticky-looking dessert.

A shadow fell over their table. "Sorry to interrupt."

Beatrice looked up with a start. "Dr Fraser, hello again."

"Just to let you know, I've given the all-clear for you to speak to the ladies who think they saw the bogeyman. Mrs Campbell is still very shaken, so don't expect too much. You may get more sense out of her companion, Rose Mason. She seems to have her head screwed on. Of course, she didn't actually see anything. Probably because there was nothing to see."

"Thanks for your permission, doctor. We'll visit them as soon as we're done here."

"Very good. Go to the infirmary reception. They're expecting you." He strode away.

Stephanakis watched him go. "What is a bogeyman?"

Beatrice stirred her coffee in irritation.

"A non-existent scary creature designed to frighten children. Dr Fraser is being very patronising. His perspective is relevant, of course, but if he discredits witnesses before we interview them, that is prejudicial. If he continues like this, we'll have to ask him to keep his opinions to himself."

After their coffee break, Beatrice and Stephanakis went in search of the infirmary, following the map they had been given. It was the first time they'd moved around the ship without a guide and soon found themselves completely lost. Stephanakis looked from the map to the signage in increasing frustration. Beatrice, as she always did on such occasions, asked a passer-by. A well-dressed man approached, wearing a navy houndstooth-checked blazer, pale trousers and open-necked shirt. He was carrying a book. Always a good sign In Beatrice's estimation.

"Excuse me. Do you speak English?"

He stopped and looked down at her with warm, light-brown eyes. "I do. Can I be of assistance?"

"We're looking for the infirmary, but seem to have taken a wrong turn. Would you happen to know where it is?"

His forehead creased and unfolded. "As a matter of fact, I know exactly where it is. You're almost in the correct place, just one deck too high. If you go down to the end of this corridor, you'll find stairs down to the next level. Double back on yourselves and you'll see the door on your left." He smiled, his tanned skin wrinkling into well-worn grooves. Beatrice smiled back. He reminded her of someone. She couldn't recall who, but it was definitely someone she liked.

"You're very kind. Thank you."

He wished them both a pleasant afternoon and continued up the corridor, stooping to duck under the doorway.

Maggie Campbell finished her story and took a moment to compose herself. Her companion, Rose Mason, reached for her hand. Marguerite and Rose. Beatrice briefly wished she'd been born in an era when it was fashionable to name one's children after flowers or precious stones. The two women could have been sisters. Both wore hyacinth shades of blue, had soft grey hair, pale powdery skin and bright eyes. Mauve shadows swelled under Maggie's eyes as she battled tears. She won. After several swallows, she was ready to speak again.

"Detective Inspector Stubbs, I'm not at all surprised people don't believe me. I still find it hard to credit myself. But I swear on all I hold dear, I saw a man throw that lady off the cliff, so help me God. I couldn't identify either of them, but she was wearing the Hirondelle uniform and she recognised him. He was tall. When he met her, she seemed relieved to see him. She wasn't surprised, though. The sort of reaction you'd have if you'd lost someone and then found them again." She scrunched up her eyes and clenched her fists. "That poor, poor woman. Dr Fraser told me she'd celebrated her eightieth birthday on board. Why would anyone do that to a harmless pensioner?"

Stephanakis met Beatrice's eyes. The four of them sat around a small table in the infirmary lounge; Stephanakis taking notes, Maggie giving her statement, Beatrice asking the questions and Rose Mason supporting her friend and gently prodding her to remember the details.

Rose spoke. "That's what the police want to find out, Maggie. So you have to help them as much as possible. Do you remember you told me one of the crew had found her? You seemed very sure the man was from the *Empress Louise*. Can you remember why you said that?"

"It was only an assumption. All I can remember is that he was a lot taller than her and wore white. Or it could have been cream, I suppose. The midday sun tends to bleach everything. I couldn't tell you his hair colour as he was wearing that hat they all wear. It looked like the white uniform and because she seemed to know him, I thought he had to be a crew member. But I definitely have no evidence for that and would want to make no accusations."

Beatrice glanced at Stephanakis, with a slight twitch of her eyebrow. He got the message and cleared his throat. "Thank you, Mrs Campbell. Can you think of anything else about the man which might help us? Did you see where he came from?"

"From below where we were sitting. But that's where all the coaches park, so it doesn't really help, does it?"

Beatrice nodded her reassurance. "Do you mind if I ask why you were up there? Why you chose to take a picnic off on your own?"

Maggie sniffed and jerked her head in the direction of Rose. "Ask her."

Rose gave an embarrassed smile. "Cruises aren't really my thing. I agreed to try it, as Maggie was so keen, but I am not enjoying the experience, to be truthful. The whole thing feels a bit stage-managed. We snatch every opportunity to go ashore and do our own thing. We try to escape the coach tours, go in the opposite direction to the herd and avoid anything that looks like a tourist spot. When we docked at Santorini, we hired a moped and took a picnic up to the cliffs, deliberately choosing a spot where we could appreciate the view, but no one else could see us. It sort of backfired this time."

"You hired a moped?" Stephanakis asked, a note of disbelief in his voice.

"Yes, I like scooters." Rose's face cleared. "They remind me of the good old times on the south coast. I used to be a mod, back in the day."

"Me too. Or at least I wanted to be. Never really had the looks." Beatrice shared a complicit smile with Rose, aware she was excluding Stephanakis. The bond and trust with the witness came first. She could explain to him later.

"Where did you get the picnic?" asked Stephanakis.

Maggie answered. "You can order them aboard and they have it ready for just after the ship docks. All beautifully presented in a wee hamper. They even remember the salt."

"And while you watched the man throw the woman through your camera, Mrs Campbell, you didn't take a photograph?"

"No. I wasn't ready... I just watched." Maggie pinched her lips together.

"And you saw nothing at all, Mrs Mason?"

Rose shook her head. "No. I'm not sure if I should be glad or sorry about that. Seeing how much it has traumatised Maggie, part of me is relieved. But I also wish I could back her up with something more concrete when people like that bully of a doctor make it clear they think she's doolally. To answer your question, Inspector, no. I was packing away the picnic and listening to her commentary. But I have no doubt whatsoever that Maggie saw what she says she saw. She was not suffering from heatstroke, she wasn't tipsy and she is in full possession of all her marbles."

The two women exchanged a look which made Beatrice soften. But she had to state facts.

"Thanks for your testimony. I have to be honest and say you are our only witnesses. Inspector Stephanakis has to find proof of what you saw or the case will be deemed accidental death. The pathologist can find no evidence of anything other than a fall. Circumstances suggest she wandered off looking for birdlife and became disorientated and she suffered from a medical condition which may have caused dizziness. Do you see why we have to explore every last detail?"

They both nodded and reached for each other's hands.

"I know reliving the incident is painful, but please, think very hard once again and if you recall anything, give one of us a call. I will be here tomorrow morning, but unless something turns up, I will have to return to London. The Hellenic Police and I really would like to help you, but we have less than twenty-four hours before this will be filed as an accident. Inspector Stephanakis and I will give you our cards."

Back in the casino, her early start, the weight of that cake, the quiet darkness of the casino and the futility of this case threw a torpor over Beatrice. Maggie Campbell's story was wholly convincing, but without proof it was a non-starter as a case.

In several of the late-afternoon interviews, Beatrice struggled to keep her eyes open. More of the coach trip passengers expressed the same platitudes – couldn't believe it... lovely woman... eightieth birthday... only spoken to her half an hour earlier. Why did that make a difference? Why did people always express astonishment at how recently they had communicated with the deceased? As if that phone call, chat in the supermarket, hug before parting conveyed special protection for at least a fortnight.

These were strangers, wedging themselves into the centre of events by dint of being a bystander. Or bysitter, as they had all been on the same coach. They added nothing to the case but much to Beatrice's misanthropy.

Last on the list were the final two Hirondelles. Miss Joyce Milligan, the trip organiser, was the first in the chair. For eighty-one, the woman was remarkable. Quick on her feet, if a little stooped, beady-eyed and with a firm handshake. They progressed through the necessaries. Couldn't believe it ... lovely woman... known her for over fifty years... eightieth birthday... only spoken to her at breakfast... family informed. Saddest Hirondelle cruise they'd ever had.

"Indeed, very sad. Especially, as you say, just after celebrating eighty years of life. Do you know if Mrs Crawford's low blood pressure ever caused dizziness?"

"Not that I know of. She never mentioned anything like that. I know she had poor circulation. Ten minutes in the pool and Esther used to go blue. Esther Williams she was not. She had tablets from the ship's doctor but didn't get on with them."

"Can you tell me a little more about the Hirondelles? How did you all meet and where does the name come from?"

Joyce looked confused for a second. "Oh, has no one explained yet? Well, I have to confess the name was my idea. Most of us, not all, were teachers at the Swallows Hall Academy in Wiltshire. Private girls' school, long since turned into a conference centre. Headmistress for twenty-two years, you know! Before I got the top job, I was originally the French mistress. Doesn't take a detective to work out what 'swallows' is in French." She gave a wheezy laugh. "A gaggle of us became good friends whilst chaperoning the girls on school trips. We had quite some adventures in those days. I could tell you stories that would make your hair curl!"

"I can imagine." Beatrice warmed to the infectious laugh. "So you've been holidaying together for a long time then?"

"We have. Many of us never married, you see. And even those who did rejoined the fold after their chaps died. It's a very special kind of club. We take good care of each other. For many of us, we're all we've got."

The piercing truth of that shook Beatrice fully awake. "I understand. And Esther..."

"Founding member. One of the original Swallows. Of all of us, she was perhaps the healthiest and most full of life. This is why it's so hard to believe. And coming so soon after Beryl, the whole group is grief-stricken and shocked. I'm organising a memorial service for them both because we have to celebrate our happy memories and all the good times we had together. It will help us overcome our sadness now and find a way of coping with future losses. I doubt I'm the only one who's aware that at our age this sort of situation will become more the norm. Every one we lose moves the rest of us further up the queue."

Beatrice looked up from her notebook. "Beryl? Are you saying another of your group died recently?"

"No one told you that either? Beryl Hodges passed away not twenty-four hours after leaving port. Just after Esther's eightieth birthday party. I really don't know if poor Esther fell or was pushed but it's not the way I'd want to go. At least Beryl went peacefully in her sleep. I'll tell you one thing, Detective Inspector, this has been the unluckiest Hirondelle holiday we've ever had."

Chapter 8

Andros Metaxas couldn't speak Greek. The few phrases he did know were delivered with no real attempt at an accent and he made mistakes most school kids would ridicule. Nikos switched to English. It was less painful.

"You're not actually Greek, are you?"

Andros held up his hands in mock surrender. "It's a fair cop, guv."

Nikos frowned. The expression made no sense.

"Oh, come on. Don't look like that! The Brits and the Yanks want the genuine article, your average Spiros from a village with olive groves, a donkey and a couple of legends. They also want someone who speaks English and understands their sense of humour. Ta-da! Andy Redmond becomes Andros Metaxas and everyone's a winner."

The guy reminded Nikos of a TV presenter. Everything he said was designed to raise a laugh or a round of applause. His long legs stretched out in front of him, he leant back in his chair, projecting the image of someone completely at ease.

Nikos kept his head down, writing nonsense notes in Greek, and allowed his other senses to take over. Andy was a smoker. The scent of tobacco mixed with something sweeter emanated from his leather jacket. His ankles twitching against one another could indicate something as innocent as nervous energy. Or not. Nikos looked at him, directly in the eyes. Bloodshot, red-rimmed and constantly shifting. All useful information to be filed.

"Your nationality is not important in itself. Your decision to create a false identity is significant, however. Is your boss aware of this deception?"

Andy pulled an exaggerated expression of stupidity. "Umm, duh, let's see. He has my passport so I guess he does. Listen, it's part of the deal. The excursion staff, the waiters, the sports coaches, the entertainers, we're all playing a role here. This is a pantomime. Glossy front, cardboard back. Give the punters what they want and everyone goes home happy."

"Not Esther Crawford. She goes home in a box."

Andy sat up in his chair. "The worst you can pin on me regarding the old girl's fall is forgetting to do the head count when they got back on the coach. When she took her tumble, I was trying to seat forty-six grandmas in a Fira taverna. I have loads of witnesses."

Nikos's attention was distracted. At the other end of the casino, Detective Stubbs gathered her things and escorted her most recent interviewee to the door.

She came back to his table with a polite nod towards Andy.

"I have to go up to the bridge. I wonder if you could take my last Hirondelle interviewee? Doreen Cashmore." She placed a manila folder on his table. "You'd better read that first."

"Of course."

She walked towards the door, then looked back and gave a reassuring wave in his direction, although her expression was grim.

He turned back to the dopehead in front on him.

"Yes. The worst we can pin on you is causing the premature death of an elderly woman by neglect. That roll call would have saved her life. Whether your omission was due to laziness, incompetence or to mental impairment as a result of consistent drug use is not for me to say."

Andy's eyes looked everywhere but at him. "Yeah right. Classic police tactics. Try to stitch me up for drugs and make me the fall guy..."

"Shut up, Andy." Nikos lowered his tone, but maintained his emotionless expression. "I can ask a staff member to search your cabin right now, and in less than five minutes, no 'stitch-up' would be required. Please understand, that is not my objective. I am here to find out what happened to Esther Crawford while she was under your supervision. Any information you can provide will be useful."

Andy's TV persona slipped away and he hunched forward. "Can I have a glass of water?"

According to the file Beatrice had given him, not seven but eight Hirondelles had boarded the *Empress Louise* just over ten days ago. Nikos wondered why no one had mentioned the name Beryl Hodges up to now. The ladies ranged in age from seventy-seven to eighty-one, all active and lively despite various infirmities. The unexpected departure of Mrs Hodges made it seven and now there were six. As if the shock of losing two of their companions wasn't enough, one death was being investigated as murder.

Fear hung on Doreen Cashmore like a damp coat. One of the youngest at seventy-seven, she told Nikos they had discussed abandoning the cruise and flying home to England.

"My son says not to be so daft and enjoy my holiday, but how can we enjoy ourselves when they're not even cold? We'll miss their funerals and we've always been there for each other. A memorial service is a nice idea, but it's not the same. Any road, no one can relax without knowing what really happened to poor Esther. Why would anyone want to harm her? She wouldn't hurt a fly."

"That's what we want to find out. It seems a silly question, but can you think of any reason why someone might benefit from your friend's death? Would there be anything in her..." Nikos stalled, searching for the word to describe the document. It wasn't testament, not bequest, it was...

"Past?" Doreen's face changed. Her eyes dropped to her hands, where she fiddled with her antique rings. Then she shook her head repeatedly, a gesture designed to be emphatically believable, which had the opposite effect.

"No. Esther and Beryl were both good-hearted, decent women and everything they did was for the best."

Confused, Nikos said nothing, processing her reaction. Doreen rushed to fill the silence.

"Not that Beryl's passing has anything to do with it. It's just bad luck and very sad to lose them both so suddenly, that's all."

The word came back to him. "Do you know if Mrs Crawford and Mrs Hodges had made a will?"

Doreen blinked. "Yes, I think we all have. We often discuss the best way of leaving our affairs in order for when the time comes."

Nikos touched her arm. "Mrs Cashmore, are you sure there's nothing else I should know? Anything from the past that might be relevant?"

She shook her head quickly and withdrew her arm. "I'm sorry. I really can't help you." She placed her hand over her eyes, pulled a tissue from her sleeve and dabbed at her nose.

Nikos recognised ham acting when he saw it. "Thank you, Mrs Cashmore. I think that's all for now. Do you want me to get someone for you?"

"No, no. The others are waiting outside. We'll be fine." She got to her feet and snatched up her handbag, eager to get away.

Nikos watched her leave, his mind replaying her words and in particular, the use of the first person plural.

Chapter 9

Captain Jensson's private rooms were situated right behind the bridge, to Beatrice's surprise. He stood in the doorway, waiting to meet her.

"Great minds think alike. I intended to send someone to find you and invite you to dine with me at the Captain's table this evening. And I would also like to discuss the issue of accommodation and movement. Please come in. Shall I arrange tea?"

"Thank you. No, I'm not thirsty just now. But I do have an urgent question. I've just discovered that Esther Crawford was not the first woman to die on this cruise."

Jensson motioned her inside, pointed to the L-shaped sofa past the desk and closed the door. Beatrice, sufficiently intimidated by the grand surroundings, sat. He pressed a few buttons on the desk phone and came to sit opposite.

"Have you ever enjoyed a cruise, Detective Stubbs? Probably not. I expect a detective is always too busy for real escape. And now, your first encounter with the concept of luxury sailing is to investigate an accidental death. That is really a misfortune."

"Captain Jensson, my question was..."

"Yes, I understand. The reason I ask is not irrelevant. Once you have experienced a cruise, you learn something about crowds. About crowd behaviour. This ship has the size and personality of a small town. I am not exaggerating. We have the same population as many small towns in Western Europe. And all that goes with that. Gossip, sickness, rumour and moods sweep through such a community with astounding speed. There is something physical at the root of this, of course. So many people in an enclosed space. But far more powerful is the psychological reason for sudden paranoia."

Beatrice's irritation grew to bursting point. "If you intend to give me a lecture on discretion, Captain, I will apologise now so we can get to the point."

He shook his head, his serene features not in the least ruffled. "No, that was not my objective. The truth of the matter is I find this collective mentality quite fascinating and hoped to share my enthusiasm. But I see now is not the time. Your question was about the earlier death. What do you want to know?"

His affable manner infuriated Beatrice. "For a start, why were we not informed? A member of the Hirondelle party dies mere hours out of port and no one mentions it when another one falls off a cliff? Surely you can see how it might have been helpful to bring this up earlier."

He got up to reach a leather-bound journal from his desk drawer. After flipping through several pages, he brought it to her. She scanned the list of names, dates, vessels and causes of death.

"Are these...?"

"The people who died under my captaincy. Although I am not directly responsible, I still feel a superstitious obligation to remember these souls. And as I captain ships specialising in pleasure cruises for the elderly, my book rarely reaches our final destination without another new addition."

Beatrice fixed her gaze on him. He gazed steadily back. In the lamplight of the casino, she had assumed his eyes were blue. Now, in the brightness of the sunlit bridge, she could see they were more of a faded green, like a dollar bill.

"What has that got to do with crowd mentality?"

"I am very pleased you asked. This is my point. Cruise ships are an exercise in collective belief. An illusion maintained by mutual will. We promise the 'ultimate luxury experience' and every effort is made to deliver precisely that. The crew are trained to anticipate your every need, catering staff spend months planning menus to suit all palates, entertainers rehearse intensively to ensure a smooth performance, the procurement department ensures a steady supply of far too much food and we all uphold the fallacy that this is the holiday of a lifetime.

"The truth is resolutely ignored and if anyone attempts to face facts, he or she is simply smiled into submission. Because the truth is, this is a sparkling, shiny, hugely expensive, floating rat run. You are given the impression of free will and endless choices, but in reality, you are shuffled from one activity to the next and gently parted from your cash at every opportunity while the message is continually reinforced: you are having such a marvellous time! In exchange for your spending money, you bank images and anecdotes as currency to distribute on your return home as hard proof that it was indeed the holiday of a lifetime."

Beatrice stared at him, speechless.

He smiled. "And you know the saddest thing of all? Many people come back. They like the fact that it's a glorified old people's home with guaranteed good weather. They are completely content with having no real decisions to make. They actually believe the hype and fork out another chunk of their savings to collect another set of photographs, dine with another group of strangers and buy another load of overpriced junk to foist on friends and family.

"Now, you asked about crowd mentality. I've just explained how it usually works. A group delusion keeps us all happy, within our closed community. As long as we all play the game. But closed communities share the same flaw. Just like sickness spreads through the ship faster than gossip, so does discontent. People do not want to be reminded of reality while they're living the dream. And there is no starker reminder of the fragile and temporal nature of our dream than dying. When the average passenger age is over sixty, the spectre of mortality casts a still-longer shadow."

Reflections of sun on water played a blithe denial of Jensson's words across the ceiling. The whiteness, the golden light, the sanitised perfection of their environment... Beatrice could understand the importance of upholding that mythology of the moment.

"So when a person dies, you try to keep it quiet rather than upset the apple tart?"

"We try to minimise disruption for everyone on board. For friends and family, we offer free transfers home and assist with transportation of the deceased. Dr Fraser is a registered coroner and we have a ship's morgue, so if an incident should happen at sea, we can begin the process of formalising the death certificate. It is in everyone's interests to try to isolate the distress and grief of those affected. With heart attacks, strokes or simply passing away in their sleep, that's relatively uncomplicated. Beryl Hodges was one of the latter. Not only that, but it was early into our voyage, and one of the easier ones to manage. However, Esther Crawford's fall set the passengers on edge, even more so when the rumours of homicide came to light. This is why I'm so keen for you to close the case quickly. This kind of atmosphere can poison an entire cruise."

"I appreciate that, Captain, but I am extremely surprised you didn't mention the previous lady's demise to me or Inspector Stephanakis. You say she died in her sleep?"

"Yes. Fraser may have a complicated name for it, but as far as I know, she just stopped breathing. I know nothing of her medical history, but I recorded her death as 'natural causes'. I myself hope for such a calm departure from this life. People fear change. And there is no change greater than death."

Jensson's melancholic world-view began to drag on Beatrice's mood. "I'll look for Dr Fraser now and get the facts. You mentioned accommodation, Captain. There's no need, as I have a hotel in Heraklion."

"Yes, that will be convenient as the *Empress Louise* is sailing to Crete tonight. Generally, we only stay one or two nights in each port, and our delay in Santorini has forced a schedule rearrangement. My question was whether you would like to dine aboard as my guest and sail with us this evening. We have fully equipped guest rooms."

It was tempting. She'd never spent a night on a ship, not even a ferry.

"May I consult with Inspector Stephanakis? I am assisting him in this investigation, so he might have other plans for me."

"Of course. And the offer also extends to him. I would very much enjoy your company. You can send a message via any member of the crew. I believe tonight's menu is shellfish, if that helps persuade you."

On the way back to the casino, Beatrice tried observing the ship through Jensson's jaded eyes. An older couple dozed on sun loungers in the shade; a group of ladies played backgammon under an umbrella and a foursome laughed helplessly as one of their party missed a shot on the crazy golf course. She looked down at the deckchairs and met the eyes of a woman around her own age, who was holding a hefty paperback and reaching out for her cocktail.

She smiled and the woman smiled back, raising her glass. As shiny rat runs go, it could be worse. She decided to stay for dinner. She was partial to a bit of seafood.

Chapter 10

Maureen, my girl, this is the last time. Never again. She even said it aloud.

"Never again, I swear."

No one could say she hadn't tried. She gave it a go but it wasn't for her. If she had her 'druthers, she'd be on a plane home already. It wasn't just the seasickness that ruined the trip. Even when she'd recovered enough to face the others in the dining-room, something she ate upset her stomach all over again. And then that nurse asking what she'd had for lunch. She'd held her tongue and just said she didn't actually know what it was, when what she really wanted to say was 'some foreign muck and rice'. So after a full ten days, she'd barely left the cabin. Holiday to remember indeed.

After all that, today had just about put the tin hat on it. Weak as a kitten, she was, and they'd had her traipsing round old ruins in the midday sun. All she'd said was a cold drink in the shade would be nice and Audrey bit her head off. Called her a Moaning Minnie. It was all very well for her; she and Pat were having a marvellous time, gallivanting around with those jolly-hockey-sticks women, while Muggins was laid up in bed.

Her mouth was dry and her nose half blocked. She sat up and reached for her glasses so she could see what time it was. Quarter to nine. She'd missed dinner. Her own fault for having a nap as soon as she got back. She hadn't really intended to sleep, it was more about making a sulky exit, but a short lie down these days could last for hours. And now she wouldn't be able to sleep tonight. It would be an idea to eat something, just to keep her strength up, but it was very complicated calling cabin service and she had no idea where her hearing aid might be. Maybe she should just take a sleeping tablet and get up early for breakfast.

In the tiny bathroom, she had a cat's lick of a wash, put her teeth in to soak and blew her nose. She took a Benadryl for her congestion, a Restoril to help her sleep, a vitamin C pill and her blood pressure tablet. *Shake me and I'd rattle*, she thought. A good night's sleep and in the morning, she'd apologise to Pat and Audrey for being such a wet blanket. That should make them both feel guilty. She filled a glass with mineral water from the mini-bar because tap water was bound to give her the trots.

Back under the duvet, she set her glass of water on the night-stand, said her prayers and switched off the light. Only another week to go and she'd be home in her own bed, with Herbie curled up on her feet. She missed him, funnily enough. But he wouldn't be missing her. Whenever she left him with Juliet, he came back fatter than ever. She spoilt him rotten. 'I can't resist, Mum. It's that pitiful miaow he makes.' Yes, he had her wrapped around his paw, all right.

A light crossed her eyelids. It took a second to register and she opened her eyes. All in darkness. The ship was lit up like a Christmas tree all night long, so she always closed the curtains. The room was never completely dark, the way she liked it at home, because those wretched floodlights were so bright. She preferred the curtains shut during the day, as the view of sea, sea and more sea got a bit dull after a while, and the glare made it harder to see the telly...

Her eyes flew open. She could smell aftershave. She stiffened and held her breath. Someone was in her cabin. The room seemed full of shapes that could be human; her jacket on the door, the shadow cast by the desk chair, that lump at the end of the bed. Then the lump moved.

She sat up with an intake of breath, her head muddled and dizzy. A man was standing at the foot of her bed. He said something she didn't catch. She reached for her spectacles but couldn't locate them. Instead, she knocked over her glass of water. He came closer.

"Don't touch me! Stay away!" Her voice sounded muffled and querulous. "Who are you?"

Her words came out indistinctly. What with no teeth and her sleeping tablet, even to her own ears she sounded drunk.

He spoke again. Although his voice was low, he sounded polite and unthreatening. She made out the words 'Waitrose' and 'best regards'. A crew member, perhaps, with some sort of delivery?

"Go away now. It's not convenient." Her neck was too weak to support her head. She rubbed at her eyes and forced herself to focus. "Do you hear? You have to go. Goodnight."

Instead of retreating, he came closer. The light spilling through the window illuminated his face. His smile seemed vaguely familiar. He sat on the bed and she noticed his hands. He wore white medical gloves. An orderly from the infirmary come to check on her progress? His smile faded as he looked into her eyes. This time she heard him quite clearly, repeating her words. "No. It's you that has to go. Goodnight."

In one swift move, he shoved her roughly back down on the bed, while clasping his right hand over her nose and mouth. Her arm flew out and hit the nightstand. Purely out of instinct, she grasped the cord of the telephone. He loomed over her and pressed his knee onto her chest. Her lungs convulsed, the impulse for air desperate. She writhed and kicked and twisted, yanking the telephone to the floor. The crushing pressure on her chest increased as she rained feeble blows on her attacker. White spots appeared in her vision and she seemed to be falling, through the mattress, through the floor, through the bowels of the ship, through the deep blackness of the sea, down and down and down to where it was finally, truly dark.

Chapter 11

Chief Inspector Voulakis sounded pleased.

"*So tomorrow you can file the report? Accidental death, unreliable witnesses, positive outcome of collaboration with London. That is music to my ears!*"

Nikos shifted the phone to his other ear as ran up two steps at a time and unlocked his front door. Karen's singing reached him from the kitchen, along with a delicious smell of roasting meat and rosemary.

"No promises, sir. But we've made a thorough investigation. Doctors, witnesses, travelling companions, crew. Apart from one lady's account, there's no evidence of foul play. Detective Stubbs is staying on board tonight, but unless something turns up tomorrow morning, we'll have no choice but to close the case."

"*Excellent! Good work, Stephanakis. By the way, the Scotland Yard detective. Stubbs. What's she like?*"

"Smart. She's really easy to work with. It's actually been a pleasure."

"*Enjoy it while you can. The next case is bound to be a bastard. Come into the station tomorrow evening and we'll have a beer to celebrate your first successful result! Have a good evening.*"

Karen watched him from the kitchen doorway, her eyes curious and a smile hovering in the wings. He replaced his phone in his jacket and put his briefcase on the chair.

"So Inspector, how was your day?" Her voice was husky. "Have you solved The Murder on the *Empress Louise* yet?" She slipped her arms around his back and pulled him to her, tilting her face for a kiss.

He obliged.

"This time tomorrow, my love, it will all be over. Voulakis will be buying me beer and I'll be celebrating my first case not only filed in Greek but also in English."

She hunched her shoulders with excitement and kissed him again. "How's it going? Is the Scotland Yard woman being kind to you? She's not sexy, is she?" Her eyes narrowed in faux jealousy.

"She's nice. She keeps reminding me that I'm in charge and doesn't play power games like most of the men I've worked with. She doesn't even correct my English when I know I'm making mistakes."

"Nice deflection. I asked you if she's sexy. How old? What does she look like?"

"No, I wouldn't describe her as sexy. But I do like her as a person. I'm not good at guessing ages. Mid fifties? She's short, but very upright and always alert, like a squirrel. Bright eyes and funny hair."

"Oooh-kaaay. So now I'm picturing a rodent in a clown wig." Her arms circled his waist.

"Not exactly. I'll find a photo on the Internet. It's a pity this case will be over so soon. I'm learning a lot from working with her. A few more days would be perfect. Why is it British women always teach me so much? Talking of which, how was your day?"

"Boring. The Director of Studies has increased class sizes, my Proficiency group wants individual feedback and the receptionist has got nits. Who cares?" She looked at him under her lashes. "My man is home. I've put lamb and potatoes in the oven, but that will take another twenty minutes. So why don't we go upstairs and I can continue your education?"

She led him by the hand up the narrow staircase. On the

landing, he caught sight of himself and his gleeful expression in the mirror. It made him laugh.

Beatrice too was grinning into the mirror. Who'd have thought the frumpy detective would scrub up so well? Despite having left all her clothes, jewellery and most of her make-up at the hotel, the ship's housekeeping staff had come to the rescue. They proved priceless. A charming lady checked her sizes and hurried off to the formal hire facility. Jensson was not exaggerating – this really was a small, perfectly equipped town. From the selection she delivered, Beatrice opted for a long black dress with a short spangled jacket. Her assistant assessed the outfit, and went off to seek jewels, shoes and a handbag. Meanwhile, the original lady made her an appointment at one of the various hair salons for a blow-dry and make-up session. In less than an hour, Beatrice was transformed into someone worthy of the Captain's table.

She tore her eyes from the glittering stranger in the mirror and looked around her cabin with some regret. It would be so indulgent to stay here, order room service and lounge around on this wonderful bed, admiring herself in the full-length mirror. But this five-star guest suite was thus named because its occupants had guestly duties. And her host awaited. She gave her reflection one last arch look, practised a gracious smile, picked up her key card and ventured onto the deck.

Halfway down the staircase leading to the Grand Dining Room, she hesitated. One could not fail to be impressed by the opulence. Chandeliers, starched napkins, gilt pillars, flower arrangements, two tiers of balconies as if it were a theatre, polished wood and the sparkle of crystal glassware managed to be simultaneously enticing and forbidding. She wanted a second to squeeze her eyes shut so she might imagine herself in the past, and also to stifle a giggle.

"Good evening. I presume this is your first visit to the Grand Dining Room? Most new arrivals need to stop at this point, if only to decide on their own responses to such flamboyance.

Some say awesome, others say awful. Have you made up your mind?"

Beatrice recognised the man as the one who had given her directions to the infirmary earlier that day, although he was now dressed in black tie. It suited him. "Good evening. I'm not sure I have. I suppose the one thing one cannot accuse them of is false advertising."

"Very true. I believe we're dining at the same table tonight, unless my guess is wrong and you are not the police detective from Scotland Yard."

"Yes, that's right. Beatrice Stubbs. Pleased to meet you."

"Oscar Martins. Likewise. Did you find the infirmary in the end?"

They shook hands and then he offered his arm in a curiously old-fashioned gesture. Amused, Beatrice placed her hand on his forearm and they proceeded down the steps.

"We did, thank you. Your directions were spot on. Lord knows how long we would have been wandering about otherwise. This ship must be full of lost souls trying to find their way home."

"A description uncomfortably close to the truth, I'd say. Here we are. Good evening, Captain Jensson. By happenstance I met Detective Stubbs on the staircase and took the liberty of escorting her."

At the circular table sat a middle-aged couple, a scowling elderly lady, and between the captain and Dr Fraser, a pretty Japanese woman.

Captain Jensson stood to make the introductions. "Mr and Mrs Simmonds from High Wycombe, Ms Ishii from Kyoto, Dr Fraser is our senior medical practitioner and this is Mrs Bartholomew who lives in Boston. Ladies and gentlemen, I'd like you to meet Mr Martins from Cambridge and Detective Inspector Stubbs, who's just joined us from London."

Beatrice followed Oscar's example, nodding and smiling around the table, with a general, 'Nice to meet you' before taking her seat. Mr Simmonds, a bland-looking individual with wholly forgettable features, rubbed his hands together.

"Lucky me. I get to sit next to Miss Marple. I've always wanted to pick the brains of a lady detective."

Mrs Simmonds giggled. "Don't be naughty, Don."

Beatrice smiled. "And I'll be happy to share whatever you'd like to know. With the obvious exception of the case I'm here to investigate, of course."

A beat of silence, then the frowning lady spoke. "We were all looking forward to hearing about your progress. It's the only topic of conversation aboard. Surely you can share a few little tidbits amongst friends?"

"It would be extremely unprofessional for a detective, lady or otherwise, to discuss ongoing enquiries. So I'm afraid 'tidbits' are off the menu tonight. But I understand we'll be dining on shellfish, Captain, is that correct?"

Jensson picked up his cue and the conversation moved onto the quality of Greek crustaceans. Ignoring the stony glares from at least three of the party, Beatrice attempted to involve the Japanese woman in conversation, but after extracting the information that Ms Ishii was a classical pianist, Mrs Bartholomew interrupted.

"Detective Stubbs, why are you here?"

Before Beatrice could gather her thoughts, Dr Fraser jumped in. "Good question. I think Captain Jensson over-reacted a wee bit. Even if you do need to take an old lady's imagination seriously, I can't for the life of me understand why you'd involve Scotland Yard. The local boys are perfectly capable of digging about, finding nothing and recording a verdict of accidental death. Waste of time and resources."

The first course arrived, an oval dish with tiny dabs of baba ghanouj and hummus, punctuated by mini falafel and dolmas, decorated with olives and a salad garnish. A waiter placed a basket of warm pitta bread between each pair and began pouring the wine.

Jensson seemed at a loss as to whether to ignore or respond to the physician's comment and the party watched the waiter's progress in silence. Finally, as the captain's glass was filled, Oscar raised his.

"Regardless of why we're here, let's enjoy fine food and good company. Cheers everyone!"

Beatrice, relieved at Oscar's gracious behaviour, lifted her glass to join the others. The lines on Jensson's forehead smoothed. The Bartholomew trout's did not but she toasted anyway. Timing was of the essence. As soon as glasses were replaced on the table, like a crack team trained in the art of diplomatic small talk, Oscar enquired as to the weather in Boston, Jensson asked Ms Ishii's opinion of the string quartet and Beatrice turned to her neighbour.

"So tell me, Mr Simmonds, what are house prices like in High Wycombe?"

The seafood platter surpassed all expectations. Shells, claws, the remnants of lemon wedges and well-used finger bowls littered the table, while compliments poured forth in abundance. Their party began to break up almost immediately. Dr Fraser was called to an emergency, Mrs Simmonds wanted to get a good seat in the auditorium for the evening's Rat Pack Repertoire and Ms Ishii excused herself, claiming further practice was required for tomorrow's recital. Beatrice felt increasingly relaxed by each departure. Oscar sat back to allow the waiting staff to clear his plate.

"My favourite kind of meal: varied, perfectly cooked, reasonably healthy and incredibly messy. Tell me, do I have any scales stuck to my face?"

Beatrice laughed. "Not that I can see, but the lighting is subdued. It really was a feast, I agree. I'm very glad I stayed for dinner. And I must remember to make a note of that wine."

"Indeed. Deceptively light, but it works its magic." He glanced in the direction of Mrs Bartholomew, whose face was flushed, but not softened as she bent the captain's ear.

Beatrice dropped her voice. "And I thought avoiding icebergs would be the worst part of the poor man's job."

"Icebergs can take many forms. Now I'm going to respect my waistline and decline dessert. However, an espresso and a digestif might round off the evening rather well. I plan to head for the Club Room. No entertainment other than some muffled Mahler, but they do decent coffee and their collection of single malts could bring tears to your eyes. Would you like to join me?"

"I would, but is that not terribly rude?" She flicked her eyes towards the beleaguered captain.

"Captain Jensson? Detective Stubbs and I have enjoyed ourselves enormously. Thank you for a truly memorable meal. We would like to round the evening off with a little dancing. Could we tempt you and Mrs Bartholomew to join us? The Kit Kat Club has an excellent jazz band."

"Thank you, Mr Martins, but I'm afraid my evening is dedicated to the usual routine checks. But I hope you enjoy the music. I am a big fan of jazz." Jensson looked genuinely regretful.

"Oh, of course. But how about you, Mrs Bartholomew?"

"Dancing? In the middle of a meal? My doctor advises nothing more strenuous after dinner than retiring to the couch since my operation. I wonder if it's conducive to digestion at any age, to be honest. No, I intend to withdraw to my cabin, order room service and enjoy my dessert in peace. I bid you all a pleasant evening."

They all stood to say goodbye. Jensson's relief at Mrs Bartholomew's departure was almost visible. Almost. He shook their hands, offered them a hint of a wry grin and hurried off in the opposite direction.

Beatrice faced Oscar. "And what if they'd said yes?"

He shrugged. "We'd have been forced to go dancing. A risk I was willing to take. It's been a while but I can still remember how to lindy-hop. Come on now, you've been rescued. Let's make the most of it."

The Club Room, as promised, was a real haven from the sensory assault of the Grand Dining-Room. Leather wingback chairs, wood panelled walls, thick carpet, green velvet curtains, hidden spotlights and a gleaming oak bar all combined to create the illusion of a traditional London gentleman's club. Beatrice even fancied she could smell cigar smoke. A few other people populated the place, the majority male and sitting alone with a newspaper or mobile phone, with the occasional couple tucked away in one of the booths. Oscar indicated a small table to their left.

"Ideally situated. Clear view of the bar, well positioned to observe newcomers and high-backed chairs to protect us against draughts."

A waiter, perfectly turned out in waistcoat and tie, appeared at their side with a drinks menu as they seated themselves. Beatrice opted for a decaffeinated coffee and chose a port wine from the extensive list. Oscar didn't need the menu, but ordered a Macallan to go with his espresso. He was evidently a familiar face, addressing the waiter by name, and nodding to a pair of bespectacled gents as they'd entered. He settled back with a contented smile and rested his gaze on her.

"So, let's hear a bit about Beatrice Stubbs. How long have you been a 'Lady Detective'?"

She chuckled. "I shouldn't get so frosty about it, really. Being called a lady detective is better than how my superior officer usually refers to me, which is either a 'bloody woman' or a 'stubborn old coot'. Let's see, I've been a detective inspector for almost fifteen years now."

"Oh, an inspector? Excuse me, I was unaware of your full title. A detective inspector from Scotland Yard. Here, on a cruise ship, in the Club Room. It's all a bit Cluedo, don't you think?"

"Coupled with the suspicious death, I suppose it is. I've never been on one of these ships before, so I'm finding it all rather an adventure. But I get the impression you are quite the seasoned cruise traveller."

"Your impression is correct, Detective Inspector. I am a veteran of these trips and have been ever since I lost my wife seven years ago. Ah, and here are the drinks. Thank you, Alex. While she was alive, we were adventurers, exploring less-travelled paths and making discoveries. After she died, adventuring seemed too much like hard work. I booked my first cruise with the aim of having everything done for me. And although I found giving up all freedom of choice too much to bear, I grew to like the itinerary being taken out of my hands. So when we dock, I hire a car and go off and do my own thing. But come back to join everyone again in the evening and sail onto the next port. And I have met some fascinating people on board. Someone like yourself would fall into that category."

Beatrice stirred a brown sugar lump into her coffee. "Nice of you to say so. Tell me, what do you do when you're not sailing the Mediterranean?"

"I'm a language historian, or a historical linguist, I'm never quite sure which. Semi-retired, in that I do very little teaching these days. But I publish in various journals and occasionally write articles for magazines, while continuing the Sisyphean task of completing my book."

"Ooh, a writer! What's the book about?"

"You'll be surprised to know it's about the history of language. Or to be precise, the death of it. I have previously completed two modest volumes, one called *Stories of the Atlantic Arc*, all about the linguistic connections between the Celts. The second was called *Mother Tongue: The Word of God*, which explores the relationship between language and religion. Hugely popular with insomniacs, apparently. Shall we toast? To inspiration and resolution!"

"I'll drink to that," said Beatrice, and lifted her tawny port towards the chandelier. The light in Oscar's laughing eyes matched the colour perfectly. They chinked glasses and held each other's gaze as they drank. *Nothing more than good manners*, she thought.

Velvety tones of sweet fat grapes danced on her tongue, a hint of sherry wood teased her nose and a gentle warmth spread down her throat and across her chest.

"Now that is an absolute jewel of a digestif. I only chose it because I liked the name, but it's delicious. What was it called again?"

Oscar checked the drinks menu. "Offley. Sounds more Irish than Portuguese. Not a name you'd forget, in any case."

"Nor a taste. Somehow robust and delicate at the same time."

A smile elevated Oscar's cheeks. "A charming description!"

The young waiter hovered at the table, his demeanour anxious. "So sorry to interrupt. Captain Jensson needs Detective Inspector Stubbs urgently. He asked if you could meet him at Cabin C343. It's on level C3. Would you like someone to show you the way?"

Oscar stood and reached into his pocket. "No need, Alex. I know C3 very well. I can escort the detective. Thank you and have a good evening." He pressed a note into the young man's hand, drained his whisky and gestured in the direction of the door. "After you, Detective Inspector. The devil waits for no man. Or lady."

Chapter 12

Typical of his luck. Instead of a successful conclusion and celebratory beers with the boss, Nikos was woken the wrong side of midnight and instructed to get to the port, ready to meet the *Empress Louise*. A second fatality had occurred during the sailing from Santorini.

This time there was no doubt. Maureen Hall had died a violent death. The telephone had been yanked from the wall, a water glass shattered on the floor and – a detail which emphasised the victim's frailty – a pair of senior citizen spectacles had been crushed underfoot. On first inspection, the doctor confirmed the body showed all the signs of having been smothered.

Nikos withdrew from the sad scene in the little cabin, leaving the forensics team to find what they could. At least Captain Jensson had been smart enough to prevent anyone other than DI Stubbs from entering after the initial discovery. She knew better than he did how to manage a crime scene. Now that the body had been removed, the little room was filled with people and light. He yawned as he turned the corner of the corridor, feeling guilty as he did so, and found himself face to face with the two ladies who had 'witnessed' the death of Esther Crawford.

"Inspector...?"

"Ladies, you should be in bed. I can tell you nothing at this stage."

The taller one interrupted. "You don't need to. Why else

would this corridor be filled with police and people so early in the morning? We know someone is dead. Sheer common sense will tell you all this fuss means it's unlikely to be due to natural causes."

"I must ask you to vacate the corridor now. I am sorry and I understand your concern, but until we find out what happened, it makes no sense to talk about it. Do you understand why I must ask you to leave?"

The little lady from Scotland shook her head in regret. "We'll let you do your job, Inspector. But please get to the bottom of this. Something is very wrong here."

He bowed his head. "I am going to do my best."

Her friend looked at him intently. "Are you on your own now? Did Detective Stubbs go back to Britain?"

"No, she's still here. It seems she will stay on a few days if she can get permission. Please can I ask you now to return to your cabins...?"

"... and lock the doors? Oh yes, we most certainly will. Goodnight, officer, and good luck."

Nikos watched them walk away down the corridor, heads bent in conversation.

They were right. Something was indeed very wrong here.

Maureen Hall. Seventy-four years old, a widow with one daughter, born in Yorkshire and lived there all her life. Confined to her cabin for the majority of the voyage due to illness. Travelling with two friends, first cruise experience. No apparent connection to Esther Crawford or the Hirondelles or anyone else aboard. Retired to her cabin after returning from an excursion at 17.50, according to the key card records. No further activity until another entry at 22.08. The telephone system indicated an attempted call at 22.14, but no number was dialled. The ship's switchboard staff, geared to anticipate the needs of its population, relayed the aborted call to the cabin attendant service, who sent a member of housekeeping to check all was well. Nina Sousa attended at 22.21. On receiving no reply, she returned to the staff room to collect her access card and notify her line manager of her intention. At 22.24, Maureen Hall's key card was replaced in the main socket which controlled the cabin's electricity. When Ms Sousa returned and entered the cabin at 22.31, she found the inhabitant deceased and evident signs of a struggle.

Nikos sat on the bridge, watching the dawn break over Heraklion, his home and a place he'd never seen before from this angle. The liner had arrived three hours ago, after sending news of the sudden death of Maureen Hall, to interrupt another night's sleep. He hoped DI Stubbs would achieve her aim in insisting the *Empress Louise* remain at anchor for another twenty-four hours. She faced a formidable opponent in Jensson. A company man, his concern was for the shareholders and stakeholders, should their schedule be disrupted. The paying customers seemed of lesser importance.

Dr Weinberg delivered the ship's medical records for Maureen Hall with a sombre greeting. Nikos appreciated it, not being one for small talk at eight in the morning either. After the quiet Austrian had departed with an equally curt farewell, he trawled through the details. Only two things the dead women had in common: blood pressure problems – but in opposite directions; one low, one high – and the fact they had both attended the ship's infirmary.

He bought a coffee from the buffet counter and took it out onto the deck. He needed some space to think. Wiltshire and Yorkshire. He pulled up a map of Britain on his phone, but saw the two counties were sufficiently far apart to make the geographical connection unlikely. He checked records of elderly deaths in each, which was when he encountered the name of Dr Harold Shipman.

The case rang a distant bell. The doctor who administered fatal doses of painkilling drugs to elderly female patients. A serial killer of 250 people, infamous in Britain, well known around the world. Nikos looked at the image and tried to imagine the motivation. None of the articles he skimmed indicated the doctor had given any kind of explanation for his actions. A twisted version of mercy killing, despite the fact so many of his patient-victims were healthy and happy? The jewellery, the savings... was his motive mercenary? Or born of altruism, a desire to save people from pain?

And here, on this peaceful, harmless cruise, why would someone wish to end the lives of these particular women? Esther Crawford and Maureen Hall led quiet lives, enjoying their retirement, until someone decided their time was up. He made a note to check the beneficiaries of their wills and ask the doctor a lot more questions about the death of Beryl Hodges.

Nikos sat back and watched early rays of sun cast long shadows across the harbour. He slugged the remaining coffee from his cup and thought back over the past two days.

Dr Fraser and his anger at everyone, including the police. The coroner, Apostolou and his quick decision regarding the fall. The clear resentment towards him and DI Stubbs from many of the staff on board. Jensson's assertion that old people tend to die. Conspiracy theories were part of a police inspector's job, but he still couldn't find the motive for any of these men to commit murder. Older people, ladies in particular, were the life blood of the cruise ship system, so killing them off would be senseless. Apostolou took care of his elderly mother himself, so he would sympathise with the hazards of old age.

He looked back at the expressionless face of Harold Shipman. No, neither the doctor nor the captain could possibly be in the frame. Even as he thought it, Nikos planned the investigation of both.

Beatrice Stubbs, despite her dramatically different appearance, looked tired and irritable as she returned from the bridge. Nikos was waiting for her outside her guest cabin, at her suggestion. The casino was not an option and both were reluctant to use the captain's office.

She gave him a humourless jerk of the head in greeting as she unlocked the door.

"What a bloody awful situation!" she said, flinging her handbag onto the table. "Please make yourself at home, Inspector, I'll just be a moment." She closed the door to the bedroom section and Nikos stood at the floor-to-ceiling windows, watching as the coastline came to life and signs of activity began in the morning light. Somewhere over there his beautiful girlfriend lay under a blue cotton sheet, her hair spread over the pillow, soon to wake up alone.

A knock brought him back to the here and now. He opened the door to a cabin attendant, who carried a tray of coffee and pastries. He thanked the man and took it with a smile. Detective Stubbs might have spent a sleepless, stressful night, but she was in no danger of losing her appetite.

She emerged from the sleeping quarters dressed in shirt and trousers with a towel around her head.

"Oh good, the coffee's here. Right, I'm ready to begin. Where shall we start?"

Nikos hesitated, but only for a second. "I'd like to hear what the immediate plans are. Did Jensson confirm the sailing time?"

"He did. The ship has to depart this evening. Their schedule is extremely tight since the hold-up in Santorini. They must set sail for Rhodes at midnight. Help yourself to milk and sugar. What about the body?"

"Taken to the city morgue for a complete post-mortem. We should have the results sometime later today. Then arrangements can be made to fly her home. I agree with your initial assessment of the scene. It looks as if the perpetrator was disturbed. On top of that, I think he was still in the cabin when the maid knocked. In the time it took her to fetch an access card, he managed to get out and disappear."

"What makes you say that?"

"I got the printout of the cabin's card activity. Inside the room there's a socket, just like this one in yours. After you open the door, you slot the key card into that socket and all the electricity works. If the card is removed, the lights don't work. It was removed at 22.08, and replaced at 22.24." He stirred his coffee. "That's not long to kill someone."

Beatrice looked up from her croissant. "Long enough. What about how the intruder got in? Any records on that?"

"A staff access card was used at 22.06. One of many used by housekeeping. They are not assigned to individuals and if you are a staff member, they're easy to find."

They both remained silent for several seconds. Nikos searched for a way of broaching his thoughts on potential suspects, but first he needed to know how much longer he would have his British back-up.

"I suppose it was too early for you to contact Scotland Yard?" he asked.

She chewed and swallowed. "No. I managed to get hold of Chief Inspector Hamilton, and I'm afraid there's good news and bad news. I am permitted to stay and work on this case, but the powers-that-be would like me to take a more active role. What happened tonight has raised the goalposts. We're talking about a potential serial killer of British citizens, albeit on Greek territory. My boss would like me to lead the investigation and unfortunately, he intends to contact your superior officer today."

Nikos tensed his jaw. He should have expected this. Voulakis would agree, of course he would. In fact, he would be stupid to argue.

"I understand, Detective Inspector Stubbs. But I hope I can continue to work with you. I'm learning a lot."

"Listen." She dusted flakes of pastry from her hands. "Depending on what your superior says, this is what I propose. A collaborative investigation, jointly led by British and Greek agents. Partners, if you like. I will need your local expertise, but I believe I can bring a certain amount of experience to bear. What do you say?"

Nerves made Nikos clumsy and he clattered his cup back

onto the saucer. "I say that is a very generous proposal. I would like that very much."

"But I do have one thing I need to get off my chest. On my return from the bridge, I met our two witnesses, Mrs Campbell and Mrs Mason. They were on their way back to their quarters in some state of alarm. Apparently, you had advised them to stay in their cabins and lock the doors. I appreciate the good intention behind your advice, but in an environment such as this, it might be better to avoid generating panic."

Nikos deliberated over what to say, aware of the heat creeping up his neck.

"DI Stubbs, I asked them to leave the corridor where we are investigating. I suggested they go back to their cabins, mainly because it was so early. They were the ones who mentioned locking doors. I can assure you I was not trying to alarm anyone."

"I see. Captain Jensson has a point. It is terribly easy to spook a flock like this, especially when they're looking for a reason to get hysterical. I'm sorry. I had my doubts but thought it best to check. And one other thing, if we're going to be partners, can we drop the formalities? My name is Beatrice."

"No problem. Call Nikos."

"Nice working with you, Nikos." She offered her hand and they shook.

"You too, Beatrice."

"Now, tell me your thoughts on how we proceed."

He was ready for this and had thought of nothing else since he'd received the call. "While we wait for the crime scene results, we research the three deaths on this cruise. We need to find out more about Beryl Hodges and make one hundred percent certain her death was natural."

"My thoughts exactly. I will call London and get them to organise a PM. I hope to God they've not buried her yet. Or worse still, she might have been cremated."

"If so, we'll have to look for the information elsewhere. Next, we seek connections between Esther Crawford and Maureen

Hall. I think we should interview the doctors again, Fraser in particular. I also want to talk to the captain. Something about that book you mentioned, his deaths record, makes me uncomfortable. And the ship's security team must have information about who we can eliminate from the crew by providing alibis. The only thing..." He tailed off, not wishing to admit it.

"Motive?"

Nikos nodded. "Exactly. I can't understand who would benefit from killing two elderly women."

"So that's what we need to work out. When we know why, we will find who."

Chapter 13

None of the infirmary's medical staff had enjoyed an uninterrupted eight hours sleep, and a large percentage of the passengers found themselves afflicted that morning by a variety of nervous disorders, requiring a visit to the morning surgery. Short fuses were to be expected. Dr Fraser's air of barely contained rage had an oddly soothing effect on Beatrice. The more he spluttered and swore, the calmer she became. Nikos impressed her by not rising to the doctor's aggression, and simply restating their requests for information.

"Just to be clear, the death certificate for Beryl Hodges was signed by you and Dr Weinberg? Did the other doctor actually examine her or did you alone determine she died of natural causes?" asked Nikos.

"You have the certificate in front of you! It's there in black and white! As senior physician and official coroner on board, I have every right to make a professional assessment without wasting my colleague's time. She died peacefully in her sleep. The woman suffered from obstructive sleep apnoea. She used a CPAP machine at home but didn't bring it with her. The condition means you stop breathing for a few seconds during the night, but then your system, or machine, kicks in and you clear the blockage. If you don't, for whatever reason, it causes oxygen deprivation, and eventually leads to asphyxia. When someone dies of asphyxia aboard, there is always a concern about insufficient ventilation, or exposure to noxious gases. So I check thoroughly. Yes, obviously for insurance, but also because I'm a professional physician and my own reputation is at stake. The truth is the woman was old, she had asthma and her lungs couldn't cope. Congestion added to the frequent blockage to her breathing and her system shut down due to a lack of oxygen."

His strident voice and expansive gestures echoed around his compact consulting room. Nikos wrote detailed comments in his notebook, but Beatrice kept her eyes on the doctor. His hostility, his easy explanation, his curious refusal to see a connection made her wary. She studied his manner. His eyes, with all the warmth of pack ice, shifted constantly between her and Nikos. He often ran his bony hands through his thick hair, dislodging flakes of dandruff onto his shoulders. While she and Nikos sat still and calm opposite him, he shifted and twitched with extraordinary impatience.

Beatrice waited till he'd finished speaking. "We believe Maureen Hall was smothered. Correct me if I'm wrong, but wouldn't an obstruction over the face asphyxiate a person in much the same way as sleep apnoea? Were there any other marks on Beryl Hodges that could support that theory?"

Fraser rolled his eyes. "How many times must I tell you people...?"

"Dr Fraser. Sorry to interrupt." Nikos sat forward, his palms open in appeal. "We are not trying to cause problems for you. Two ladies died in a similar way, one of whom was murdered. Police procedure is to seek any connection which leads us closer to finding who killed Maureen Hall. As we have another suspicious death to add to this case, the job of the police is complicated and difficult. We want to work with other professionals as a team, not make enemies."

Fraser considered, his physical fidgeting in abeyance. "Fair point. It's just this calling of my professional competence into question... Look, there was no need for a detailed post-mortem on Beryl Hodges. As I explained, her sleep disorder coupled with asthma explained why she stopped breathing and I had no reason to look any further."

Beatrice gave a sympathetic smile. "Understood. And as it was over ten days ago, I doubt you'd remember any unusual injuries."

Nikos shot a sly glance sideways at Beatrice and bent his head over his notebook.

"The problem with women of that age is their susceptibility. Their bones are fragile, their balance is unreliable, their digestive system is inevitably problematic and their skin... their skin can tell many stories, but we don't know which is which. By that I mean injuries heal far more slowly than they do in the young, they bruise easily, and often tend to cause themselves more damage than others."

"By which I gather Beryl Hodges bore some marks you could not explain?" asked Beatrice.

Fraser ran his hands through his hair once more. "There was a certain amount of bruising to her face, especially the left side of her jaw. Any number of explanations for that, so it wasn't worth including in my report. Cause of death was clear."

"I see." Beatrice closed her files. "Doctor, can I ask you, when you have a minute, to think about that incident once again? In the light of what has just happened, and the pathology report on Maureen Hall, I think it might be worth turning every stone. Even those already turned."

"Yes, I'll think about it in the unlikely event I get a minute. Now I really need to start on the backlog of paperwork." Fraser picked up a pen and Beatrice noticed his hands were unsteady.

"Just for the record, doctor. You left the captain's table at around quarter to ten. I believe you were called to an emergency?"

"Are you telling me I need to provide an alibi?" His grey-blue eyes were incredulous.

"Only so we can eliminate you. Or we wouldn't be doing our job," said Nikos.

"There was no emergency. I just had to get away from that

Bartholomew woman. Her accent drove me up the pole."

Beatrice could understand that. "So where did you go, if you don't mind my asking?"

"Back to my cabin. Stayed there the rest of the night." The man spoke through clenched teeth.

"Thank you. We'll let you get on."

"About bloody time."

Exhaustion aside, Beatrice's respect for the young Greek inspector kept growing. He showed great timing and excellent instinct, even though he'd been dragged out of bed in the small hours. Nikos Stephanakis, she decided, was destined for great things.

Beatrice and Nikos split up to interview the nurse, Sister Bannerjee, and Assistant Physician Dr Weinberg. She sat opposite the weary little nurse who was so washed out even her bindi looked faded. Beatrice began her introductory speech.

"Sister Bannerjee, the only reason I am here is to clarify..."

"Detective Inspector, I am very sorry for my rudeness and for my disloyalty but I have to tell the truth to a police officer. Dr Fraser is not a good doctor and makes many short cuts. The routine here is 'P and PO'. Excuse my language, but this means 'Prescribe and Piss Off'. We have to push the medicines of our sponsors, encouraging injections and vitamin supplements and we send our patients away with a packet of pills and no idea of the root cause of their problems. I have spoken to the captain about this issue on several occasions, but this whole enterprise is only about making money from the weak and vulnerable. DI Stubbs, on this ship, something is rotting. Now at last, it eventually floats to the surface."

The sincere face opposite astonished Beatrice. Beneath the mask of friendly efficiency lay an anger and passion which had found its voice.

"I see there is a great deal to discuss. But first, Sister, I have a question regarding Beryl Hodges. Did you happen to see her body? Dr Fraser tells me there was some bruising to her face."

The horizontal frown lines on the nurse's forehead contracted into sympathetic verticals. "I assisted at the medical examination and yes, I saw the bruising. Chiefly on the left side, on her cheek and jaw. Older people bruise easily."

"So you didn't think there was anything suspicious about her death?"

The woman's eyes widened and Beatrice detected a flash of anger. "Let me guess. He told you about the bruising and the fact she was asthmatic. Did he say anything else?"

"Anything else regarding the body? No, I don't think so."

"Perhaps he forgot to mention the Emerade."

Beatrice stopped writing and lifted her head very slowly to meet the nurse's eyes.

"I beg your pardon?"

"Mrs Hodges had several doses of Emerade in her cabin's fridge. It's an adrenalin auto-injector. People who are at risk of anaphylactic shock, those with allergies to insect stings or certain foods, need to be prepared to inject epinephrine or adrenalin directly into their systems to counter the effects of anaphylaxis."

"The sort of swelling-up and can't-breathe effects?"

"That's part of it, yes. Asthmatics are a particularly high-risk group. Dr Fraser performed tests on her lungs to ensure there was no inhalation of toxic fumes but did not test for symptoms of anaphylactic shock. To be fair to him, it would have required laboratory conditions and a full post-mortem. He said it was unnecessary and saw no need to add it to the report."

Beatrice put down her pad and thought. Then she walked over to the examination table in the spotless nurse's station.

"Sister, I am going to lie down here and I want you to attempt to force something into my mouth. Let's do this in slow motion. Remember, I am old and feeble and probably asleep. How would you do it?"

Sister Bannerjee stood, blinking for a moment. Then she exhaled sharply with a nod.

"OK. First thing, Mrs Hodges had an interior cabin on B1.

That means her bed was against the cabin wall. You need to turn the other way. If I was going to attack her, I would have no choice but to come at her from the right." She placed herself at the foot of the examination table. "One minute please, I need to lower it. This table is much higher than the beds on board."

Adjustments made, she gestured for Beatrice to get into position.

"She would have been sleeping on her side. I think. On the back is the worst way for someone with her condition to sleep. Now, I come into the cabin and..."

She pulled Beatrice's shoulder gently, rolling her onto her back. Beatrice opened her eyes. The nurse pressed her left arm against Beatrice's windpipe and used her right hand to steady Beatrice's jaw. She lifted her left hand and prised Beatrice's teeth apart, picked up an imaginary object and poked it into her mouth. Beatrice, in character, bulged her eyes, struggled weakly and began to choke. Sister Bannerjee used her body weight to hold Beatrice down and brought her right knee up to press on her victim's chest. They made eye contact and the nurse's fierce expression of concentration dissipated. She released Beatrice and stepped back, straightening her uniform.

"Perhaps I should have locked the door before attempting to kill a police detective," she said, an awkward smile surfacing.

Beatrice swung her legs off the table and sat up. "You're right-handed. Any marks made by your fingers would be on the left-hand side of my face."

"Yes, but anaphylaxis rarely works that quickly. It depends what allergies Mrs Hodges had, but if that is what killed her, it is far more likely she was stung by something or ingested a trigger at least an hour earlier. Leaving her time to get up, inject herself and call for help."

"So why would someone need to hold her face?"

The nurse opened her palms. "I just don't know. She might have even made the marks herself. Who knows? Now it's too late to do a complete post-mortem examination."

"Perhaps. Thanks for your assistance, Sister. I think I should talk to the senior physician again. One last thing..."

She shook her head. "No. Dr Fraser is left-handed."

Captain Jensson did his best to persuade Beatrice to stay another night on board, dangling the offer of a place at his table, but she remained steadfast in her determination to return to her hotel. Even lamb kebabs could not sway her. There was the meeting with Nikos's superior to be navigated, she had several phone calls to make and if the truth were told, the atmosphere on board was stifling. As she followed Nikos down the endlessly looping gangway, she reflected on the ridiculousness of such a feeling. On a ship where she'd got lost twice, she felt boxed in. It was purely psychological, she knew, but the sense of lightness as she stepped onto the dock and into the police car was absolutely real. The *Empress Louise* would sail at midnight, destination Rhodes. Beatrice and Nikos would join them tomorrow, hopefully finding the same number of passengers as when they'd left.

The journey though Heraklion – the frenzied traffic, errant mopeds, graffiti on corrugated tin, blasts of music from passing cars, the scent of a fish stall, a jumble of vegetables outside a shop, children chasing each other round a fountain, an unruly cypress tree reaching out from a park – all grounded Beatrice with a reassuring sense of real life unpredictability. Here, anything could happen and she felt all the safer for it. When a rain shower spattered the windscreen, she rolled down the window to inhale the smell.

Meanwhile Nikos relayed the limited results of his interviews with the housekeeping crew, outlined Dr Weinberg's opinions and shared his own reaction to the showdown with Fraser.

"Anyone who works on the ship can access those cards. The only record they keep is who signed for which card for security purposes. If there are any accusations of stealing, for example.

The card used to open Maureen Hall's room had not been signed for and it hasn't been returned. No surprise. Weinberg has very little respect for Fraser, although he was complimentary about the nurse. As for Fraser's behaviour, I'm not sure if it's his professional reputation he's trying to protect or if he's hiding something, but he behaves like a guilty man. Did he apologise for being so rude to you?"

"Eventually, and with bad grace. Yes, you're right to say he has something to hide, but as to whether it's connected to criminal activity or just incompetence, I'm not sure."

Nikos flipped open his notebook again. "Something else that doesn't add up. He said he went back to his cabin. I checked. His access card was used to enter the infirmary at 21.53. He didn't return to his own cabin until 22.37."

"Good thinking," Beatrice said, in with genuine admiration. She hadn't thought to check the doctor's alibi. "Right, I want to talk to Fraser again tomorrow and I'll also ask Jensson about him. There's something unhealthy about the captain's unquestioning acceptance of everything Fraser does. If both Weinberg and Bannerjee doubt the doctor's methods, Jensson really has a responsibility to take it seriously. But he allows himself to be bossed and bullied by the man."

"Yes, he does. But you don't," said Nikos, with an amused respect in his tone. "I think you made both of them very nervous by saying they were still under suspicion."

"So they should be. Heads in the sand, hoping the problem will go away. Unless they wake up to what is happening and start to cooperate with us, both their careers are likely to end in under a week. They're typical of people who've been in a job too long. Bored and resentful, going through the motions, wishing they were somewhere else..."

She stopped, aware how cynical she sounded. "Now, tell me about Inspector Voulakis. What kind of man is he?"

Nikos looked out at the activity on the street for a few seconds.

"He's been in the job too long. He's bored and resentful and going through the motions, wishing he was somewhere else." Nikos echoed Beatrice's words with a rueful smile. "He's deadened by administration – always hoping for a bit of action, as long as it doesn't involve hard work. He sometimes likes to divide people or encourage tension between his officers. I don't know how he will react to you, Beatrice. He's a real Anglophile but..."

"But what? How do you advise me to play this?" Another battle with someone else's baggage was the last thing she needed.

He shrugged, with an apologetic grin. "One one hand, you are exactly the kind of exciting challenge he loves. On the other, you represent a whole pile of problems."

She grinned back. "Story of my life, Nikos."

Chapter 14

Rose was right, it was time to get out. Maggie knew her reluctance to leave the cabin was becoming unhealthy. After two days of sympathy and room service, she'd sensed Rose's patience beginning to fray. Even Joyce Milligan's kindness in visiting twice, as a representative of the Hirondelles, only made it plainer that life went on. Rose was bored, and if Maggie were honest, so was she. There was only so much entertainment to be gained from people-watching, and as their inner balcony overlooked the pool the scenes below had grown repetitive and dull. Rose told her they were turning into curtain-twitchers. Time to get out and do their duty, she said. Detective Inspector Stubbs needed their help, she said. Rose could be very persuasive.

"Between five and seven is the best time to venture out. The excursions have returned and will be either resting or refreshing in their cabins." Rose made it sound like an adventure. "Fewer folk on deck. The crew tend to use the facilities more at that time, so we can keep our eyes peeled for someone of the right height and build. The man we're looking for is tall..."

"Yes," Maggie agreed. "A good six-footer. Although Esther was a tiny woman. He may have looked bigger beside such a wee thing. But tall and strong, of that I have no doubt." She suppressed the image of the jerky body in freefall.

"So we go for a walk, greet anyone we meet, keep our opinions to ourselves and watch. Avoid the Hirondelles if at all possible, and dine at The Sizzling Grill. We'll find none of those biddies in there."

"Don't be rude, Rose. I hope I have as much energy as Joyce Milligan when I'm her age. And we're not far off biddies ourselves. I'll just say again, if it feels too much, if I start to feel panicky, I'm coming back here. No arguments."

Rose sat in front of the dressing table, dabbing lipstick onto her bottom lip. "Yes, of course, but that's not going to be necessary. You're the observer, collecting information on all the male crew members on this ship. You're the only one who's seen this man. You have to give DI Stubbs something to go on. Especially after Maureen Hall."

Maggie, standing by the door, gathering all her courage, stepped back into the room and sat down on the ottoman with a thump. Maureen Hall. That poor elderly, infirm and ailing woman, smothered in her sleep. *How could anyone, why would anyone...?* her thoughts began the same futile circuits as before, so she called a halt. Rose was right. Time to get out.

The heat came as a surprise as did the brightness and the noise. Squeals and shrieks of laughter from a group of youngsters in the pool competed with a group singing *Happy Birthday* from the deck above. Maggie recoiled, only to meet the resistance of Rose's guiding arm and positive voice.

"Fresh air! I feel better already. So, let's start with a walk around the deck – right or left?"

Maggie pointed away from the pool and Rose led the way. A few people dozed on the loungers and chairs, paperbacks or magazines propped on their chests. Maggie's paranoia subsided as she saw that no rubber-necking mob of ghouls was camped outside her cabin. In the first few minutes, no one took any notice of her at all. Maggie relaxed her shoulders, raised her head and gazed out to sea. The sun sank, filling the sky with ripples of colour; tangerine, violet, blush and scarlet reflected in a mercury sea. An outrageous display enjoyed by covetous eyes for the briefest of moments, but never captured. Like the flash of a Moulin Rouge underskirt.

She looked at Rose. "The world doesn't care, does it?"

Rose's optimistic expression faded.

"No, no, I mean that in a good way. Whatever tragedies and dramas we endure down here, the world turns, the sun sets and life goes on, relentless and oblivious. As it should be." Maggie reached out to squeeze Rose's hand briefly. "I know I've not been much fun these past few days. So I'm giving myself a good shake. Look."

She shook herself from head to toe, wobbling her cheeks for comic effect. "From this moment on, I stop feeling sorry for myself and do everything in my power to identify the man I saw. It's the least I can do for Esther, for DI Stubbs and for you. Shall we start by the staff pool?"

Many staff and crew members used the quiet period between passengers' daytime activities and evening entertainments to swim, sunbathe or use the gym in their own private, less well-equipped section of D deck. Rose and Maggie positioned themselves in the shade and watched the high jinks as waiters, maids, chefs, entertainers and sailors let off steam in the water. The age-old signs of flirtation had not changed, Maggie observed, as she watched the interaction among the young. A bunch of men organised an impromptu water volleyball match, hastily unrolling a net across the pool and yelling instructions at each other.

A great hairy individual Maggie didn't recognise clambered out of the water and fetched a ball. She assessed his build and height, and nudged Rose. "That's about the size of him."

"That one? But he has a beard. You'd have spotted that, wouldn't you?"

"I'm not saying it is him. But he was about that size. And at that distance, I couldn't see his face at all clearly, although I can't picture a beard."

Rose pulled her sunglasses down her nose to observe the

big man leaping into the pool after the ball. "Some people have more than their fair share of hair."

Maggie looked over her shoulder and recognised a passer-by. "And others were at the back of the queue. That language fella should either wear a hat or put some sunscreen on his bald patch. I'll mention it at dinner."

They both watched Mr Martins walk along the deck, jacket over his arm, purposefully making for the Reception Area.

Rose spoke. "Make that breakfast. By the look of him, he's off out for the night. Plus you and I agreed on The Sizzling Grill for dinner, to avoid any nosey parkers and... Oh hello, Captain Jensson!"

Maggie jumped at the unexpected presence of the captain.

"Good afternoon, ladies. I'm very happy to see you out and about. How are you both?" The captain's smile was as glittery as the pool.

Maggie assumed a smile. "Better every day. Just trying to get back into the swing of things."

"I'm very happy to hear that. And your timing is perfect, because tomorrow we arrive in Rhodes. So much unforgettable history to experience, you really shouldn't miss it. Could I invite you to the Captain's Table tomorrow evening?"

Rose stepped in. "We're not yet up to braving the dining-room, but thank you for the invitation. This evening, we're going to the grill. Small steps, you see."

"I quite understand. The food at The Sizzling Grill is deli-cious, incidentally. Kostas takes extraordinary pride in the freshness of his selection. An asset to our team, who works hard and as you can see, plays hard."

He gestured to the pool.

"That hairy one is a chef?" asked Maggie.

"Most certainly. But I can assure you he wears clothes in the kitchen." The captain winked and departed.

Maggie watched him move along the deck, stopping to greet the occasional passenger with a friendly observation. She could spot a poor actor a mile off and his false bonhomie galled her. She turned to Rose.

"Similar heights, the captain and that chef. And I feel sure as eggs is eggs, the man who threw Esther Crawford off the cliff had no beard."

"The captain? Now, don't get paranoid. He has to be above suspicion. He spends all day and every day on board. Still, we can keep our eyes peeled for lookalikes."

"Hmmm. I'm fed up with watching this lot and their tomfoolery. Let's go up onto the observatory deck."

The way the world had tilted on its axis reminded Maggie of September the eleventh, 2001. The shock of those attacks in America changed how she looked at the world, and not for the better. Aircraft, usually nothing more to her than noise or vapour trails, had taken on the form of instruments of death. The rhetoric of 'terrorism' and 'war' left a manipulative taste of political engineering in her mouth, but the images had made their mark. September 11th changed the way she saw the world. The way she saw the sky.

Two days ago, what she'd witnessed changed the way she saw people. Now every smile hid a hint of ill intent and everyone wore a shadow. Words like 'evil' floated like storm clouds through her mind. A crew member's good manners in allowing them right of way on the steps appeared predatory; a fellow passenger's comment on the weather rang an ominous note. Her nervous system was yet to disable the alarms.

She and Rose leaned on the railing and gazed out at Crete. As the evening darkened, lights sparked into life across the port of Heraklion. Restaurateurs would be readying tables, bands tuning up, taxi drivers preparing for a busy night. A peculiar sadness stole over Maggie. She wanted to rush down the gangway and fling herself into the midst of it all, but at the same time she was happy to hide, appreciating the ship's protection, the distance from real life. She sniffed, mostly in disgust at herself.

Rose inclined her head. "Funny how a view changes as you get older. Here's you and me, standing here looking at a beautiful Greek island. Look at all the others here, all gazing out at exactly the same place, at exactly the same time. But I'll bet not one of us is seeing the same scene. What are you seeing?"

"Life," said Maggie, without hesitation. "Or rather other people's lives. I'm standing here, imagining how much fun they're all having. I'm envious and a bit of me wants to hurry down there and join them. And another part of me is saying 'Go home, old lady. Jigsaws and knitting is all you're good for.' That's what I see. How about yourself?"

Rose's brow twitched, somewhere between concern and annoyance but before she could speak, another voice interrupted.

"In which case, you should run down there this minute and throw yourselves into the middle of the action. Which would be just the thing to fill you with lust and life and mischief. For one thing, it would kick all that 'too old' business into a cocked hat. The downside? You'd miss my show. Which is something else to fill you with lust and life and mischief. Especially lust."

The man was tanned, smiley and had eyes worthy of Frank Sinatra. Maggie found herself smiling back.

"I recognise you. You're Toni Dean. 'The Man with the Golden Voice.' I've seen your picture on those posters."

"Hush now. We don't talk about *those* posters." He darted a glance behind him. "Oh you mean the ones for the show? Fair dos." His eyes danced with teasing fun. "As for the Golden Voice, that wasn't my choice of marketing line. I wanted 'The Voice of an Era.' See, I don't sing any of the modern stuff. All classics - Tony Bennett, Dean Martin, Tom Jones, Howard Keel, Paul Anka, Bing Crosby... they don't make 'em like that any more. Have you two charming ladies seen my show?"

Rose's expression brightened along with each name the man quoted. "No, not yet. We've spent a lot of time ashore and haven't had a look at the entertainment. But we're just beginning to take advantage. Did you say you'll be singing tonight?"

"Nine o'clock, The Empress Grand Ballroom. Consider it a first step. Tonight, music and laughter. Tomorrow, another island and another day. And Rhodes might be an inspiration. You'll feel brave enough to go exploring and find an adventure!"

Maggie's smile was a weak effort, she knew, but she'd had her fill of adventures. Rose's response held far more enthusiasm.

"Nine o'clock, then. If we're still full of beans after our dinner, we'll come and hear you sing."

"If you're full of beans, don't you come anywhere near me!"

Rose laughed, almost a giggle. "You know what I mean. See you at the ballroom."

He bowed like a typical showman. "Look forward to seeing you there. And even if you don't make it, promise me you'll remember this: You are never too old. If you feel like it, do it. That goes for jigsaws or gigolos!" With a mock-shocked face, he waved and backed off towards the steps.

After he'd descended from sight, Rose gave Maggie a nudge.

"What do you think? He's just like an old-fashioned Redcoat, or one of those Saturday Night at the Palladium entertainers. Old-school with the personal touch. It might be good fun."

"Yes. Exactly what I feel like tonight. Something familiar and unthreatening. Not to mention an hour or so in the dark. I'm game."

"Me too. Adventures can wait till tomorrow."

They linked arms and headed downstairs to The Sizzling Grill.

Chapter 15

Chief Inspector Voulakis and Detective Chief Inspector Hamilton. Her stiff, unsmiling, immaculate boss seemed worlds apart from this amiable chap with his large belly, loosened tie and five o'clock shadow. He carried a peculiar but not unpleasant scent about him, which Beatrice could only associate with roast potatoes. Where Hamilton projected a judgemental chill, this man radiated warmth and bonhomie. Hard to imagine as it was, the two had been great pals for sixteen years, according to Nikos's voluble superior.

He greeted Beatrice with a huge smile and shook her hand in both of his. He showed surprisingly little interest in the details of the case and accepted Beatrice's suggestion that she and Nikos Stephanakis should work as a team without demur.

"Why not? If you are happy to share the role, who am I to argue? I know this will be a great learning experience for Inspector Stephanakis. I myself learned so much from working with Hamilton in that one year alone. I will never forget how much I improved as a detective. You know, we were two of the first officers to award an ASBO. They'd only just been introduced and we used them to break up two hooligan firms associated with Millwall FC. Ground-breaking work."

"I didn't know that, sir. Congratulations. Although I'd say we no longer think of ASBOs as 'awards' these days."

The man's grin just grew wider. He sat back with his arms behind his head. Beatrice looked away from the sweat patches and spotted a leather cord around his wrist, threaded through a single blue bead.

"Ha! My English police vocabulary was never the best. Yes, I am sure you will teach Stephanakis much. I wanted to send him to London, you see, but secondments like mine are much harder to finance these days. This will be the next best thing. I owe Hamilton yet another debt of gratitude for sending you. How is he, by the way?"

"Very well, if a little bad-tempered. He expected me back in London this week, but that is unlikely to happen now."

Voulakis burst into laughter, smacking his hand on the desk. "His loss, my gain. He will never do me a favour again in his life. Tell me, is he still a confirmed bachelor or has he found a lady friend yet?"

Beatrice hesitated. She abhorred rumours and speculation about her colleagues' private lives, having seen first-hand how damaging it could be. But as the two men had a personal connection, it might appear rude not to pass an innocent comment.

"As far as I know, sir, DCI Hamilton prefers to remain independent. But I am not the best informed on office gossip."

He sighed, shaking his head and gazing into the middle distance. "Such a shame. You know, he is the reason I married my wife. That's where I met her, in London! She was a second-generation Greek immigrant and a neighbour of Hamilton's. He introduced us, thinking it would cheer me up if I could speak Greek with someone. Cheer me up? I fell in love! Every time he comes to visit, I try to find a nice woman for him, but it never works. You know the expression, 'he bats for the other side'? Well, that's what my wife thinks. But that is not the truth."

Despite herself, Beatrice's curiosity took the bait. "Really, sir? Several of my colleagues would agree with your wife."

Voulakis folded his hands over his substantial stomach and shook his head. "No. It's a sad story. He doesn't often talk about his private life, but one night we drank a bottle of brandy, and he told me he'd fallen in love. The lady was unavailable, unfortunately, but his feelings never changed. Every time I ask him if he's met someone else, he says no one ever comes close. Perhaps one day he will forget her and move on. It's never too late."

The temptation to snort arose, but Voulakis wore an expression of such heartfelt sincerity, that Beatrice opted to change the subject instead. How people love to extrapolate, turning a probable brush-off into an operatic tragedy.

"Captain Jensson has offered both Inspector Stephanakis and myself accommodation aboard for the rest of the investigation, as the ship needs to proceed with its itinerary. Is that acceptable to you?"

Voulakis widened his eyes. "To me, yes, but Stephanakis! What about your girlfriend?" He winked at Beatrice. "She's British as well, you know. Very romantic. She was his English teacher and she fell madly in love with him."

Nikos rolled his eyes, but softened the gesture with a smile. "Karen will understand the practical reasons for staying aboard. And it's only for a few days."

"Perhaps not even that long," Beatrice said. "I want to wrap this up quickly and return to Scotland Yard. But looking at it realistically, we think have a serial killer on our hands, so we'll need to keep a close ear and an eye to the ground. So aboard the *Empress Louise* is where we should be."

"Are you going back tonight?" asked Voulakis, his question apparently born of enthusiasm rather than supervisory rigour.

Nikos replied first. "No sir. We'll join the cruise tomorrow. Tonight, I would like to prepare for a few days away and tomorrow DI Stubbs will check out of her hotel. We both need some rest after last night and I think a few hours away from the ship will do us good."

Tired, tetchy and a little claustrophobic, Beatrice looked over at Nikos and mentally transmitted her gratitude.

It was quarter to five. The sun filled her hotel room with butterscotch light and threw intersecting triangles across the tiled floor. With every intention of explaining the reasons for her extended stay to Matthew over the phone later that evening, Beatrice took a shower, drew the curtains and lay on the sheets to get an hour's rest. She checked her phone and picked up a voicemail.

"*Message for DI Stubbs. Dr Bruce of Beech Avenue Surgery, Salisbury here. Bad news, I'm afraid. Beryl Hodges was buried on Friday. No post-mortem carried out, but I did examine the body, at the family's request. Cause of death determined as asphyxia brought on by anaphylactic shock exacerbated by asthma. The lady had suffered previous violent reactions to shellfish, so in my estimation, that was what provoked the allergic response. Hope this information is useful, call if any questions.*"

Which brought her no closer to deciding if Hodges had been killed deliberately or had made a mistake with her choice of starter. If the woman had medication in her fridge to counter such a reaction, surely she'd be extremely careful? In which case, how would someone make her eat the very thing that might kill her? She imagined trying to poison someone with prawns, recalled an episode of *Masterchef* involving fishcakes and her eyes closed.

When she awoke, the clock said half past eight and her stomach said dinner-time. She decided to go out for some food and call Matthew on her return. Due to the time difference, he'd barely be home from work yet and she needed a bit more practice on her breezy update.

The lobby, which had been awkwardly full of guests checking in earlier, was now peaceful and almost empty as she made for the exit. She handed her key to the receptionist, clearing her throat to disguise her growling stomach.

"Good evening, Mrs Stubbs. Your visitor is waiting in the bar."

Beatrice raised her eyebrows. "Sorry?"

"He said not to disturb you and he would wait until you are ready. Through there."

She followed the pointing finger and entered a small room, dimly lit and sparsely populated. At the bar, a familiar figure sat reading a paperback, an almost-empty glass of red wine at his elbow. She approached, feigning a frown.

"And what do you think you're doing here?"

Oscar Martins's face passed from surprise to puzzlement to pleasure as he brought himself back to reality. She could identify with that feeling, so lost in a book that reality comes as an intrusion.

"What do you think I'm doing here? Stalking you, of course. I ruthlessly pumped Inspector Stephanakis for the name of your hotel. But I'm on a break right now, so the time seemed right to enjoy a glass of the local grape. Can I tempt you?"

"Certainly not. On an empty stomach and three hours' sleep, I would be swinging from the chandeliers. I was on my way out to find something tasty and substantial. With chips. Have you eaten?"

"No. I saved myself in case I happened to bump into you. My Machiavellian plan was to track you down and invite you to dinner." He slipped his book into the right inside pocket of his jacket and Beatrice recognised the cover. *An Empty Vessel*, by Vaughan Mason. One of Matthew's favourites. She made up her mind. She'd refuse to be drawn on any aspect of the case, but some company and discussion on literature wouldn't hurt.

"Come on then, let's waste no more time. You're due back on board at eleven. I'll ask the concierge for a local recommendation."

"No need. I found the perfect place, just around the corner. A good stalker should do his homework. I do have one request, if you don't mind?"

Beatrice tilted her head to indicate she was listening.

Oscar clasped his hands under his chin and lowered his brow. "I must ask you not to talk about or allude to your investigation in any way. I warn you now that if you should attempt to share sensitive details about this case, I shall stick my fingers in my ears and sing Demis Roussos until you stop."

"I rather like Demis Roussos. But thank you, I accept your terms. Can we go now? I'm absolutely starving."

"This way."

Oscar's evident pride in having found a charming little local taverna was somewhat punctured on their arrival. Dinos spotted her instantly and rushed to kiss her on both cheeks.

"Again! You come back! You love my food! Welcome, Police Lady! Welcome, mister. Sit, sit!"

A flush of happy anticipation suffused Beatrice as they sat at a battered table, but she sensed Oscar's confidence had lost some of its ease.

"Inspector Stephanakis brought me here for lunch when I arrived. You obviously have an eye for the right kind of eatery. If the *stifado* is on the menu, I'd strongly recommend you try it."

His face creased into a knowing smile. "And you have a knack for tact. Not to mention notoriety. It seems you're not easily forgotten."

Beatrice glanced across at Dinos behind the bar, who was roaring with laughter at one of his own jokes. The whole room turned to watch, his laugh an entertainment in itself.

"I believe Dinos is what we'd call a local 'character' and one of his quirks is a peculiar fascination with the British Royal Family. That's why a London detective is likely to stick in his mind. Now, why are you lurking about hotel bars when you could be attending the 'Introduction to Rhodes' lecture on the *Empress Louise*?"

Oscar stroked an imaginary beard. "I was paralysed by choice. What should I do? The lecture on a place I have visited three times before, aqua-aerobics in the main pool, a retro sing-a-long in the piano bar or fifty percent off having my legs waxed? When you have so many opportunities, sometimes it's easier not to decide. Plus, our conversation from last night remains unfinished. You were..."

"Meatballs!" boomed Dinos. "Special today, very good. Yes?" He plonked a basket of bread and carafe of red on the table and rubbed his hands together. "Yes?"

Oscar shrugged helplessly while Beatrice laughed.

"Meatballs. Yes." She waved a finger between herself and Oscar to indicate they would both succumb to the house special. She had every reason to trust their host.

"Very good!" he bowed and gave the thumbs-up.

Beatrice watched him roll back to the kitchen, the loose sole flapping from his trainer. A man in his element, at home in his world. Not rich in the conventional sense, but respected for himself, and apparently happy with his lot. She compared him with Jensson, whose job ascribed greater status and certainly accrued greater wealth. And yet the outlook of the two appeared diametrically opposite. She checked herself. Making assumptions about two men she'd met a couple of times. The worst kind of mindset for a detective.

She focused on her dining companion. "I hope you didn't mind my ordering for you. Well, acquiescing for you. Dinos seems to be rather a steamroller, so I just gave in. I also tend to trust the dish of the day when all the locals are tucking in."

Oscar poured wine into two beakers. "Me too. And I'd never have been brave enough to argue even if I had wanted *stifado*. So let's toast going local. Cheers!"

"Cheers!" The wine, like Dinos himself, was rough, unpolished, full bodied and warming.

Oscar took a sip and his eyes widened. Instantly his tanned cheeks began to glow.

"Oh dear," said Beatrice. "Do you hate it? We can order something else."

Oscar shook his head and drank again. "No, not at all, I like a wine that gives you a bear hug. I feel more manly with every drop. And what better partner for homemade meatballs? As I was saying, our conversation was interrupted by last night's incident. And, if I may make so bold, rather unfair. I told you about my profession, my marital status, my cruise habits and my shameful habit of writing books. You, with classic professional cunning, revealed nothing more than your full title. Well, I'm not a man to give up easily. Tonight, DI Stubbs, I'm asking the questions."

The meatballs, as predicted, were a triumph. The second carafe slipped down smoothly as more and more people packed the taverna. Departing diners struggled and wrestled their way to the door. Heat and condensation increased, yet tempers remained friendly and cheerful, while the noise level made any conversation less than shouting impossible.

Oscar paid the bill, claiming it as his treat. Dinos insisted on taking a group selfie and bestowing more kisses in their effusive goodbyes. Beatrice didn't argue with either of them, but expressed her thanks with absolute sincerity for an excellent evening. Once on the street, the night air cooled her cheeks and she slipped into her jacket. Traffic, people, lights and music seemed to spill across their path, flowing, bouncing, bumping and perpetually moving. Oscar shielded her from a group of shrieking girls tumbling from a bar, but Beatrice's sense of goodwill remained unshaken. She smiled at the girls, at Oscar, at the world. Dinos's house wine should be available on prescription.

"Your hotel, madam. Thank you for your company and I will see you tomorrow, I'm sure. Good luck with the investigation, not that you'll need it. I should hurry and get a cab. Look, here's my card. Give me a call. Sleep well."

He took her hand, drew her to him and kissed her lightly on both cheeks.

"Goodnight, Oscar, and thank you. Yes, it's getting late. Don't miss the boat!"

He gave a surprised laugh. "My sentiments exactly."

He stepped into the street and hailed a taxi immediately, causing a cacophony of horns behind the cab. He turned for a last wave and ducked inside. Beatrice waved back and watched the vehicle careen off into the direction of the dock.

She released a happy sigh and looked at her watch. Half past eleven. In Devon, it was half past nine, a perfectly reasonable time to call someone. Then she should pack, perform ablutions and bed. The flight to Rhodes was due to depart shortly after seven. She tucked Oscar's card into her pocket and picked up her key from reception. As she made for the stairs, she congratulated herself. Not only had she relaxed and stopped thinking about the case, but she'd made a new friend. For someone who'd spent the whole previous night awake investigating a murder, it was a respectable night's work.

"Good evening, Professor Bailey speaking."

"Matthew, it's me. Sorry to call so late."

"Hello, Old Thing. Didn't recognise the number. How's Greece?"

"The place itself is very pleasant. However, the case itself has taken a turn for the worse. There's been another fatality and this time, I'm afraid there is no doubt."

"Oh dear, that's most unfortunate. I understand you can give no details, but from a purely selfish perspective, I presume it means you won't be back on Wednesday."

"Highly unlikely. The aim is to clear this up in the next couple of days, but you know how unpredictable such a situation can be."

Matthew's voice, when it came, was profoundly weary. *"So long as you hold Hamilton to his word and insist on days off in lieu. We need some uninterrupted time together."*

"I will try. The only thing is, he wants me to take over another operation, so I'm not sure how flexible he'll be."

She stood at the French windows, watching the patterns of lunar light on the ocean. A moon bridge, from this world to another. Seconds passed as she waited for his response.

"Matthew?"

"What takes priority, Beatrice? Really, it's a genuine question. Are Hamilton's needs more important than yours? Than ours?"

She pressed a hand over her eyes and grimaced. "No." Her buoyant mood leaked away, leaving an uncertain void. "As a matter of fact, I broached the subject of early retirement. He wasn't happy and told me to forget the idea for next year. But the year after, I'm sure he'll be fine, because he'll have two detective sergeants in..."

"*To be completely frank, I could not care less about Hamilton's problems. I'm more concerned with ours. I begin to feel you actually prefer our being apart and have no inclination to change that. My attempts to discuss our future are met with evasion or absence. For my part, let me be clear. I would very much like to spend my dotage with you. Ideally in the same house, but I'd settle for the same county.*"

"Matthew..."

"*What do you want, Beatrice? That is not a rhetorical question. Think about it and give me your answer on your return. Whenever that may be. I wish you a goodnight and a swift resolution to your case. Take care, Old Thing.*"

Beatrice returned his wishes, put the phone down and leant her forehead against the window. Her relaxed and positive frame of mind had been ousted by a malign and familiar unease. She was being irresponsible, hiding her head and hoping the problem would stop knocking. She winced at the idea of identifying Matthew as a problem. The one person who had loved her, supported her through the worst of times, made so many sacrifices and only wanted a future together. What was wrong with her?

She thought about his question. What did she want? The best of both worlds. Matthew's love and companionship, Hamilton's respect, her own peace of mind and equilibrium. Even if it came in the form of medication. There had to be a compromise. All she had to do was find it. But before that, she had to call James. Her counsellor of two years was unfailing in his patience yet unforgiving in his persistence, never letting her twist off the hook.

Yes, she would call James. It was not quite a decision, but a decision to decide, which would have to suffice.

Chapter 16

Winds buffeted the city of Rhodes, shaking trees and whipping tourists' hair into their faces. As they drove along Papagou, Nikos pointed out the Palace of the Grand Master of the Knights of Rhodes, just visible through the trees of Platia Rimini. Beatrice seemed impressed, exclaiming her admiration of the ancient edifice. They drove under an arch in the city walls and alongside the harbour, where the wind flailed masts and whipped flags. He kept up his tourist guide commentary, but his mind was elsewhere. He had mixed feelings about this place.

On the island of Rhodes, Karen had changed from being his teacher to his lover over one highly charged weekend. Incredible memories he hid away so as not to wear them out. Yet Rhodes was home to a piece of shit he'd rather forget. There were several people on this planet Nikos never wanted to see again, but only one he actively wished dead. Demetrius Xanthou, schoolmate, colleague, rival and now an inspector for the South Aegean Region of the Hellenic Police. Acid roiled in Nikos's gut.

The awe-inspiring architecture changed in stature as the police vehicle turned away from the beach and rolled down Akti Sachtouri into the commercial port. Three vast cruise ships dominated the skyline, anachronistic and intrusive, like contemporary hotels in mediaeval towns.

By the time they arrived at the *Empress Louise*, breakfast had finished and many of the cruise passengers were descending the gangway, keen to begin their exploration of the island. Nikos took a deep breath and with a nod to Beatrice, led the way onto the boat in the opposite direction to the silver-haired tide.

Captain Jensson looked less than rested. When he greeted them at the bridge, he reported no disturbances other than a great deal of seasickness amongst the passengers. High winds had made the sailing the most turbulent so far.

"We weren't even sure if we'd be able to dock. So the medical team have their hands full. I don't think Dr Fraser will be able to spare you much time today, if any. How do you want to proceed, detectives?"

Nikos looked at Beatrice, but she gave a minuscule nod for him to take the lead. So he did.

"DI Stubbs received news last night that Beryl Hodges died from anaphylactic shock, very likely a reaction to seafood complicated by her asthma. This may be coincidence, but we have to keep in mind the possibility someone knew of her allergies. Our plan is to search for links between the dead women and identify potential suspects. We'd like to interview their companions, talk to you and your team once again, and we will need to speak to Dr Fraser at some stage. Do you mind if we use the casino again?"

"The casino is available for today, but then we will need to make other arrangements. As for another interview, I'm not sure what more I can add. I rarely do more than pass the time of day with most passengers. And the Hirondelles, travelling as a group, would not be invited to dine at my table. Not out of any kind of prejudice, but we don't like to split up a party."

"Did you meet Beryl Hodges?" asked Nikos.

"No. The Hirondelles arrived in the afternoon, held a birthday party in one of the restaurants for Mrs Crawford that evening, and unfortunately, the Hodges woman died during the night. I never even saw her."

Beatrice jumped in. "Do you know which restaurant they chose for their party? It could be relevant, given cause of death."

"If I remember correctly, that would have been The Sizzling Grill. Esther Crawford told me she had a particular fondness for the Sticky Chicken Wings."

Nikos wrote 'grill' and 'chicken wings' in his notebook and would find out how to spell the other words later. "Did you have any contact with Maureen Hall?"

"Mrs Hall was sick for most of the voyage. I'm afraid I hadn't even spoken to her."

"But presumably Dr Fraser had seen her, as she would have been a patient?" asked Beatrice.

Jensson frowned. "Usually the nurse sees to everyday problems such as nausea and blood pressure issues, so I doubt it."

"Well, that's something we can check with him personally. We'll let you get on, but perhaps you might find time for us later this afternoon?" Beatrice's voice, while polite and friendly, contained an underlying firmness Nikos admired. A fleeting frown crossed Jensson's face.

"Detective Inspectors, I don't mean to be difficult and obviously I want this situation resolved. But I have received a succession of visits since you left us in Crete. Firstly our Human Resources manager, delivering a series of complaints from staff about police intrusion. Then Nurse Bannerjee, representing herself and Dr Weinberg, whose workloads have increased substantially. Apparently, many passengers no longer wish to be treated by Dr Fraser as he seems to be the focus of the enquiry. Finally, the head of entertainment would like to have the casino back. He has not been able to keep up his regular maintenance and cleaning since you've been here. Morale amongst the staff is visibly low, everyone has their suspicions and the atmosphere is becoming sour. I urgently need to demonstrate some progress before this gets out of hand."

Nikos resisted the urge to look at Beatrice. "Believe me, Captain, our aim is to solve this as fast as we can. But we cannot demonstrate progress if we don't make any. We can give you an update later today if you like."

A uniformed crew member hovered behind Beatrice, trying to catch Jensson's eye. When he succeeded, he pointed to his watch.

Jensson raised a finger in acknowledgement. "I have to go. My afternoon break is at 15.30. I can see you then."

Nikos watched him walk away and return the sailor's salute, back straight and head high. One of those men who had an innate authority and commanded respect without even trying. Nikos wondered if he would ever get to that stage.

One of the worst things about interviewing friends and relatives of the recently and suddenly deceased is ascertaining the root cause of their guilt. Because they are all guilty. In Beatrice's experience, that guilt could be as pertinent as having wielded the murder weapon or as irrelevant as being less than complimentary about that morning's pancakes.

Audrey Kean and Pat George, the travelling companions accompanying Maureen Hall, were most definitely guilty. They outdid each other in self-recrimination, seeking and finding more reasons to feel terrible about their friend's unfortunate end. But they didn't kill her. Beatrice knew that from the outset. What she had to do was assume the role of grief counsellor while plucking the occasional useful nugget from the cascade of self-flagellating misery.

Maureen, a widow, had lived her entire life in Yorkshire. She had no connection with Esther Crawford or Beryl Hodges and had met none of the Hirondelles. Seasick, and probably homesick, for the majority of her first cruise, she'd been cabin-bound for almost a fortnight. Her only trip ashore was on Monday. The heat and exercise were too much for her and she'd complained. Which, according to Audrey, led to 'words'. The threesome had parted ways on their return to the ship. That was the last time they saw her.

After the women left, tearful and wretched, Beatrice took a few minutes to order her impressions and knowledge of the facts. Cabins of the deceased in completely different areas. Two women belonging to the same party, the third with no connection. Two very different methods of killing, one very narrow age range. But was this really a serial killer? Or simply a series of coincidences which made two deaths and one murder appear connected? Beatrice lay back on the banquette, covered her eyes with her hands and started all over again.

The ship's records on who was aboard and who disembarked at each port had been rigorously maintained. Nikos ran several reports on the data and noted the vast majority of passengers who left the ship at every port joined official excursions. A tiny percentage chose to make their own way, including Rose Mason and Maggie Campbell, a small group of architects and a few individuals, such as Oscar Martins. For each possible murder, Nikos cross-checked the locations of the individuals concerned. Everyone was aboard when Beryl Hodges expired. When Esther Crawford plummeted into the sea, the tourist buses were parked outside the tavernas, the architects were attending a lecture on archaeological reconstruction, Rose and Maggie were picnicking, and only Oscar Martins was somewhere on the island alone. No one else remained unaccounted for. When someone smothered Maureen Hall, most people were dining in the ship's restaurants, including the architects. Oscar Martins was in the Club Room with Beatrice, and Rose and Maggie had ordered room service in their cabin.

But that only narrowed down passenger movement. The person who took the housekeeping key card to Maureen Hall's room knew where to go and what to get, indicating a level of inside knowledge. And as for who was where and when in terms of staff and crew, Nikos needed help. He stood up and looked across the silent expanse of casino to Beatrice. No one there. She hadn't passed him so she must have gone to the bathroom. He folded up his laptop, tucked it under his arm and set off for the bridge.

A deadly combination.

Lying down in a darkened room, with a firm cushion beneath her after nights of insufficient sleep, it was no wonder she'd dozed off. Beatrice blinked up at the ceiling, massaged her face and checked her watch. 11.40. She'd only been asleep for around twenty minutes and just hoped her catnap had not involved snoring. Still, Nikos was far enough away not to have heard. She held her breath and listened. Not a sound. She lifted herself onto her elbows and peered across the room. No sign of him. He'd obviously taken a break.

She flopped down onto her back and tried to relocate her thought-process regarding connections between the killings. But her stomach released a creaking, snapping groan, as if an alligator had opened its jaws. A scanty breakfast of yoghurt and fruit at six in the morning was barely enough to keep body and soul together. She was starving. Another creak, this time from the end of the room. Good. Nikos was back. She'd propose an early lunch over which they could share notes. She shoved herself upwards again, her eyes at table level and blinked into the darkness of the casino.

A man, much taller than Nikos, was pacing silently along the bar. He scanned the room and bent over Nikos's table, turning some papers to face him. With a brief check back at the door, he then withdrew a phone from his inside pocket. Beatrice squinted but the light from the bar rendered the individual nothing more than a large silhouette. He tilted the phone over the table and Beatrice understood.

"Can I help you?" she yelled, the volume of her voice even scaring herself. The man shot backwards and was out the door before she'd even got her feet on the ground.

She hurried after him and burst out into the corridor, startling an elderly couple walking past.

"Sorry, didn't mean to alarm you. A man just came out of here, did you see him?"

They looked at each other, back to her and shook their heads, like nodding dogs in the negative.

"Did someone pass you? In a hurry? Someone tall?"

They shook their heads once again. Then the woman spoke. "We didn't see anything. All we heard was a lot of noise. Just now, down there." She pointed at the opposite end of the featureless corridor.

Beatrice ran, assessing the risk of leaving the casino, her laptop and notes, against getting a description of whoever wanted to photograph police evidence. She turned the corner to see a maid collecting the contents of a cleaning trolley from the floor and muttering in some Eastern European tongue.

"What happened?"

The maid's irritation segued into apology. "Sorry, madam. I leave my trolley here and someone comes round this corner too fast. Knocks everything all over the floor. I am in the cabin, changing the towels and I hear a big crash. So I come out here and look at this mess! Nothing wrong with my trolley. This is correct parking according to housekeeping rules."

"Did you see who it was? Can you describe the person?"

"No. He is gone when I come out. Hear feet running. Big man, for sure, and he says a lot of bad words. Some passengers don't know nothing about good manners."

She picked up her feather duster and mini-shampoos, shaking her head in disbelief or disgust or possibly both.

Beatrice thanked her and returned to the casino.

Coincidence could now be ruled out. Whoever had targeted these three women was on the ship and not only aware of the investigation, but watching them. How else did he know Nikos had left the casino?

On her return, the cavernous, shadowy room was quiet and suddenly sinister. The shadows and recesses now made her skin prickle and she wished for Nikos's reassuring presence. His table was empty, but all his papers were still there. She didn't touch anything, aware of the possibility of fingerprints, but bent to see what had interested their visitor so. The uppermost page listed the Hirondelles: name, age, home address and cabin number.

Chapter 17

Rose had been waiting forty minutes by the time Nurse Bannerjee called her name. In that time she'd grown increasingly uncomfortable among so many sickly faces, most with a greyish pallor.

An elderly man with a dressing over one eye released regular sighs, the hairy chef held a bandaged left hand against his chest while using his right to press buttons on his phone, two middle-aged women with dyed blonde hair held a whispered conversation, interrupted frequently by the smaller of the two's frame-shaking cough. All eyes assessed Rose with curiosity, as she appeared perfectly healthy. She jumped to her feet on hearing her name and left the waiting room in relief.

"Come in, Mrs Mason. Close the door. How is Mrs Campbell today?"

Rose folded her hands in her lap. "Much better. I feel bad for taking up your time when I can see you're rushed off your feet, but Maggie needs some more sleeping tablets. She's doing fairly well during the daytime, but still having restless nights. It's only a repeat prescription I'm after."

The nurse made a note on the pad in front of her. "She couldn't come herself?"

"She slept badly, partly to do with the rough crossing. She's getting some rest, so I said I'd come on her behalf."

"I see. Mrs Campbell is Dr Fraser's patient. Shouldn't you see him?"

Warmth crept up Rose's throat. It would be tactless to say she didn't want to bother him, but she could hardly tell the nurse the truth – that Dr Fraser was rude and aggressive and she hated dealing with him.

She cast around for a suitable reply, but Nurse Bannerjee didn't seem to expect one.

"I'll get her files from his office," she said.

"There's no need, I know the sort she takes. I brought the packet with me."

"I'll need to record it, Mrs Mason. Wait there."

Rose did as she was told, feeling more uncomfortable than ever. She hated to be a nuisance. The nurse was usually cheerful and pleasant, but today she seemed uncharacteristically short-tempered. After last night's crossing and the stream of patients, that was to be expected. *It's not all about you, Rose*, she told herself. *You're just the latest in a long line of irritants.*

Sister Bannerjee took a long time and Rose found her thoughts wandering, so that when the door swung open, she actually jumped.

"Sorry for the delay, I couldn't find the file. But Dr Fraser has signed a prescription for your friend's medication and agreed to release it to you. Here you are."

The scrawled handwriting was difficult to decipher, but Rose could read it well enough to see the name was different to the packet she had in her hand.

"Oh, this is not the same. Is this a weaker dosage, do you know?"

The sister took the piece of paper and the empty carton and compared. "No, it's a bit stronger if anything. I'm not sure why he'd do that. Well, today is extremely busy, so I'm going to write Mrs Campbell a repeat for the time being. I'll keep this and talk to Dr Fraser later, when we've located these missing files. If we need to change anything, I'll let you know."

Rose waited while the sister wrote the prescription, thinking over what she had said. "Is there more than one file missing?"

"Not really missing. Just been put in the wrong place, I expect. It happens when we're very busy. Don't worry, everything's on database, so we can always make a copy. Here you are."

She held out the chit.

"Thank you. On Maggie's behalf as well as mine. I'm sorry to be a nuisance, but the missing files don't include the ladies who recently passed on, do they?"

The nurse shook her head. "No, no. It seems we've misfiled a few under the letter C. Mrs Campbell, Mrs Cashmore and Mr Chester have all gone walkabout. They'll turn up, don't you worry. Give my best to Mrs Campbell."

Rather than returning to their suite, Rose went in search of the casino. She argued with herself all the way, but the voice of reason drowned out the whispers of self-doubt. And even if they did see her as a flapping, paranoid old woman, it would be better than not saying anything. She knocked lightly on the door and waited until the young Greek inspector opened the door. Although he was very nice and friendly, she persisted in her request to speak to Detective Inspector Stubbs. He advised her to wait on deck, as his colleague was conducting an interview. Rose did as she was told and had just sat down on a deckchair when DI Stubbs arrived. She greeted Rose warmly, despite looking worn and harassed.

"Thanks for coming, Detective Inspector. I really am sorry to drag you out of an interview."

"No problem at all. I needed a break. Inspector Stephanakis says you might have some information."

"It's probably nothing. But it struck me as odd and I thought you should know. I picked up a prescription for Maggie at the medical centre this morning. Her file has gone missing, along with a Mrs Cashmore and a Mr Chester. The nurse thinks they've been mislaid."

The detective nodded and waited for her to continue. Rose swallowed. "Now normally I wouldn't think twice about something like that. But the name Cashmore rang a bell. I had a quick look at the passenger list again and realised who she is. Doreen Cashmore is a member of the Hirondelle party."

The detective didn't clap her hand to her mouth or go goggle-eyed. Instead she lifted her face to the sunshine and closed her eyes. "This weather is sublime. Such a change to rush hour in wintry London."

"I'll bet it is. Shame you're here for so brief a stay."

"I have a feeling it will be just about right for me. Thanks for letting me know about the ship's medical files. I will check them myself. No detail is insignificant, and I'm glad you spotted that. How's Maggie?"

"Better every day. Now it's just the nightmares. She had a bad night so she's napping as we speak. Most of the ship was up last night, though. Dreadful crossing. I'm glad we have two days on Rhodes to recover. We're planning to go ashore tomorrow. It looks like a lovely city."

"Good idea. Can't miss an opportunity like this and they say the architecture is worth the trip in itself. Thanks for the tip-off, Rose. I'll keep you posted."

Rose lay back in her chair as the detective's heavy shoes clumped along the deck. She'd done her duty. There was nothing in it, she was sure, but her whole body felt lighter for having relayed her concerns. Now, time to get back to Maggie.

After the initial explosion, Dr Fraser's bluster and outrage had blown itself out. The computer records held by the reception-ist indicated that of the 243 registered visitors to the medical centre, only 232 physical files could be located. Those missing included one member of the staff, German swimming instruc-tor Hans-Rudi Burkhard; retired couple Ken and Pam Miller, on their second honeymoon; Jonathan Chester, an IT engineer suffering from burnout; and Maggie Campbell, witness to the death of Esther Crawford. The others belonged to the six remaining Hirondelles.

Nikos and Beatrice faced each other over the printed spreadsheet. Her frown carved two deep vertical grooves in her forehead as she used a highlighter to mark the absent folders. Nikos watched the pattern emerge.

Beatrice looked up. "I think you're right. Whoever took the files was in a hurry and grabbed those he wanted, accidentally picking up a few extras in the process. Look. Deirdre Bowen and Doreen Cashmore, both Hirondelles, were alphabetically separated from one another by Burkhard and Campbell. Chester was next to them. And Mr and Mrs Miller happen to be the only names between Vera Melville and Joyce Milligan. The other two gaps are Nancy Palliser and Emily de Vallon, the remaining Hirondelles. The person who took these has no interest in the swimming instructor or the honeymooners or the IT chap. But I do wonder if Maggie Campbell was entirely accidental."

Nikos lifted his head to look over Beatrice's shoulder. "As the one person who actually saw our suspect, probably not. She needs protection and under the circumstances, I'm not comfortable with using any of Jensson's crew. I want to ask Voulakis for some support. For her and the Hirondelles. I think we now have evidence someone is targeting that group."

She frowned again. "If it is a single individual, and I'm not sure it is, then Maggie's not the only person to have seen him. The man in the casino? I could only see his silhouette, but I was a lot closer than Maggie."

"True. So we need to be very careful. I will act as protector for you, but we can't ensure the safety of these women without more officers."

"Would it not make sense to use some of the local force?"

Nikos wrestled with himself. Personal loathing should not get in the way of an efficient investigation.

"Yes, possibly. I'll make some calls and see if we can have at least two uniforms."

"Jensson won't like that."

Nikos shrugged. "No, but any more deaths and he'd have to

cancel the cruise. His choice."

"He might have to anyway." Beatrice folded up the spread-sheet. "There are no secrets on this vessel. The news about the medical centre is all over the ship already, and it's likely to fuel suspicion and hostility towards Fraser. Nikos, I suggest we take him ashore to 'help with enquiries'. For his own benefit, and because I strongly suspect more than one person is involved in these deaths."

"Good idea. Maybe we should offer the same opportunity to Maggie Campbell? She'd be easier to keep safe on the island."

Beatrice revolved the highlighter pen in her hands, her gaze distant.

"Beatrice? You don't agree?"

"What? Oh yes, absolutely." She placed the pen on the table and stretched as if she'd just woken up.

"Let's get Maggie and Rose off the boat and under protection. It's better to divide our chickens. I just can't understand where Maureen Hall fits in. I have to talk to the Hirondelles again. Firstly, to warn them of the seriousness of this. And to find the connection. There has to be one. Have we talked to all of them?"

Nikos consulted his notes. "Between us, yes. One woman I interviewed didn't actually say anything but I got the feeling she wanted to."

"Doreen Cashmore."

Surprise at Beatrice's astute guess made him sit up straighter in his chair. He tipped an imaginary hat in her direction. She smiled and inclined her head in acceptance.

"Yes. Doreen Cashmore. It's only an instinct, but I know she was lying." He replayed their conversation in his mind. "I wanted to ask her about Mrs Crawford's will, but couldn't recall the word. I asked if there was anything in her... and she finished my sentence with the word 'past'. Why say something like that? She's another one hiding something, but I don't think she'll tell me. You might have more luck."

"I can but try. Perhaps if I talk to her unofficially?"

It amazed him how Beatrice seemed not only on his wavelength but one step ahead. In a feeble attempt to keep up, he shared his latest discovery.

"There's one other thing. Beryl Hodges didn't get to use cabin service much in her first few hours aboard, but after she left the birthday party, she ordered a drink. I checked the records. A glass of warm milk with a sachet of Ovomalt was delivered to her cabin at 21.49. The cabin attendant's name was Vicky Morton. Nothing special about her, apart from the fact she is the current girlfriend of Andros Metaxas."

"The tour guide who forgot Esther?"

"Yes. His real name is Andy Redmond. I need to ask some more questions."

"We both do." Beatrice tapped the pen against the back of her hand. "Where do we go from here?"

"How about this for a plan? I'll call Voulakis and the South Aegean Force, while you tell Fraser we're getting him off the boat. You find Maggie Campbell and persuade her and Rose to leave. I'll talk to Andy and his girlfriend separately. I want to get a feeling for how much loyalty there is. Talk to the Hirondelles together and ask if they too would like to leave in the circumstances. Then get Doreen Cashmore alone, while she's feeling scared and vulnerable. Offer support, a safe place to hide and all the help she needs if she can just give us some idea of why they are under threat."

Beatrice's smile stretched across her face as she nodded her approval. "You, Nikos Stephanakis, have all the makings of an excellent inspector. And a devious human being. Let's go."

Chapter 18

Beatrice and Jensson compromised. He gave permission for two South Aegean sergeants to come aboard only after Beatrice had agreed they should operate in plain clothes. The two officers worked with the *Empress Louise*'s own security staff to identify any crew members without an alibi for one of the three deaths. It was not a substantial list. Nikos made a rota of interviews for the sergeants while he escorted a subdued Dr Fraser ashore, along with Maggie and Rose. The two women had jumped at the chance to leave the ship and Beatrice detected as much enthusiasm from Rose as from Maggie.

She spent forty minutes trying to persuade Joyce Milligan to take her Hirondelle party ashore, but they seemed determined to stick it out. Not only that, but a memorial service was imminent so there was no question of leaving. The Hirondelles extended a most cordial invitation for Beatrice to join them.

Under a cloud of reluctance and defeat, Beatrice returned to her cabin to change into her grey suit. A little on the warm side for this weather, but suitably sober for the Hirondelles' memorial service. The *Empress Louise* had a multi-faith place of worship. No full-time chaplain or priest was attached, so it operated on an ad hoc basis. Occasional ordained passengers consented to hold services such as Mass or Shabbos, if sufficient interest existed.

Joyce Milligan, with indefatigable determination, had rooted out a Church of England priest willing to say a few words and persuaded a couple of the entertainment staff to sing some carefully chosen songs for the two departed Hirondelles.

The ladies were already seated when Beatrice arrived at the small room on E deck. She made a rough calculation and determined the room would hold no more than forty people. Currently, it hosted half that number. Four rows of pine benches took the place of pews and a neutral altar provided a point of focus. Someone waved. Maggie and Rose were sitting behind the main party along with half a dozen individuals Beatrice didn't recognise. She waved back and parked herself on the end of the last bench so as to observe proceedings. No sign of Captain Jensson, which she found disappointing. The priest, Reverend Melvyn Price, had just begun to welcome the congregation when the door eased open and a man sneaked in and stood by the gauze curtains flanking the doorway. Toni Dean, the crooner from the Rat Pack Revue. Oh dear, thought Beatrice, a Sinatra impersonator at a funeral can only mean one thing.

In front of the altar, another low table bore three photographs, propped up against white wooden cubes. The central picture was a group photograph of the Hirondelles, in a formal pose, all wearing their bowls-club style uniform of A-line skirt and peony-blue blazer, with a stylised swallow on the pocket. To the left, a less than distinct image of Esther Crawford laughing at the camera. Her short, neat haircut gave her the appearance of an ancient elf. The picture of Beryl Hodges, on the opposite side, was better technical quality but lacked atmosphere. Owlish glasses, a worried expression and standard issue set-and-blow-dry. She looked like half the occupants of the ship.

The priest, who'd caught a bit too much sun in the past week, read some endearing memories about each lady and invited mourners to pray with him. One of the young entertainers sang *Amazing Grace* in a pure, uplifting soprano. Several of the ladies reached for tissues. None of this breached Beatrice's defences. Then Joyce Milligan gave a short reading.

"*Not, how did she die, but how did she live?*
Not, what did she gain, but what did she give?
These are the units to measure the worth
Of woman as woman, regardless of birth.
Nor what was her church, nor what was her creed?
But had she befriended those really in need?
Was she ever ready, with words of good cheer,
To bring back a smile, to banish a tear?
Not what did the sketch in the newspaper say,
But how many were sorry when she passed away?"

The words, the rhythm and the sentiment might all have left the casual observer unmoved. Yet Joyce Milligan's voice, fighting emotion to deliver a powerful, heartfelt eulogy to her friends, had goose bumps creeping over Beatrice's skin by the second line.

The priest thanked her and introduced the last element of the service. 'One of Esther and Beryl's favourites'. He signalled to the back of the hall. The latecomer made his way down the aisle, bent to shake hands with all six of the Hirondelles and expressed his condolences with sincerity. Beatrice watched him operate. Blond hair, a deep tan, a charming if somewhat feigned manner. He took his position behind the photographs and nodded at the priest, who pressed a button on the CD player. The intro to *My Way* burst thinly into the space and Beatrice's toes curled. Then Toni Dean began to sing and her cynicism melted into chocolate marshmallow with caramel on top.

"Beautiful service. Lovely idea. Such a touching way to say goodbye. Thank you for inviting me. So sorry for your loss. Beautiful service. Very moving. Not at all, happy to be of help..."

The litany continued as the party milled about before the dead women's photographs. She praised the young soprano and admired Joyce Milligan's reading. She was working her way towards Doreen Cashmore when Toni Dean stepped into her path.

"Detective Inspector Stubbs. Just wanted to say hello. Toni Dean, entertainer. Very pleased to have you with us even on such a sad occasion. If today tells us anything, it's how much these dear ladies touched lives. I wish you great success with your investigation."

"That's very kind. I enjoyed your song very much. You do have an extraordinary voice."

"Thank you. When Miss Milligan asked me to sing this song for this occasion, I bit her hand off. It's a lovely way to say goodbye to someone you..."

Over Dean's shoulder, Beatrice saw Joyce Milligan and Doreen Cashmore leading the way to the exit.

"Indeed. Nice to meet you. Thanks again," she said and hurried off in their wake.

Doreen Cashmore was happy to join in the general approval of the service, compare the detail with other funerals she'd attended and reminisce about Beryl and Esther, but separating her from the rest of the Hirondelles proved a challenge. Ostensibly as a supportive gesture, the women had made a vow – that none would be left alone – not even with an officer of the law. Gentle persuasion and an emphasis on Beatrice's own role as protector met with polite resistance from the surviving ladies. She chose not to insist, although she had every right in her investigative role, as she wanted to elicit the information without recourse to pressure. Despite all the friendliness and encouragement to attend the service, Beatrice registered the atmosphere of closed ranks. Less vulnerability, certainly, and less chance of anyone veering from the party line. An opportunity would arise, eventually. All Beatrice needed to do was keep her eyes and ears open.

By teatime, Nikos had still not returned to the boat, but the South Aegean sergeants were ready to report the results of their interviews, such as they were. Of the fourteen individuals who had left the ship in Santorini, only five could not prove their movements; two women, three men. Yet when Beryl Hodges and Maureen Hall died, Efthakia Dellas was at her post in the communications room, Toni Dean was running through his Rat Pack repertoire onstage in the ballroom, Kostas the chef was in the kitchen, and senior stewards Lukas Karagounis and Susana Iliou were supervising evening service in the Grand Dining Room. No single staff or crew member remained without an alibi for at least one of the deaths.

Beatrice sat alone in her guest cabin, her focus switching fruitlessly between the various PDF versions of the ladies' wills, the spreadsheet of suspects on her computer and the view of the Aegean. No surprises in the list of beneficiaries. Children, grandchildren, a cancer charity, a sister. She had put in a request to the Wiltshire police to see if they could establish any connections but held out little hope.

Two methods of murder. Two people? One favours smothering and chest compression. You don't have to be especially strong to suffocate an octogenarian, so this person might have quite a different build to the man seen on the cliff. It could also be a woman. Experience had taught Beatrice the danger of gender assumptions. The cliff man had greater brute strength and a sense of opportunism. One ensures the alibi whilst the other performs the act. At least one might be staff or crew, explaining access to key cards. She made a note to cross check the alibis and anything linking all five staff visitors to Santorini.

If a passenger were an accomplice, it would make sense to observe the police investigation. The Hirondelles had not sought her out, but accepted her presence with a similar skittishness as a flock of sheep might show towards a collie. Apart from Maggie and Rose, only Oscar had made any friendly overtures. Yet he had actively prevented her from discussing the case and asked no searching questions.

Whether the killer was a passenger or ship employee, whether he worked alone or with a partner, the fundamental question remained. Why? Precedents existed, such as the Californian woman who killed and buried her tenants then claimed their benefits. The Tunisian who murdered more than fifteen elderly women in Southern Italy eventually confessed to sexual gratification as his driving force. As for The Stockwell Strangler, whose oldest victim was ninety-four, his motivations were both financial and sexual. None of the women on the *Empress Louise* had been molested, and if there were no monetary advantage, what would make someone go to such lengths to end the lives of ladies enjoying the third age?

The telephone in the cabin lit up and emitted a purr.

"Hello, this is DI Stubbs."

"*Hello Beatrice, Oscar here. Congratulations! We thought we'd given you the slip in Crete, but you tracked us down.*"

Beatrice smiled. "Elementary, my dear Oscar. Equipped with a detailed itinerary and scheduled arrival times, tracking this great white vessel was a doddle. How are you?"

"*Frazzled. Been out exploring and actually feeling my age. I'm planning a nap, can you believe? But before I surrender to The Sandman, I wanted to enquire as to your plans for dinner. Last night's conversation, scintillating as it was, seems unfinished. Especially as bellowing over the background row of the average taverna tends to obscure the nuances. Could I lure you ashore, or failing that, into one of the less pretentious eateries aboard?*"

Beatrice considered. He really was good company and helped her forget the case. Which was currently the last thing she needed.

"I'd love to. I really would, but tonight I plan to treat my partner to dinner in return for picking his brains. Perhaps another evening?"

"*Ah, the handsome Inspector Stephanakis. I stand down. I could never compete with such rugged good looks. I wish you an educational evening. And should our paths cross tomorrow, I would consider myself blessed.*"

Beatrice's laughter was genuine. "Talk to you tomorrow,

Oscar. Bye for now."

She focused once again on her spreadsheet, only to be interrupted by a knock at the door. She opened it to see a pretty blonde girl in a cabin attendant's uniform.

"Hello?"

"Detective Stubbs, my name is Vicky Morton, Cabin Attendant Service Personnel. I spoke to Inspector Stephanakis earlier today about the death of Beryl Hodges."

Beatrice remembered. The tour guide's girlfriend. "Oh yes, I know. You delivered her drink."

"That's right. I did. I wasn't much help, I'm afraid. Anyway, Inspector Stephanakis said if I thought of anything, any detail I could remember, I should let him know. But I can't find him."

"He's gone ashore. If you have something to say, you can talk to me. Come inside. Does this mean you've remembered something?"

Vicky followed her into the room and closed the door. "Sort of. When Mrs Hodges let me into the cabin, she was in her nightgown and she'd already taken her teeth out. Ready for bed, I thought. So I put the milk on the table and I saw a slice of birthday cake."

"Yes, she'd been to Esther Crawford's eightieth birthday party."

"Right. But she wasn't going to eat cake without her teeth. She told me to put the milk on the bedside table and draw the curtains for her. I asked if I should put the cake in the fridge and she waved her hand, you know, like the Queen."

Beatrice said nothing. The girl had thirty seconds to get to the point or would be noted as a timewaster.

"I wrapped it in a plastic bag and popped it in the fridge. It was the only thing in there."

"And? Why do you think this is relevant?"

"Inspector Stephanakis mentioned that Mrs Hodges was allergic to seafood and kept an EpiPen in her fridge in case of a reaction. Thing is, when I put that cake inside, the fridge was empty. I mean empty, like it had never been used."

"There could be several reasons for that. She had only just arrived, so she might not have unpacked it yet. Or if the injection device needed to be chilled, perhaps it was in the mini-bar instead."

"That's what I thought, but Inspector Stephanakis definitely said the fridge. Anyway, I just went down to G Deck and asked the cleaning crew. They were the ones who cleared the room after the body was removed. They told me they found four of those EpiPens on the top shelf of the fridge next to a slice of cake. What I'm saying is they weren't there at half past nine the night before. If she had a reaction in the night and went looking for her medicine in the fridge, it wouldn't have been there."

Chapter 19

Of all the crappy luck. Two years after he thought his nemesis had gone for good, his very first case as inspector had to involve Rhodes, the South Aegean Region and Demetrius Xanthou. It was as if Fate was laughing at him.

Once Mrs Campbell and Mrs Mason were settled in their hotel, he drove Dr Fraser to the police station with dread in his stomach. However, an interview room was prepared, the desk clerk expected him, an English-speaking sergeant was waiting to assist and Xanthou made no appearance. Nikos began to hope they might actually avoid each other. The second surprise was Fraser's willingness to talk. He hadn't expected much more than a repeat performance from the defensive Scot, so his humility came as a shock.

"Inspector, you should know that my career as a physician is now over."

"If that is the case, I'm sorry. I'm afraid we had no choice but to remove you from the ship. It was a decision made jointly with the cruise line management."

"I know. Jensson told me. You were right to do it; I'm not stupid enough to deny that. To be honest, I'm relieved. This situation has gone on too long and is not sustainable. When it begins to harm others, it's time to face the problem." He fiddled with his coffee cup but did not drink. "I have an addiction, Inspector. OxyContin, an opoid-based painkiller. It's the only thing that gets me through the day."

Nikos took a second to process that information. "How long have you been dependent?"

"Since a back injury in 2009. It happens a lot. I'm not the only one. Doctors are trained to look out for the repeat prescription seekers. Whereas doctors themselves don't need a prescription and we hold the keys to the medicine chest, so there's nothing stopping us."

Nikos tore off a sheet of paper from his notepad. "Please could you write down the name of the drug for me?"

Fraser scribbled something and then wrote several more words in block capitals beneath. "Medical name and brands. Over five years, I've not paid for one pill but this has cost me everything. My marriage fell apart, my career atrophied, I lost several jobs, the offers dried up, my colleagues in the medical profession avoid me and I know I've been guilty of negligence."

Nikos, scrambling to comprehend, tried to formulate a question but the doctor hadn't finished.

"My kids would rather I didn't visit and most of my friends have drifted away. Not Jensson, though. We met years ago, doing the Norwegian routes. Great man, full of ideas and intelligence. We played chess when we could and enjoyed the occasional debate. Our paths only crossed once in a blue moon, but we kept in touch. He's a pal, the kind of friend you call when you're up Shit Creek. He put his own neck on the line to offer me the Senior Physician post on this cruise. He trusted me."

A strange chill blew across Nikos's neck and he knew without doubt Xanthou must have entered the observation room behind the mirrored glass. He tried to push those judgemental eyes from his mind and focus on the man opposite.

"Do you feel you deserved his trust?" Nikos asked, wishing the other person in the room was Beatrice, not a blank junior officer, and that his interviewee would speak simple English.

Fraser clenched his hands together as if in ferocious prayer. "From the minute I wake to the minute I lose consciousness, one single thought process dominates my brain. How to get it, when to take it and how to hide it. No, I didn't deserve this post; I'm barely competent and better practitioners than me are still in medical school. As for the deaths of these ladies, I take full responsibility for a less than thorough post mortem on the Hodges woman. That's all. I didn't kill her. I can hardly focus on the conveyor belt of habitual daily complaints, let alone plan a succession of murders."

"Do you think you misdiagnosed the death of Beryl Hodges?"

"Very likely. And in doing so I lost any chance of redemption. Worst of all, I've probably lost the only friend I had left." His head dropped onto his knuckles and Nikos gave him a moment.

"Dr Fraser, you're free to go now. I'd like you to stay in Rhodes for the time being while I corroborate your story with Captain Jensson. Please leave contact details and the name of your hotel with the desk clerk. Thank you for your time. And good luck."

Fraser stood up and held out his hand. "Thanks to you too. I'll be in touch. All the best."

The sergeant escorted him out and Nikos collected his notes, waiting for Xanthou's big entrance and the dick-waving show-down, which could only be seconds away. The door opened.

"Nikos Stephanakis! Good to see you again! How long has it been, three years?"

Someone once told Xanthou he looked like John Travolta. Nikos often wondered who it was, as he would like to hunt that person down and punch them in the face. The most misguided statement ever, not least because it was absurdly far from the truth. In full ignorance of the fact that Travolta was at least half a metre taller, Xanthou had taken it to heart, growing sideburns, combing back his hair and dyeing his eyebrows. Now, in jeans, black shirt and denim jacket with the collar turned up, he looked like a low-rent Elvis impersonator.

Nikos mentally rolled up his sleeves and donned his super-hero mask.

"Demetrius Xanthou. Two years, I think." Neither man

offered his hand.

"Really? Feels longer. Congratulations, by the way. I hear you finally made inspector." (*ZAP!*)

"Thanks. Yes, really pleased with my first case. Teamed with a senior inspector from Scotland Yard." (*ZIP!*)

"So I hear. Having a woman as your boss? Very modern. How's Karen?" (*POW!*)

"Great. Karen and I are a team, equal partners, in the same way I'm working with DI Stubbs. Pretty effective together." (*WHACK!*)

"Yeah. Which is why you need the help of the South Aegean force. I have to get on, but if you can't cope, you have my number. Give my love to Karen. Wait, I have her email, I can do it myself! Those days, huh? Happy memories." (*KAPOW!*)

Xanthou was out the door before Nikos noticed his interview notes were crumpled in his clenched fist.

He found an empty office, forced himself to relax and called Beatrice. She answered on the first ring.

"Nikos. Where are you?"

"Still at the station. I made sure Rose Mason and Maggie Campbell checked in OK, and then interviewed Dr Fraser at the station. Interesting outcome. He's addicted to prescription drugs. A painkiller called OxyContin."

"I know it. Same sort as Vicodin and that has plenty of fans. Yes, that explains some of his behaviour."

"He functions, at a basic level, but got sacked from several previous posts and it's damaged his personal life. Jensson is an old friend, so this position was a kindness and a last chance for Fraser."

"Wouldn't painkiller addiction make him less mentally adept?" Beatrice asked.

"That's what he said. When he's had his fix, yes. When he needs more, it makes him agitated and aggressive. Neither situation fits the profile of the calm, well-planned serial killer we're looking for. I'll check out his story, just in case."

"*Yes, better had. Addicts can be very cunning. Still, his planning and methods will have an entirely different target.*"

"Exactly. I can't see a motive either. I really don't believe Fraser's connected. Did you talk to Doreen Cashmore?"

"*I've not been able to get her alone. The Hirondelles are joined at the hip. But I got the results from your South Aegean colleagues.*" She conveyed the unexciting outcome of the crew interviews. Nikos listened intently, occasionally asking for clarification and making notes.

"OK, thanks. I agree with checking for connections and testing those stories. I'm just going to Pathology for the forensic results on Maureen Hall's cabin and the papers he touched in the casino. Then I'll be back."

"*Let me know as soon as you get anything. Do you have plans for dinner tonight? I thought we could chew over theories and a steak at The Sizzling Grill.*"

"Good idea. Let's talk to the stewards and the communications officer before dinner, say hello to Kostas the chef, and then attend the Rat Pack Revue. That way, we can cover all those alibis."

"*Sounds like quite a plan,*" said Beatrice. "*But I've had my fill of crooners today, so might seek out Mrs Cashmore and leave you to enjoy Ol' Blue Contact Lenses.*"

"He certainly looks the part. So I'm interested to hear if he can actually sing."

"*He can sing, I'll vouch for that. He did his bit at the memorial service. Apart from his voice though, everything about the man is fake, from tan to accent.*"

Nikos looked up at the police personnel board. Xanthou's face smirked back at him. "I know exactly what you mean."

As he left the station, he got a text message alert. Karen.

Missing you. Any news? How's Xanthou? Kxxx

He stopped on a street corner to write back.

Miss you too. Some progress. Still an arsehole. Nxxx

Chapter 20

The only hole in any of the alibis, at least so far, seemed to be Kostas's assertion he had been in the kitchen all evening when Beryl Hodges and Maureen Hall were killed. As *chef de cuisine*, he was responsible for all dishes leaving the kitchen, and personally approved each plate before it went through the swing doors. Yet service ended at 10pm, leaving only desserts, supervised by the Pastry Chef. Kitchen staff turned their attention to cleaning surfaces and storing unused food, while Kostas took a break. According to the *commis chef*, he usually disappeared for half an hour to forty minutes, returning to approve the standards of cleanliness. Plenty of time for a cigarette, a drink or even a visit to an old lady's cabin.

Beatrice dawdled over her chocolate mousse and coffee, chatting to her waiter and digesting her conversation with Nikos. His assessment of motive was rather astute. Elderly women and sudden death usually suggested money. Or less commonly, revenge. The absolute lack of forensic evidence in Hall's room and on the documentation in the casino had bothered Beatrice more than she liked to let on. He'd worn gloves. There was nothing haphazard about the way this man operated.

Nikos had left just before nine in order to catch the opening number of the Rat Pack Revue. A wave of diners had departed around the same time. A new batch descended shortly afterwards and Beatrice was reminded of Jensson's words.

You are given the impression of free will and endless choices, but in reality, you are shuffled from one activity to the next and gently parted from your cash at every opportunity while the message is continually reinforced: you are having such a marvellous time!

The thought depressed her and she made Rorschach patterns on her napkin with spilt coffee. A vampire bat, a cross of thorns, a broken heart... my, she was morbid tonight. She paid the bill, left a generous tip and went in search of Doreen Cashmore.

To her surprise, the cabin door was opened by Joyce Milligan, who wore a lilac leisure suit and a hairnet.

"Detective Inspector Stubbs? You're either here because you've heard the rumours about my cocoa or you have arrested a suspect. Have you got someone?"

"I'm afraid not. I'm sorry to disturb you so late, but wanted to check all was well and have a quick word with Mrs Cashmore."

Joyce shook her head, like a horse refusing a jump. "Not right now, Detective Inspector. She's had the most dreadful day. Poor Doreen suffers with her nerves, you know. Under the circumstances, we thought a milky drink and an early night best. I'll stay with her. We look out for each other, you know."

Her huge hand, with bony, veined knuckles, rested on the cabin wall. A relaxed posture, but one which also barred entry. Strangler's hands, thought Beatrice.

"Of course. You're very lucky to have each other."

"And lucky to have you looking out for us. It was jolly decent of you to come to the service today. We all feel better for having said our goodbyes."

"It was extremely touching. Your reading and Mr Dean's Sinatra both had me welling up."

"He's got a fine pair of tonsils, hasn't he? I was quite overcome by his generosity when he approached me and offered to sing. I'd never have dared ask."

"Ah, I thought it was all down to your powers of persuasion.

Give Mrs Cashmore my very best and I hope you both sleep well. Goodnight."

"Same to you, hope the bed bugs don't bite."

Beatrice returned to deck and stood watching the shore as she considered the possibility the Hirondelle Hunter could be one of their own. The idea was totally ridiculous. Joyce Milligan was eighty-one years old. The sort who may well have wrestled bullocks in her youth, but nowadays, she was nothing more than a protective mother hen.

Laughter rang out from a table at one of the bars on the entertainment deck, generating a spike of envy in Beatrice. In one of her rare sociable moods, she had no one to talk to. Nikos would not leave the show till ten and then he would tail Kostas, so they'd agreed to debrief in the morning. She could return to the cabin and call Matthew. Except she really didn't feel like any more intensity. Her mind was all over the place and she had the urge to do something. Her mother's voice whispered on the Mediterranean wind, 'The Devil makes work for idle hands'. Beatrice hunched her shoulders against the breeze and turned in the direction of her cabin. She'd watch some television, empty her mind and take one of her pills, as several signs of rapid mood cycling were in evidence.

Pills. The news of Dr Fraser's addiction had sparked a nagging concern, once again. James had assured her more times than she could count that her mood stabilisers were not an addiction but a necessity. The alternative, allowing her condition to dictate her life, was much more alarming than taking one tablet a day. This she knew. This she understood. She fought a daily battle with her thought processes and with the recurrent urge to miss a day. Just to prove she could do without. It inevitably backfired and she'd regret it, but the temptation to rebel, to revolt against what was best for her returned again and again. Grow up, woman, she told herself. Get back to your cabin, take your tablet and reattach your stabilisers.

As she ascended the stairs, she heard rapid footsteps from

the deck above and when she arrived at the top, she saw Oscar hurrying in her direction.

"Quick! This way!" he hissed with some urgency. He turned her around, guiding her by the elbow, and they trotted back down together. At the bottom, he took another sharp angle, drawing her with him until they were tucked side-by-side under the steps in a dark alcove. He pressed himself back into the shadows and listened.

Deck lights between the rungs threw horizontal stripes across his face, making her think of film noir and Humphrey Bogart. Beatrice looked at him for an explanation and was just about to open her mouth when Oscar boggled his eyes and pressed a finger to his lips.

An American woman's voice carried on the night air. "... usually found in the Club Room after dinner. Well, if Mohammed won't come to the mountain..."

"The Club Room? Wouldn't you need to be a member?"

"Perhaps. If so, we'll join. It's only a question of greasing palms. Do you know, I found a concierge service in Boston..."

Two pairs of feet clanged down the metal steps and a rustle of evening gowns brushed past their faces. The ladies proceeded, still talking, across the deck below. Beatrice left Oscar in the shadows and tiptoed across to the railings. Mrs Bartholomew and another woman marched towards double doors diagonally opposite without a glance behind.

Beatrice looked over her shoulder and laughed to see Oscar flattened against the wall. "What does she want with you?"

Oscar closed his eyes with a mock shudder. "She has some 'totally awesome' family stories which really should be in my book. Or maybe this material might merit a book all its own. I'd have to sign a confidentiality agreement, blah, blah ... oh spare me, please. And now my sacred retreat, The Club Room, is off limits. I always said there should be a door policy. I am cut adrift."

"Don't be so dramatic. There are plenty of other cafés and bars to hide in. You're spoilt for choice."

"I beg to differ. For an old codger who desires good conversation in a peaceful setting with a quiet glass of something elegant, there are precious few."

Beatrice spoke without thinking. "The ship's guest cabins each boast a substantial mini-bar, muted yet tasteful music and I was quite fancying a nightcap. Or would our reputations be forever tarnished if we were to withdraw unchaperoned?"

"My good lady! Let us make haste and to hell with the rumours. Which way?"

Lamps lit, a bottle of red opened, a concerto wafting from the speakers and Oscar relaxing in the armchair; the scene soothed Beatrice. She kicked off her shoes and sat on the armchair diagonally opposite him, so they both faced the panoramic window and the city, which from this distance looked strung with fairy lights.

"Does that happen a lot?" she asked.

"Being pursued by women? All the time," he said, with a regretful shake of his head.

She raised her glass. "Cheers. I meant the offer of material for a book."

"Cheers. Oh, I say. That's fruity. Yes, sadly, all too often people believe an apocryphal anecdote about their granny's comical expressions is worthy of inclusion in a serious academic study on language. I've fallen victim to this phenomenon so many times, I now flee at the first warning signs. Mrs Bartholomew sent a summons for me to join her after dinner, including the details I mentioned earlier. I politely declined, claiming a prior engagement. But the woman is indefatigable. She made a bee line as soon as she saw me down cutlery, and I had to quit the dining-room with unseemly haste. I knew I should have gone ashore. It's always on the last leg of the journey when one's fellow passengers become insufferable."

"Oh dear. What will you say when she finally catches up with you? She will, you can guarantee it."

"I'll deny all knowledge of running away, or claim forgetfulness. I cultivate that air from first impressions. Sitting at the wrong table, unable to recall people's names, searching for my glasses when they're on my head. The dotty professor act."

"You didn't fool me."

"I didn't try to. What is this wine, please? It's quite lovely."

Beatrice fetched the bottle and handed it to him. He removed his glasses to read the label.

"Ah, a Portuguese Dão. I went on a tasting tour up the Douro valley two years ago. Loved every drop. Have you been?" He looked up at her. Lamplights reflected in his hazel irises and dark lashes framed his eyes, surprisingly naked without his glasses. She returned to her seat, leaving him with the bottle.

"No, but it's on the list. Last time we went wine-tasting was to Hungary. That was a revelation."

"I'm sure it was. I've heard great things." He sprang out of the chair in a supple movement and placed the bottle back on the table. Whilst on his feet, he approached a print depicting a Greek fishing village. He stood in front of it with his hands folded behind his back, in the style of Prince Phillip.

"I must say guest suites certainly have the edge. Wine, space, artwork and soft furnishings are all quite superior. But I suppose the view is the same for us all. And what a view it is." He replaced his glasses and walked to the window. Beatrice felt a peculiar sense of relief at having a barrier between her and Oscar's eyes.

She joined him to gaze at the Palace of the Grand Master of the Knights of Rhodes, as imposing a sight over the city as Castle Rock over Edinburgh. They sipped their wine in appreciative silence.

"You said '*we* went wine tasting'. I presume you're referring to Mr Stubbs?"

She shook her head and returned to her spot, tucking one leg under herself, wishing the conversation would take another turn. "There is no Mr Stubbs."

"I'm so sorry."

He sat in the armchair once more, waiting for her to continue, his brogues keeping time with the Brahms.

"No, no. I meant we're not married. Matthew and I have been together over twenty years but never..."

"Got around to it?" offered Oscar.

"No, no. Made it official, I was going to say. I'm sure marriage is a wonderful thing for some people. It just never appealed to me."

The piano and cello reached a crescendo, as if attempting to score the conversation. Oscar rested his chin on his hand and studied her. She scratched her temple, swilled her wine around the glass and willed him to look away.

He smiled, as if sensing her discomfort. "So that poor man, besotted by this elusive and brilliant butterfly, proposes every year on Christmas Eve, hoping in vain to capture the object of his desire. But no. She flutters into his garden, accompanied by sunshine and rainbows, stays awhile, but refuses to be netted."

The wine had gone to her head and she flushed. "I'll tell him about that image. He'll find it hilarious. Especially the butterfly bit. One of his daughters refers to me as Beatrice the Bull Elephant ever since an awkward incident in a Totnes delicatessen. We were admiring a display of exotic spices in a glass case. Unfortunately, a rather forceful sneeze took me by surprise. My forehead hit the glass and it shattered, exploding colourful spices everywhere. That was seven years ago and I still occasionally find grains of turmeric in my ear."

Oscar threw back his head and laughed, a warm, deep sound. His shoulders shook and his stomach bounced.

"If I could exchange all the money I paid for this cruise just to have been present at that moment, I would do so twice. Those shopkeepers are probably still telling that story."

"I wouldn't know. Unsurprisingly, we've never been back."

Oscar got to his feet. "I feel duty-bound to have one last glass of the Dão before leaving you to your rest. You will join me, DI Stubbs?"

"I should coco. A wine like that cannot be ignored. Are you peckish? There's nuts and whatnot in the cupboard."

He offered the wine and she held out her glass. He kept his eyes on the carmine stream, only glancing at her as he finished. Again, she felt the jolt of adrenalin. Danger, yes. But what kind? He settled back in his place and refilled his own glass, still with a slight smile.

"Thank you, but after bolting three courses to escape The Boston Badger, not even nuts and whatnot could tempt me. How about you? Did Inspector Stephanakis enjoy dinner with the boss? Where did you eat?"

"I'm not his boss. We're equals on this one. We went to The Sizzling Grill. We both had the ribs but with different sauces. I never want to eat anything else. Ever."

Oscar's face creased into another laugh. "My wife used to say the same thing. After every holiday, every memorable meal, every concert she'd enjoyed. Always vowed to move there, or eat, drink and listen to nothing else." He gazed into his wine, his face soft in recollection.

"If you don't mind my asking, how did you meet her?"

Oscar looked up in surprise. "Many people start a question the same way, but they want to know about the end, not the beginning. As always, Beatrice Stubbs is different." He raised his glass in an ironic toast, then sipped.

"She was a mature student. Not one of mine, I stress. I had rules about that sort of thing. But she assisted me at a couple of conferences. One evening, I wanted to return to my hotel room to prepare some slides. She challenged me. Language, she said, is a living thing. You cannot study it from behind a microscope. Come out in the city with me, let's listen and talk and get Jane Goodall with the natives. She bullied me out of the library and into an all-night cafe in Copenhagen. We continued adventuring for sixteen years until bowel cancer took her in 2007. Without her, I have regressed to my natural state. Playing it safe."

The CD came to an end and silence swelled to fill the space.

Beatrice realised she had deflated the mood.

"I'm sorry you lost her so early. I'm also glad you found someone so remarkable and enjoyed her company for many years."

His smile was that of a weary child. "Yes, I know how lucky I've been. The problem is that she showed me the joy of life. Now I'm back behind the microscope, observing but not getting involved. My daughter despairs of me and still holds out hope that someday I'll meet someone to break through the glass. Good Lord, we've turned maudlin. I'd best cede the floor to you as your spice cabinet mishaps are far more entertaining."

"Mishap. It was only the once. Thank you for being so honest and I'm sorry if I dragged up old wounds. Shall I tell you the story of the time a bee flew up my trouser leg?"

He smiled but shook his head. "Fair's fair. I told you mine. Now I want to hear about Not-Mr-Stubbs. How did you meet?"

The words were out of her mouth before she'd decided to speak.

"I stole him."

Chapter 21

Beatrice looked at her wine glass as if it had betrayed her. Several well-rehearsed fabrications lay at her disposal, and other than those directly involved, few people knew the reality. She'd not even told Adrian. So why this sudden impulse to share the less palatable elements of her past with a near stranger? After twenty-four years, the burden of truth didn't get any heavier. If James were here, he would ask her to examine her motives before saying any more. But he wasn't here. It was just her and Oscar.

He set down his glass, crossed his legs and folded his hands around his knee. A patient listener. She took a large swig of wine and began.

"I grew up in the Gloucestershire countryside. Stone walls, quaint towns and charming hedgerows. Quiet, just the way my parents liked it. They had accepted their childlessness and I believe they had begun to enjoy it when I came along. I was a solitary child; content to read, listen to adult conversation or play with an elderly Labrador called Horace. On my first day at school, I sat next to a pretty blonde girl called Pamela Pearce. Without even asking my name, she informed me she was an only child and her two favourite things were steamed pudding and picking scabs. With so much in common, we naturally became immediate friends. Ersatz sisters, I suppose, throughout our school days.

"When we got older, she attended my graduation ceremony and I was her bridesmaid. She was the first person I called when I was accepted into the CID. She made me godmother to her eldest. While I thrived on the daily battle that is life in London, she was content to be a housewife and mother in the country, joining the school committee and all that. Her husband was a university don and a lot older than us, but he seemed pleasant enough. Pleasant, if rather dull. I liked visiting for the occasional weekend, seeing the girls, enjoying Pam's company, although I was always relieved to get back to my little flat in the East End. Pam travelled up to see me once and was terribly anxious the whole time. What's the phobia where you are afraid of crowds?"

"Agoraphobia."

"Is it? I thought that was open spaces. Well, she had the most awful time and we both agreed it was better if I did the visiting."

Oscar listened with complete attention, not even touching his wine. Beatrice took another swig and pressed on. The story seemed desperate to be told.

"In 1988, Professor Matthew Bailey gave a series of weekly lectures at The British Museum. Pam pleaded with me to look after him. I think she was projecting her own experience, because he was perfectly at ease alone in the city. He actually preferred his own company. I made excuses the first couple of times, but then caved and took him to the Docklands. A bunch of art students had put on an exhibition in the Port Authority Building. I thought he'd hate it. He didn't."

"You mean...?"

Beatrice brought herself back over the decades and focused on her companion.

"Yes. No one had any idea how significant it would turn out to be, least of all me. Anyway, I bought him fish and chips and felt I'd done my duty. Of course, his typical old school manners meant he had to return the favour, and pretty soon it became a weekly event. He'd come up on the train, give his lecture and then we'd do something cultural and argue about it. It's hard to explain. He was so different. You see, my life was made up of answers. Matthew was all about questions."

She fell silent, recalling how reluctance, by imperceptible degrees, shifted to anticipation and eagerness.

Oscar's voice almost startled her. "You fell in love." His tone was comprehending and sympathetic, with no hint of judgement.

"Yes. It sort of crept up on me. One evening, as we said our polite goodbyes at Green Park, I saw the same thing in his eyes. Nothing happened. No passionate kisses in the rain or a tearful flight across a photogenic bridge; it wasn't a bloody Richard Curtis film. I just looked at him and knew this was it. The best and worst thing in my life. I'd fallen in love with my best friend's husband, so my choices were destruction or destruction."

Oscar stood and poured a little more Dão into her glass. "An impossible position. What did you do?"

Beatrice realised she was scratching at the scar on her wrist. She laced her hands in her lap. She had to finish the story and get Oscar to leave. Her desire for solitude whined like the spin cycle of a washing-machine.

"I stopped seeing him. I told him I was too busy, volunteered for overtime, spent every waking hour at work, refused his calls, the whole five yards. It was agony. His lecture series finished and I thought I was in the clear. Then Pam invited me to Marianne's first communion."

"Your god-daughter?"

"Yes. I couldn't refuse. I spent weeks counselling myself and practising detachment. The second I saw him, everything fell apart. I was so jumpy Pam even asked if I was taking anything. Can't recall anything of the communion, just a blur of white dresses, singing, fizzy wine, ribbons and this pulsing presence I had to ignore. Matthew was supposed to take me to the station. He said nothing but drove us instead to a beauty spot by the river. We sat on a bench and talked. He loved me, I loved him and neither of us had done it on purpose, but there it was. A few days later, he told Pam, and then the girls. He moved out to a cottage nearby. I stayed in London and we gave the relationship a trial period, just seeing each other at weekends. That trial period has lasted twenty-four years."

"And Pam?"

An ancient pain, like a once-sprained muscle, flared into life.

"She never spoke to me again. After a period of ugliness and spite, things settled down. Now we take turns at family events. The girls ensure our paths never cross. I always intended to build a bridge once the dust had settled. But what words do you use to say 'I'm sorry I had to ruin your life to find mine'? I'm still searching."

Oscar rubbed his forehead, pushed himself out of his chair and stood at the window, facing the view. Beatrice joined him, her stomach inexplicably fluttery.

"Look, I'm sorry about all that. I normally lie when people ask me that question. Other than those involved, you're only the third person I've ever told all the details. And one of those was paid to listen. Tonight, it just all whooshed out, for some reason. I have no idea why."

Oscar kept his eyes on the lights of Rhodes but a faint smile smoothed his face. "I think I can hazard a guess. This is a genteel form of sabre-rattling. You are fluffing your feathers, shaking your quills or baring your teeth. The entire display, possibly not even on a conscious level, is designed to make me retreat. The message here is two-fold. Firstly, you belong to another. And secondly, you want me to think badly of you, as The Other Woman. Either way, your unusual candour is a warning. I understand. And I'll back off."

A rush of anger erupted in Beatrice. She stalked to the table and refilled her glass, counting to ten in her head. Rather than having the intended calming effect, the numbers fuelled her temper.

"In point of fact, I pay a professional counsellor to help me analyse my behavioural patterns. He's very good at guiding me towards an understanding of my own motivations. The one thing he never does is tell me why I act a certain way or attribute a gesture to his own deeper comprehension of my psyche than I have myself. So when I share a secret with someone who then imposes some cod psychology on my words, intimating my embarrassing truth is nothing more than some primitive fan dance, I find it infuriating to say the least. If I wanted you to piss off, Oscar, believe me, I would have no hesitation in saying so!"

His expression, backlit by the lamp, was unreadable. Another surge of emotion swelled as she debated asking him to leave. The problem was, now she didn't want him to go. He came towards her and placed his hands on her shoulders.

"Beatrice, I'm sorry. That was incredibly arrogant of me. For you to share what you describe as 'the embarrassing truth' must have been painful and I should have been more sensitive to the compliment. But with classic egotism, I interpreted your honesty only in relation to myself."

His eyes searched her face. She replayed his words and understood what he was saying. Her anger collapsed. Her voice, in complete contrast to her most recent outburst, was hushed.

"I wasn't telling you to back off because I didn't realise you were..." she discarded several alternatives and still the right expression eluded her.

Oscar's lips twitched. "Coming on?"

She couldn't reply, her senses muddled by the heat of his hands, the scent of his cedar wood cologne and the expression on his face.

He shook his head, his gaze never leaving hers. "In that case, I'm seriously concerned about your skills of observation." His pupils expanded, a few fireflies of colour floating on the edges.

A pulse beat at her throat as his thumb brushed her collarbone, sending whispers across her skin.

"Can I just clarify one thing, Detective Inspector? Do you, or do you not, want me to piss off?"

A voice in her head began making a series of statements. *This is the perfect time to laugh, apologise for shouting and tell him not exactly to piss off but that it is getting late. Your moods have been erratic all day and you have not yet taken your stabiliser. Sudden flares of lust and lack of good judgement are, as you well know, sure signs of your condition. Break his gaze and speak, woman.*

The roaring in her ears drowned it out. When Oscar bent to kiss her, her body moved to meet his, as if she had no say in the matter. The touch of his lips triggered a simultaneous liquefying sensation and intoxicating euphoria so that his steadying hands on her shoulders seemed the only things keeping her upright. She released a huge, shivery breath as his mouth moved to press butterfly kisses on her neck and the diminished voice in her head floated clean away.

Then he stopped. He lifted his head, looking over her shoulder. "There's someone outside the door," he whispered.

An envelope lay on the mat. Oscar broke the clinch, wrenched open the door and looked both ways up the corridor. Beatrice, light-headed and dizzy, picked up the white *Empress Louise* stationery.

"No one there," he said.

"They can't have got far. You go left, I'll go right. Quick!"

She rushed barefoot along the corridor, shaking with a maelstrom of emotions. As she turned the corner, the envelope clutched in her hand, she collided heavily with someone coming the other way. Doreen Cashmore had the air of a wild animal exhausted by the hunt.

"Mrs Cashmore, are you all right?"

"I changed my mind. I was coming back to get the letter. I shouldn't have written it. It's not my place but it's been on my conscience, you see. That poor woman had nothing at all to do with it. I can't, I just can't..." Her face screwed into a wretched grimace and she began to weep dry hitching sobs that sounded like a gate blowing in the wind.

"Come. Let's sit down and sort this out. You really shouldn't be wandering about alone, especially not at this hour. This way."

Doreen allowed Beatrice to manoeuvre her back along the corridor and pulled a tissue from her sleeve to blow her nose.

"I couldn't get out before. I had to wait till Joyce went to bed. But she was playing cards on the computer till late and... oh!"

As they approached the guest cabin, Oscar stepped out of the door, glancing quickly at the elderly lady and back to Beatrice.

"Ah. I was just coming to find you." His eyes locked onto hers.

Beatrice's stomach effervesced and she forced herself to look away. "Mrs Cashmore, this is a friend of mine, Oscar Martins. Oscar, Mrs Cashmore is a bit upset, so we're going to have a chat in my cabin, if you don't mind."

"Of course not. I'll leave you in peace. I hope you feel better soon, Mrs Cashmore. And perhaps we can continue our discussion tomorrow, Detective Inspector?"

Mrs Cashmore was still blinking at Oscar so didn't spot the transformation of professional police officer into fourteen-year-old girl.

"I... umm... well... yes, that's a distinct possibility. See you tomorrow then."

"See you tomorrow. Sweet dreams. Goodnight, ladies."

They watched him walk down the corridor until Beatrice came to her senses and ushered Mrs Cashmore inside. While making her guest some tea, she splashed cold water on her face, took her stabiliser and prepared to concentrate on the job. She'd save thoughts of Oscar till later.

Chapter 22

Finding a place to make a private call with no danger of being overheard by the police patrol or anyone else was impossible. In the end, Nikos walked all the way back to his cabin to call Karen.

It might make him late for the cabaret, but it was worth it. Of all people, Karen would understand why today's encounter with Xanthou had got under his skin. With her usual perceptive analysis, she said Xanthou's behaviour showed him to be insecure and threatened. His problem, and no one else's. No, she'd received no emails from the cocky little git, but if she did, she'd delete them. She wanted Nikos to come home. She missed him and when he got back, she would chain him to the bed to stop him leaving again. By the end of the call, he felt warm, righteous and a little bit horny.

He checked his watch. The show had already started. He hurried back to the entertainment decks and The Man with the Golden Voice. Fortunately, the ballroom was laid out in cabaret, rather than theatre style, so Nikos's late arrival caused the minimum of disturbance. A waiter showed him to his seat and took his order for still water. Toni Dean was coming to the final chorus of *King of the Road*. Behind him, spotlights picked out the backing vocalists, two tuxedo-clad men and a woman in a black sheath dress singing into a single microphone, while two showgirls in sparkling swimsuits and an abundance of feathers struck poses every few bars. The band, at the back of the stage, consisted of a piano, drums, a trumpet and a saxophone, along with a double bass and a synthesiser. Dean swayed from foot to foot, convincingly Sinatra-sounding, flashing his teeth at every opportunity.

Nikos settled back and wondered what wicked observations Karen would make if she were here. She could always puncture the artificial and pretentious with a well-chosen barb. She'd have something to say about the showgirls' eyelashes and fixed grins, for sure, not to mention Toni's perma-tan. She insisted on watching the Eurovision Song Contest every year, 'for comedy value'. If only she was here. He loved the way she reduced Xanthou so effectively to a 'cocky little git'. Voulakis, when he'd been their senior officer, could see there was a problem, but laughed it off as professional jealousy. In fact, he used to fan the flames, in the misguided belief that competitiveness would make them both work harder. He had no idea how personal and destructive Xanthou could be.

Toni (Frank) was introducing the cast with a showman's patter. The crowd applauded and whistled as 'Sammy Davis Junior' and 'Dean Martin' strolled onto the stage to join in with a rendition of *A Lovely Way to Spend an Evening*. Nikos, already bored, browsed the glossy programme and realised that each entertainer would have a section of the show to himself, beginning with Frank and ending with a finale involving all three. So what did Toni Dean do while his colleagues took the stage?

Nikos made some rough calculations and decided to leave at the interval and miss the start of the second half. He'd just have time to find out what Kostas got up to after ten o'clock before returning to watch the offstage movements of Toni Dean. He sat back to listen to *My Kind of Town* and found himself humming along.

Kostas, clearly in a hurry, left the kitchen with a bag. Nikos almost lost him a couple of times as he slipped around corners and through doorways. Tailing an experienced staff member round a cruise ship without alerting said individual to his presence – Nikos could remember easier gigs. The chef, whose familiarity with layout far exceeded his own, ducked into a crew elevator and the doors closed. Nikos waited several seconds before approaching to watch the numbers descend. G Deck. Below sea level and where crew quarters were housed. Kostas was staff, so certainly had a cabin on A Deck or above. All staff and crew facilities, including mess, buffet and recreation facilities were in A Deck. The only things on G Deck were laundry, refuse, engines and the lowliest quarters. What would he need down there?

As a senior member of staff, Kostas had access to all areas. Crew, staff and passenger facilities were at his disposal. So what would draw him to visit the most basic, below-sea section, where engineers slept on bunks and shared a toilet? In the same crew lift he'd seen Kostas take, Nikos pressed the button for G Deck, wondering if he'd emerge into a full-fledged ceilidh with Kate Winslet dancing the polka.

He didn't. The gangways stood silent, every door closed and apart from the far louder sounds of the engines and the smell of cooking fish, no different to six levels above. He turned left, for no other reason than he sensed that was where the smell came from.

The first open door led to an empty cabin, with two unmade beds and laundry hanging from a makeshift line across the sink. The second opened into a communal area, where a few men played cards and others argued or laughed in small groups. They turned to stare as he crossed the threshold. One man shook his head and pointed towards the ceiling.

"No place for you. Go back upstairs." Nikos withdrew, opting not to use his police badge. Kostas was nowhere to be seen. He retraced his steps to the lift and decided to turn one last corner in the other direction, before abandoning hope of finding the vanished chef.

Storerooms and offices. Each bearing an abbreviation: HT/

HR Office, LC/LS Store G2, IT/ITS, PLCPO, C/S/C Storage. Nikos tried every door. No indication as to meaning or usefulness and each one locked. A fruitless exercise and now he'd have to hurry not to miss the Rat Pack changeover. Back to the elevator. As he watched the numbers descend, he heard a door open, a soft goodbye in Greek and footsteps coming his way. Kostas started at the sight of the inspector. Nikos noticed the chef's jaw harden and saw the bandage on his hand. He assumed a relaxed pose to counteract the chef's folded arms and greeted him in Greek.

"Yeah, I followed you. It's my job. I have to check each staff and crew member's alibi. Yours, in the kitchen from six till eleven, didn't stand up. I know you leave during dessert and only come back to check the cleaning. I can't remove you from suspicion until your alibi is proven. You're not being persecuted. You're not the only one."

Kostas cursed under his breath. "No such thing as privacy. Just like a TV show. Performing, all the time."

"I don't know. Not my area of expertise. What did you do to your hand?"

"Cut it. Meat cleaver slipped. Do you want to see?"

"No. All I have to do is make one hundred percent sure that you were somewhere else when three elderly ladies died. You told the Rhodes sergeant you work in the kitchen till eleven pm. You don't. See my point, Kostas? I need to know what you do between ten and half past."

"Come." Kostas jerked his head back up the corridor. Nikos checked his watch. 'Frank' would be handing over to 'Sammy' about now, and heading off to do what exactly? He shrugged and followed the chef.

Kostas rounded the corner and knocked on a cabin door and called out. "Tsampika? It's me again."

The door opened and a tall, gaunt woman peered out. Her expression darkened when she saw Stephanakis and looked to the chef for reassurance.

"This is Inspector Stephanakis. He's not interested in you, he's checking my alibi. He wants to know what I do in the break. Will you tell him?"

She addressed Nikos with a resentful glare. "He visits me. Every night."

Stephanakis could guess the reason but had to get confirmation. He winced at the indelicacy of the question.

"Can I ask why?"

Kostas answered. "It's the only chance I get to see my sister."

"Your sister?"

"Yes. Tsampika is crew, on the laundry team. Since her husband lost his job and their savings got swallowed by rent increases, she has to work. On the ships, she earns enough to keep her family by leaving them for two weeks every month. It's not the worst job in the world. I gave her a reference, but not as her brother. Some people down here know we're related but the powers-that-be don't know anything. Crew are not allowed on passenger decks, so if we spent time together on A Deck, it would raise eyebrows. That's why I visit her in her cabin and bring her some decent food when we both have free time. She doesn't have much."

"Food or free time?"

"Both."

"I'll need your full name, Tsampika. I won't cause you any problems, I'll just check this out quietly."

She chewed her thumbnail and looked up at her brother.

Kostas lowered his brow. "I'll give you her name, but know this. If you tell any senior management or anyone at all in HR, she'll lose her job. Mine could be in danger, too."

"I will make sure your sister is not implicated in any way and will keep my investigations general. I don't want to cause harm here. I just want to stop someone killing the passengers."

He thanked Tsampika and wished the siblings goodnight. While he waited for the elevator, Kostas caught him up. They rode in silence to the entertainment deck.

Nikos spoke. "Kostas, you're an experienced cruise veteran. In your view, is the person who's targeting these women a passenger, a member of staff or crew?"

Several seconds passed and the lift doors opened. They stepped out onto the deck and Kostas paused.

"It's not anyone on the crew. They all know these people are our livelihood. Staff? Many of us could happily kill the occasional passenger, of course, but how stupid would we be to bite the hand that feeds? Passengers, I couldn't say. In my experience of eighteen cruises, at least fifty percent are borderline crazy."

"Thank you. I'll leave you now and I promise to be discreet."

"That would be most welcome. Goodnight, Inspector."

Nikos held out his right hand.

The chef shook it.

Backstage at the Ballroom was surprisingly shabby. Worn carpets, peeling photographs of earlier performances, empty coffee cups and labelled rails of costumes. Nikos knocked twice on Toni Dean's door but no one answered. He tried the door, which was locked. The Stage Manager was unconcerned.

"Gargling in the bathroom? Gone out for fresh air? He's a wanderer, that one. The entertainers spend so much time indoors in the dark, soon as they get more than five minutes break, you'll usually find them on deck. With Toni, he's a free spirit. He's a biker, you know. When we're docked, every chance he gets, he's off out on his Harley. Couple of times he's only just made it back in time for the show. Gives me grey hairs, that one."

A pressure lifted. Subject to checks, the chef was simply a loyal brother and the crooner relished a bit of freedom from routine. Not only that, but Nikos was growing increasingly convinced the predator was a passenger. He made a note on his phone: Oscar Martins – any history?

He ascended the stairs to the observation deck, scanning the strolling passers-by for a man with a tan and extraordinarily white teeth. The evening air, cool and fresh, energised him.

Somehow, he felt secure. It had taken a while, but he was now an inspector. He'd encountered Xanthou and risen above any attempt at patronisation. Despite being promoted two years later than his rival, he was working his first case with an experienced detective from Scotland Yard, who treated him as an equal. Best of all, he'd got the girl. Karen, his fantasy woman, had chosen him. Perhaps it was premature but the world looked pretty good to Nikos Stephanakis.

A man was smoking at the end of the deck, looking out at the island. Nikos approached, gauging the man a little short to be his target, although the tuxedo looked familiar. As he approached, he spotted the goatee beard, the paunch and the round glasses. Not Toni Dean, but Dr Weinberg. No wonder he was hidden from sight. A doctor with a cigar?

"Good evening, Doctor."

Weinberg acknowledged him with a half nod and continued his contemplation of the city of Rhodes. "A man could never get tired of Greece, I'm sure."

Nikos leant his arms on the rail beside him and tried to see the view through foreign eyes. "Not sure. Give me another thirty years."

Weinberg laughed, a gentle, restrained sound from one side of his mouth, blowing smoke away in a considerate gesture. "To live here, in the lap of the Gods, with history and beauty and knowledge surrounding you. You are fortunate to be born Greek, Inspector."

"Thank you. I think so. Though the general atmosphere, at the moment, is not one of feeling lucky."

"Are you referring to the situation on board or the morale of Greece as a whole?"

"I was thinking about my country," Nikos replied, preparing his defences.

Weinberg exhaled downwind and fanned the smoke away with his hand. "With good reason. The current climate is to be expected when austerity measures weaken the vulnerable still further."

Surprised, Nikos checked the doctor's face for sarcasm.

The ship's floodlights reflected in Weinberg's glasses as he turned to meet Nikos's stare. "Oh yes, Inspector, I'm serious. I cannot claim comprehensive knowledge, as my interest is medicine. But I follow the news in my field. I know about the increase in HIV infections, the malaria outbreak, the infant mortality rates and number of male suicides. What has happened to Greek healthcare in the past five years is a retrograde step. This makes me sad. Sad and very angry. You see, when I'm not working, I volunteer with *Médecins Sans Frontières*, or used to."

"Why did you stop?"

"I didn't stop. But I had to stop working in Greece. My last tour of duty was in Mozambique. Very different, but another beautiful country."

"I don't know it. Why can't you work in Greece?"

The doctor extinguished his cigar. He used a small tin cup complete with lid to dispose of all traces of his habit. "Some people, including many members of the crew, blame Germany for the EU bailout conditions. As an Austrian, I'm regarded as more or less German as well. The accent, you see. So I am the enemy. Today, they had no choice. But I think both the engineer and the chef would have preferred Nurse Bannerjee to me."

"A chef? Was that Kostas, from The Sizzling Grill?"

"Correct. Broken finger. Easily set with a splint."

Nikos's phone, switched to silent since entering the ballroom, vibrated. He checked the screen. Number unknown.

"Excuse me, Doctor. I have to take this call. It was good talking to you and I wish you a nice evening."

He walked across the deck and answered professionally. "Stephanakis?"

"*Inspector Stephanakis, I'm sorry to disturb you. This is Captain Jensson. Could you please join the emergency team in Deluxe Cabin 254 on the Aegean Deck? It seems there has been another attack.*"

Nikos began running and talking at the same time.

"On my way. Another of the Hirondelles?"

"*The lady in question is a member of the Hirondelle party, but fortunately the attack was incomplete. An alarm alerted neighbouring cabins and the man escaped before help arrived.*"

"Where's DI Stubbs?"

"*Here. One moment. I will pass her the telephone,*" Jensson said.

"*Nikos? Where are you?*"

"On my way. Who did he attack? Doreen Cashmore?" He rushed up the stairs to the next level.

"*No, because Doreen was in my room. He assaulted Joyce Milligan. But she fought back. Her injuries look pretty nasty, but she'll survive. By God, I hope so. Nikos, listen. Doreen's spilled the beans and now I know why. The only thing we don't know is who.*"

Chapter 23

Dear Detective Inspector Stubbs

I am writing to you because I feel there is something important you should be aware of regarding the Hirondelles and Swallows Hall. I apologise for not talking to you earlier, but we thought it best not to speak of the matter as it seemed irrelevant. However, recent circumstances have convinced me that it is most definitely something the police need to know. Not all my companions agree, which is why I am writing this letter rather than coming to you in person.

When I secured a position as house mistress at Swallows Hall in the winter of 1961, Joyce Milligan was Head. It was a prestigious school and we were all proud of our reputation for academic standards and propriety. It was the place for nice girls. Several of our pupils came from important families and two of the girls' fathers were MPs. In the spring of 1965, Eva Webber, a fifteen-year-old whose family were well-respected landowners in Surrey, came to me with a problem. She was pregnant.

I consulted with Joyce immediately and we held a teachers' meeting to decide the best course of action. If the news became public, it would be a disaster for all concerned. The girl would lose her good name and stain that of her family. Parents the length and breadth of the country would doubt Swallows Hall as an appropriate moral institution for their daughters. The child was too young to marry and in any case refused to reveal the identity of the father, who could and should have been prosecuted. As a Church of England school, we could not consider terminating the pregnancy. Even if we had, she was too far along.

We were lucky in one respect. The school hosted day girls and boarders. Eva was one of the latter, which made it easier for us to keep her condition quiet. We told her to write to her parents asking permission to join summer school and stay over the holidays. I had the task of accompanying the girl to the French Alps, to a sympathetic convent school where we used to take our winter sports holidays. She spent the rest of her confinement there, and as far as I could ascertain, maintained her education. In the meanwhile, Joyce and Esther located a private adoption agency to find a family for the baby.

Eva gave birth on the first day of July. Thankfully, without complication. Although the nuns had experience in midwifery, several other teachers and I travelled to Isère just in case. Joyce and Beryl took the child back to England as quickly as possible to minimise upset for Eva. Unfortunately, she had already formed a bond with her child. Removing the little boy was a deeply upsetting experience all round. I remained with Eva until she had recovered in both body and mind, then we returned to school and tried to put the episode behind us.

It is my belief our actions brought a curse upon us and we are being punished for what happened in 1965. Moreover, I believe that the killing of Maureen Hall was a terrible error and it should have been me. I became Mrs Cashmore in 1972. Before that, my name was Miss Doreen Hall.

Yours sincerely
Doreen Cashmore

Dr Weinberg would not be drawn on a prognosis until he had seen the X-rays. Joyce had a suspected broken collarbone, and possibly a broken rib, plus extensive bruising to her face as a result of her defensive injuries. After consultation with the staff at Andreas Papandreou Hospital, it was decided she would be better served by a smaller private clinic in Sgourou, where security would be easier to arrange. Exhausted, frustrated and shaken, Beatrice watched the ambulance leave and returned to the bridge.

At first glance, she assumed the man in conversation with Nikos was one of the entertainers. Leather jacket, quiff and old-fashioned sideburns. She picked up the tension as soon as she saw Nikos's face.

"DI Stubbs, this is Inspector Xanthou from the South Aegean Region of the Hellenic Police. Xanthou, this is Detective Inspector Stubbs of Scotland Yard."

The man's eyebrows arched and despite being the same height as her, he managed to look down his nose.

"Right." He shook her hand with minimum effort and turned away to continue speaking Greek.

Nikos interrupted. "Xanthou, this investigation is a cooperative effort between the UK and Greek forces. So that everyone can understand, we speak English."

"Fine. I'll repeat myself in English. I find it amazing that two senior officers, supported by two of my own men, cannot protect five old ladies. My resources are stretched to the limit, so I can't offer you any more assistance. This is a farce."

Beatrice had an urge to giggle. A farce indeed. This ridiculous bantam cock of a man, attempting pomposity while dressed as if he were busking in a skiffle band.

"Pleased to meet you, Inspector Xanthou. I fear 'five old ladies' is a serious underestimation of the task. This ship carries two thousand passengers, all of whom deserve our protection. Your sergeants understand that much and have patrolled the entire vessel. My suggestion, if you're in agreement, Inspector Stephanakis, is to entrust the protection of Joyce Milligan to Inspector Xanthou, whilst we proceed with our investigation. Let's hope the South Aegean force can protect one old lady." She faked a laugh and prodded Xanthou's shoulder, for no other reason than she knew he'd hate it. "Excuse me gentlemen, I need to talk to Captain Jensson."

By the time she'd finished discussing the logistics of removing the Hirondelles with Jensson, Xanthou had left. Nikos stood outside, talking on his mobile. When he saw her, he signalled for her to follow. He led the way to the empty cafeteria and bought two coffees from the vending machine, still conversing in Greek. They sat at a window table and he ended the call.

"Well?" he asked.

Beatrice cradled her coffee. "Jensson's staff will book six seats on a charter flight to London Gatwick for lunchtime today. Five Hirondelles and myself. We'll need an escort to the airport and specialised transport for the ladies. From there, I'll hand over to the Wiltshire police. Can you arrange for a briefing room at Gatwick where I can talk to those officers and any relatives we can get hold of?"

"You're leaving?"

"No. Just ensuring the ladies get home safely, then I'll be back. Someone on this ship is our man and we are this close to finding him." She held up finger and thumb in a narrow pinch.

"You said Doreen Cashmore told you what all this is about. You went to her cabin?"

"She came to mine. She delivered a letter around the same time Joyce was attacked in Doreen's room. The first thing you should know is Doreen's maiden name was Hall. She is firmly convinced that Maureen Hall's death was a case of mistaken identity and that she was the intended victim. She thinks the Hirondelles are cursed because of something which happened almost fifty years ago."

"Cursed? Come on."

Beatrice took a sip of coffee. "It might not be as far-fetched as it sounds. They're called the Hirondelles..."

"Because of the school. I know. Swallows Hall."

"Yes, a girls' boarding school. An underage pupil fell pregnant in 1965. Obviously a scandal in those days. Not just for her but also for the school. The teachers, under the direction of Headmistress Joyce Milligan, hushed it up. They hid the girl away until she reached full term and gave the child away for adoption. Doreen believes they're now being punished."

Nikos snorted, blowing foam off his cappuccino. "By whom? The mother would be in her sixties now."

"Yes, and unlikely to be a serial killer. Doreen's conscience led her to keep an eye on the girl after she left school, but she hasn't seen her for several years. It seems the woman suffered from depression and became an alcoholic. I have the last known address, which I intend to check while I'm in London. I'll also visit the adoption agency which took the baby."

"What about the father?"

"They don't know who the father was. The girl wouldn't say. The only men the girls had contact with worked at the school. All the teachers were female, so that left only a caretaker, a priest and two gardeners. Doreen thinks it could have been a local boy she met while in town. Why would he suddenly pop up after fifty years?"

"Hmm. How about the child they gave away? Who would be forty-eight, forty-nine? The HR department must be able to give me a list of employees of that age."

"Definitely worth checking, because we have a birth date. 1st July 1965. You'll also need to check where our suspects were at the time of the attack."

Nikos made a note on his phone. "I will. I made progress with Kostas, but still need more information on Toni Dean and Oscar Martins."

"I can help you with the latter. Oscar was having a drink with me last night."

Nikos's head snapped up. "Where?"

"In my cabin." She tried not to sound defensive.

"You had Oscar Martins *and* Doreen Cashmore in your cabin?"

"Oscar first, who left when Doreen arrived." She picked up her coffee cup to hide her discomfort.

Nikos tapped his phone against his chin. "So he knew Doreen was with you and Joyce was alone. He could easily have gone to their cabin and attacked Joyce Milligan."

"It's not their cabin, only Doreen's. He didn't know Joyce was there. I only knew because I went to talk to her after dinner and Joyce opened the door. So the person who attacked Joyce was looking for Doreen."

"You sound very convinced," Nikos frowned. "I don't understand why you would invite a murder suspect to your room."

Beatrice finished her coffee. "I wanted to find out a little more about the man, that's all. Anyway, he's ten years too old to be that adopted child."

"You didn't know about that then."

"No, I didn't. Fair enough. Go ahead and interview him again. Should we get back to the bridge? I have a batch of calls to make then I'd like to grab forty wings before we leave for the airport."

"You're hungry?"

"What? No, I just need a short nap, you know, rest my eyes."

Nikos sat back and appraised her. "If there's anything going on, it might be better to tell me now, for the sake of this case."

"There's nothing going on. Yet I get the feeling that is not true of you and Inspector Xanthou of the South Aegean Force. Is this something more than local rivalry?"

"Nice deflection. Yes, there's history, but it has no bearing on this case. If it did, I'd tell you."

His chin lifted, dark with stubble. Beatrice held his eyes and heard a faint echo of James's voice. 'So would you say that when you are emotionally pressured, you tend to look for a scapegoat?' A pang as familiar as thirst plucked at her and she had a thought.

"Nikos, I apologise. It's none of my business and you're right. Only when the personal affects the professional is it worth discussing. We have a job to do, so let's get on with it. I plan to spend about twenty-four hours in Britain, so with a following wind, I'll be back tomorrow afternoon. Meanwhile, this end of the investigation is in your hands."

He rested his cheek on his fist, all the defiance gone out of him.

"Yes, of course. I'm sorry for being suspicious. I guess we both need some sleep. Why can't serial killers keep to civilised hours like the rest of us?"

"Civilised hours?" She thought about it. "Yes. He works late and sleeps late. Bear that in mind when you're checking alibis. You know what, that bastard is probably tucked up in bed right now."

"Wish I was."

"Me too. But first I need to make sure Joyce is all right. Can we trust him to look after her, do you think?"

"Who?"

"Danny Zuko. Sorry, I meant Xanthou. He seems to be pursuing another agenda."

"He's got ego issues. But I think he'll make a point of protecting Joyce Milligan. Who's Danny Zuko?"

Rarely had Beatrice been so relieved to hit the tarmac. Fretful and querulous without the steadying presence of Joyce Milligan, the five Hirondelles in her charge behaved like a flock of giddy geese, vacillating between alarm and absent-mindedness, with Beatrice as the hapless gooseherd trying to guide them safely home. Even the stewardesses' patience had frayed.

By the time the little beeping airport trucks deposited them at the conference centre after a protracted toilet break, Beatrice was ready to snap. However, seeing the emotional reactions of the families and the efficient organisation of the briefing, she managed to remain professional and helpful throughout. She kept to the vaguest of terms regarding the investigation. The Wiltshire detective, on the other hand, went into fine detail of how the relatives and carers should keep their charges safe.

At first, his pedantry irritated Beatrice, but the effect on the families was a panacea. She answered several questions, ranging from naive to aggressive, then at a signal from the detective, called a halt. She made a hurried general farewell, thanked the representatives of the Wiltshire force and rushed out across the terminal to the taxi rank.

"Can you take me to Islington? I have an appointment in Upper Street. Just across from the Hope and Anchor."

The driver folded his paper. "Course I can, darling. What time's your appointment?"

Beatrice clambered through the rear door, amused and reassured by the casual endearment. "Four o'clock."

"Plenty of time! Sit back and relax."

She did as she was told. Her head fell back against the seat and she took three deep breaths, intending to open her worry box in a moment. Within minutes, she was fast asleep.

When she awoke, it took her a few moments to orient herself. The taxi was parked but the driver was absent. Islington flowed past the window and James's practice was across the street. She checked her watch. 15.43. Despite a stiff neck and dry mouth, she actually felt better. She sat up straight, checked her purse and mobile - both present - and found a packet of wet wipes to refresh her face. She was smoothing her hair in the wing mirror when a mechanical click announced the unlocking of the doors.

"She's awake! All right, sweetheart? Didn't mean to scare you, just thought I'd let you sleep for a bit. Your appointment's in a quarter of an hour, so I fetched us both a coffee." He handed her a cardboard cup and placed his own on the roof.

Beatrice blinked in disbelief. "That's very kind of you. How long have I..."

"We got here about half an hour ago. I'm not in a hurry so I thought I'd have a break and let you get some kip. You'd only been asleep an hour, see. Bad time to wake someone. My daughter, she's cabin crew with BA, told me how it works on long-haul trips. Forty-five minute cycles, innit? Have a nap for minimum three-quarters of an hour. Or if you got time, an hour and a half. The old 'grab an hour's shut-eye' is the worst. You wake up even tireder, see? How you feeling?"

The milky coffee, cheerful chatter and kindness from a stranger comforted Beatrice so easily, she wondered if her appointment with James was as urgent as it had felt several hours and another country ago.

"I feel vastly restored. It really is very decent of you to let me rest, not to mention bringing me a coffee."

He grinned. "As my missus always says, do as you would done by or dooby-dooby something or other." He raised a hand as another cabbie tooted.

"Well, I'd like to pay you for your time." She glanced at the meter, which was switched off.

"Let's call it forty quid. Cheers my darling. You have a good afternoon, now, all right?"

Chapter 24

James had changed receptionists. Another good sign. No matter how sanguine these discreet, polite people were, Beatrice always managed to rub them up the wrong way. She knew the endless reorganisation of appointments and short-notice cancellations was a nuisance, but on top of that the urgent requests for a last-minute slot meant she invariably became one of their least favourite patients. This one, a young man with Joe 90 glasses and too new to be jaded, gave her a pleasant smile and told her to go on in.

Not for the first time did Beatrice feel a surge of relief and affection on seeing her counsellor. She quelled the urge to rush over and give him a hug.

"Beatrice. Right on time. Did David offer you coffee?" His gentle smile and cool blue eyes acted like a cold flannel on her forehead. She couldn't wait to begin.

"I just had one, thank you." She settled into the chair. "And I appreciate your making time for me, despite the fact it's unscheduled."

"Yes, we do have our regular slot next Wednesday, but I assumed you had something pressing you'd like to discuss."

In an instant, the weight of all the time she'd known James seemed oppressive and suffocating. He knew everything about her relationship with Matthew, always advised truth in emotion and set great value in trust. How could he do anything but judge her? After all, she'd even judged herself. Once again, she wondered if she should change counsellors. Maybe someone closer to her own age. Silence dragged on and although there was no clock in the room, Beatrice heard ticking.

James spoke. "If you don't feel ready to discuss what brought you here, could we begin by dispensing with the formalities? How is the medication working for you?"

"James, I am a horrible person. Selfish, immature, greedy, unbalanced and just plain horrible. I can no longer bear to be in my own skin. If only I were religious."

He watched her, attentive and concerned. "How would religion help, do you think?"

"Because it's always so black and white. This is right, that is wrong. Punishment on earth, rewards in heaven. Actions count, not feelings. But if you have no system telling you how to behave, if you're carving out your own code of conduct, you only have yourself to blame."

"Hmmm. That's an interesting choice of word. 'Blame'. Something I tend to associate with judgement."

Beatrice studied him for a second. She really did wonder if he could read her thoughts.

"Or responsibility. You do something wrong. You accept the consequences. You take the blame."

"OK. Can we return to that in a moment? I ask because I feel I've missed a stage in your reasoning. You said 'do something wrong'. If we're not applying the rules of religion or law, who makes that call?"

"I do. According to my own principles, which happen to tally with those of most civilised people, I have done something wrong. Therefore I am culpable."

James tugged at his earlobe, a deceptive gesture Beatrice knew well as signifying serious thought.

"I'm wondering where I fit in, Beatrice. As both defendant and jury in the High Court of Stubbs, you have reached a decision and accepted your own verdict. Would you like me to pass sentence? I'm happy to do so, but feel the penance must fit the crime. As yet, I'm unaware of the deed, the motivation behind it, any extenuating circumstances or other offences to be taken into consideration."

It took her almost half an hour to tell him. Not least because he constantly interrupted her statement of facts to enquire as to her feelings. Unusually for one of James's sessions, she didn't cry. She squirmed and winced and fidgeted, but would not allow herself the indulgence of tears. She didn't deserve them.

Finally she stopped and James left a pause before speaking again.

"Can you see any correlation between recent events in Greece and what you think Matthew is planning?"

Beatrice stared out at the traffic on Upper Street. "God, I am so tediously predictable. Kicking against the traces at my age. It's pathetic."

"Pathetic, predictable, horrible, selfish. I think it's time the tenor of the language changed. You may feel angry about your behaviour, but I cannot allow you to be abusive to one of my clients. Even if it is yourself."

"Don't you ever get bored, James? Is it not bone-wearyingly dull listening to all these people, each of whom thinks they're special, who make the same set of clichéd mistakes as everyone else?"

"That's almost the exact opposite of how I see my profession. I also recognise your question for what it is – a classic Beatrice wriggle of evasion to avoid taking the last step. You've told me what happened and how you feel about it. You've acknowledged the thought processes which led you to behave in a way you deem reprehensible. The unaddressed issue is how you plan to deal with it."

A sigh so deep it was practically a groan escaped her. With the inevitability of the phases of the moon, here was the last part of the pattern. She wanted James to tell her what to do. He wouldn't. She'd sulk and then finally, if there was any time left in their hour, she'd face the fact she had to clean up her own mess. This time, she'd just skip to the end.

"I will separate my ego from my emotions. I will tell Oscar I made an error of judgement and keep my distance. I'll say nothing to Matthew and instead engage in a serious conversation about our future. And I'll stop trying to hide."

James nodded as the speakers emitted a soft sound, waves or rain or somesuch, but it was the indication that their session was drawing to a close. "Definite progress, Beatrice. I will ask two more questions, if I may? The medication?"

"No side effects and so long as I take it at the same time, the swoops are softer. Still there, but softer."

"Good. Let's keep the dosage the same and talk next week. You still want to honour next week's appointment?"

Beatrice stood up. "Definitely. I have to go back to Greece tomorrow but I expect everything to be done and dusted by Sunday. Monday latest. See you next week and thank you so much."

"You're welcome. You did all the work. One last thing I'd like you to think about between now and Wednesday. To what extent are your fears about marrying Matthew related to your fear of becoming Pam? One to chew over. See you next week and good luck in Greece."

Rush hour had begun and Beatrice battled through the crowds towards the Tube. Dusk was falling and the gloomy onset of evening mirrored her mood. Becoming Pam? Where the hell had he got that from?

Chapter 25

DEATH STALKS THE AEGEAN!

Three women dead, one hospitalised at the hands of the Cruise Killer!

One of the most reassuring sights is a Chevalier Cruise Liner sailing majestically along our coastline. These leviathans of the Mediterranean represent luxury, comfort, five-star service and the best way to experience the joys of the Greek islands for visitors — and let's not forget, a steady source of tourist income for residents.

Strangled in their beds! Thrown from a cliff!

Since the *Empress Louise* sailed from Athens two weeks ago, three elderly ladies have been brutally murdered in shocking circumstances. Two smothered in their beds, another thrown from a cliff top in Santorini. And last night, the killer tried to strike again. Joyce Milligan, 81, fought off her attacker and rang the alarm, alerting the ship's crew. Doctors at Sgourou's Kalithea Clinic say her injuries are serious but she is comfortable. A source close to the case said the cruise has been abandoned,

Nikos laughed. "Oh, stop it. I don't find you intimidating so drop the menacing looks. Act like an adult for just a few minutes. Look, I can tolerate all the digs and snide remarks, even if I think there's something quite sad about you still crowing two years later. Yes, you're younger than me. Yes, you got promoted before me. Yes, you're Karen's ex-boyfriend. Get over it. I have. This is not about some puerile jostling for position any longer. We have to work together to catch a serial killer who is still at large. And thanks to you, now has the name of the hospital in which his latest potential victim is still recovering. Going to the press to criticise the Cretan Regional Force is sabotage. Is your ego that desperately fragile that you'd rather make me look bad than prevent any further deaths?"

Xanthou tilted his head to one side in a gesture of sympathy. "It really is eating you up, isn't it? Jealousy becomes paranoia."

"Don't patronise me. Who else knows as much about the case and stands to benefit from bad-mouthing the Cretan police?"

"Well, let's see. The failure of an expensive collaboration with Scotland Yard has upset a lot of people. Could be the press, the ship's crew, the cruise line management..."

"The collaboration is not a failure and I know damn well this leak has your fingerprints all over it!" Nikos stopped, aware he was shouting.

"If you can't control your temper, I'll have to ask you to leave my office. The journalist could have got that information from a number of sources. For the love of God, you only have to hang around the bar of Hotel Kyrios and buy that drunken doctor a whisky. He tells anyone who'll listen how he was wrongly accused."

Nikos hesitated. Dr Fraser had not even crossed his mind.

Xanthou pressed home his advantage. "So, better get back to that extensive list of suspects, bring them in here and let's start interrogating. Because to be honest, Nikos, you're wasting my time."

"There are only three suspects, but I'll interview them on

board. The ship sails to Athens tonight, and I'll be on it."

"No. The ship is impounded and will stay in Rhodes until we make an arrest."

Nikos rolled his shoulders to release the tension. "This is not your case. You are assisting. DI Stubbs and I make the decisions. I'm going back to the ship and if I make an arrest, I'll bust my balls to make sure the suspect is taken to Athens. Or Crete, or even London. Anything to avoid being hamstrung by you and your ego."

"This may be a bad time to mention it, but I've filed a report on your mishandling of this case and registered a vote of no confidence in you and DI Stubbs. Thankfully, your behaviour today confirms my judgement as correct. Sorry, Nikos, but you just aren't inspector material. I need to make some calls so I'd like you to leave now."

Nikos sat back, his arms behind his head. "Maybe you're right. If all I had in my life was my job, I really would consider myself a failure. Have a good day, Xanthou."

His smile lasted until he'd closed Xanthou's door.

Hotel Kyria had seen better days. The bellboy, smoking in the shade of the awning, did not lift his eyes from his mobile as Nikos passed. Inside, the interior decor was what Karen would call 'Louis d'Hotel', faux grand, ornate, gilt but most of all, dusty. A sign indicated the way to the bar, which was empty but for a solitary figure with a newspaper and a glass of orange juice. He spotted Nikos and straightened in anticipation.

"Good afternoon, Dr Fraser. No news yet I'm afraid. Hopefully we'll make an announcement later today."

The light in the doctor's eyes dimmed and his face sagged. He suited the shabby atmosphere perfectly, as did the newspaper, a two-day old copy of *The Daily Telegraph*.

"If there's no news, this must be a social call." He caught the barman's eye. "Anything for you, Inspector? Spiros squeezes a mean orange."

"Not for me, thanks. The reason I'm here is to find out how the press got hold of the *Empress Louise* story."

"The press?"

"It's the lead story on the main Rhodes newspaper site, *Dimokratiki*."

The barman placed a fresh drink on Fraser's coaster.

"*Efharisto*, Spiros."

Nikos waited for him to drink and continue.

"Yes, I can say 'thank you' in Greek, but that is the extent of my knowledge. I've not read the paper or its website, but I heard the story's out. So you put two and two together and decided the Scottish addict must have been rambling to some hack."

"On the contrary. In fact I'm sure the information came from another source. I just need to be able to prove that."

Two young men entered and sat at the bar, each performing an elaborate handshake with Spiros.

Fraser took a long draught of his juice and licked his lips. "Chevalier Cruises cancelling this particular trip is a shame for the grannies. Bit of a bugger for staff and crew, too. Still, the worst they'll suffer is a couple of weeks unexpected holiday before the next batch of pensioners arrives and it all starts over – hopefully with fewer deaths, mind. The one person who'll struggle to recover from this is Jensson. His captaincy is tainted and his career is just about over. That man has been a solid friend to me. Why would I shoot the poor bastard in the foot?"

Nikos inclined his head. "You knew the cruise had been cancelled?"

"Jensson called earlier today to ask if I wanted to sail with them to Athens at ten this evening. I refused. I have a flight home on Sunday and I'm checking into a clinic. I can't help you, Inspector. Yes, I had the opportunity. Journalists drink here regularly and I drink with them. You could even say I had a motive. Bitter that my career is over, I wanted to destroy my friend's. The fact is that I didn't and I wouldn't. But I how can I prove that?"

"I think you just have. You know the ship is sailing tonight. The person who leaked the information didn't." Nikos rose from his seat and held out his hand. "Doctor, I wish you all the best."

Fraser heaved himself up and returned the handshake. "Same to you, Inspector. Listen, I wrecked my own career. Jensson doesn't deserve to crash and burn because of some sick bastards who are out to get old ladies."

"Bastards? You think there's more than one?"

"I don't know. But if it is just one man, I hope to God I never meet him."

Chapter 26

The 18.39 from Waterloo disgorged its passengers at Bookham Station just before seven. By the time it had pulled away, the platform was empty. Commuters hopped into waiting cars or unlocked their bikes or trotted off up the lane. Everyone had a purpose and knew where they were going. Beatrice checked the map on her phone and set off through the cool, damp evening air towards Church Street. Well-lit pavements, people walking dogs, a hairdresser's, an art gallery and neat front lawns; here was suburbia at its finest. Fife Way lay to her left and the house was easy to find in the quiet cul-de-sac. To Beatrice's relief, the lights were on. Repeated calls had received no response.

She withdrew her badge and knocked on the door. Seconds passed with no sign of movement within. She knocked again and listened. After today's discovery that the adoption agency no longer existed, this was her last hope. She was bending down to look through the letterbox when a voice behind her made her jump.

"Can I help you?"

A woman in her late thirties wore a padded jacket over a Co-op supermarket uniform and held a heavily loaded carrier bag.

"I'm looking for Eva Webber. I understand she lives here."

"What do you want with her?"

Beatrice held up her badge. "DI Stubbs, CID. I'd like to ask her a few questions in relation to an investigation I'm conducting. I believe she might be able to help."

The woman tilted her watch to the street light. "Should've come earlier. You won't get much sense out of her now. She just called up for more supplies." She raised the carrier bag. "Smirnoff, tonic, fags and a sliced white. Come on; let's see what we can do."

She moved a miniature watering-can from the windowsill and picked up a key. The *Eastenders* theme came from the living-room as forcefully as the stench of cigarette smoke and stale air. Eva Webber lay on the sofa, a knitted patchwork quilt over her legs. Beside her stood an occasional table, almost entirely hidden under an empty plate, two remote controls, a mobile phone, a bottle of vodka with a third remaining, two empty tonic bottles, a packet of Marlboro Lights, a lighter, an ashtray, a dirty glass and a pile of magazines. Her slow gaze flickered over Beatrice and came to rest on the Co-op carrier bag. The room was uncomfortably warm.

"You are good to me, Jen. How much do I owe you?" Her voice, hoarse and low, had an indistinct looseness, as if she'd just woken up.

"Receipt's in the bag. We'll sort it out tomorrow. Eva, this lady is a detective from the police. She wants a word."

Eva blinked slowly. "About what?"

Jen shot a sympathetic look at Beatrice. "Nothing to worry about, I'm sure. I'll be off now and pop round in the morning. Good night, DI Stubbs, and best of luck."

As the door clicked shut, Eva began pouring herself another drink.

"Please sit down, officer. How can I help?"

The affected sobriety struck Beatrice as the most illogical behaviour when all evidence pointed to the contrary. She sat, taking in the room. The dust, the stains on the carpet, the gas fire and old-fashioned cushions piled on every chair.

"I'm sorry to call so late, Mrs Webber."

"Miss." She pulled the kind of haughty look only a drunk can manage.

Beatrice made a rapid decision. "I'd like to talk to you about what happened at Swallows Hall."

The trajectory of glass to mouth did not falter. She sipped twice and cradled the glass to her chest as if afraid Beatrice might steal it.

"Swallows Hall? Haven't thought about that place in years. What do you want to know?" Her gaze rested on the flames of the gas fire.

"I want to know about your baby, the one they made you give away."

Eva's expression did not change. "Jen's very good, but she never thinks to get the tonic from the cold cabinet. There should be some ice in the freezer compartment."

The kitchen was messy, but not actually dirty. Beatrice found a clean teacup, popped out the last three ice cubes and opened the back door for some fresh air. When she returned, Eva was lighting a cigarette. She tipped the ice into her glass and swirled the contents with such little coordination that some spilt onto her lap.

"Thank you. You'd better tell me why you want to know."

A blanket of tiredness overcame Beatrice, exacerbated by the warm room, fug of smoke and lack of sleep. She wanted to walk out the door and leave this wretched woman to drink herself into oblivion. Instead, she turned off the television.

"That's not how it works. I ask the questions, you give me answers. If you don't want to talk, we'll go down to the police station. Of course, you'll have to leave the bottle behind. I know about your pregnancy, what the teachers decided, who was involved and how your baby was given up for adoption. What I don't know is anything about the child. I want you to tell me if it was..."

"He. Not it. I had a baby boy." She stirred the ice cubes with her middle finger, a tinkling sound providing a counterpoint to the pings of the gas filaments. "I never even held him."

Something in her tone checked Beatrice's exasperation. The woman wasn't talking to a police detective, she was talking to herself. Beatrice would need to sympathise, tease out, engage and encourage – but never demand.

"It must have been very hard for you. You were so young."

"I was fifteen." Her face collapsed into a grimace and Beatrice scrabbled in her bag to find tissues. By the time she'd found them, Eva was blowing her nose on an ancient handkerchief.

"I understand it's painful to bring all this up again. I wouldn't ask if it weren't important."

"They ruined my life. And his. I'll never stop wondering what might have been."

A thin line lay between emotional truth and maudlin sentimentality. Beatrice had to keep the woman focused or all she'd get would be a series of country and western clichés.

"I suppose you still think about him, wondering where he is now."

"I know where he is." For the first time, Eva looked directly at Beatrice. The rain cloud of grief left her face, leaving an expression of beatific joy in its stead. "He found me."

Her words pulsed through Beatrice like a shot of caffeine. The chill breeze from the kitchen pierced the stale air. Still in uncertain territory, Beatrice knew she was very near to getting the information she needed.

"How extraordinary! It's much harder to do that via private adoption agencies. He must have been very determined."

"He was. He said he'd never tried before, but he'll be fifty soon, so he decided to find me before it was too late. Fifty years." Eva was shaking her head as she reached for the Smirnoff.

Beatrice seized her opportunity. "How did he contact you?"

Her eyes were unfocused as she looked past Beatrice with a soft smile of reminiscence. "He came here. He sat right where you are sitting now."

"I cannot imagine how it must have felt to meet your son

after all these years."

Tears spilt from Eva's glassy eyes as she laughed. "Nor can I. Not really. He turned up late and I'd had a few. When I found out who he was, I had a few more. I must have fallen asleep, because when I woke up, he'd put a cushion under my head and a blanket over me. He'd gone. I didn't get to say goodbye."

Beatrice tried to halt the slide into self-pity. "What can you remember, Eva?"

She sniffed. "He asked a lot of questions. He wanted to know why I gave him away. I didn't! Not willingly, I never had any choice! I told him that. I told him the truth about what they did."

"Did you tell him who was involved?"

Eva broke eye contact and shifted her focus back to the fire. "I don't remember. I said a couple of things, but..." The downward pull of her mouth reversed suddenly. "I tell you what, though. He's a looker. A real heartbreaker. Tall, handsome and he looks just like him."

"Like who? His father?"

Eva scowled and narrowed her eyes. "You're all the same, aren't you? They tried that. They tried every trick in the book. Threats and bribes and trying to catch me out, just like you. Didn't work. I didn't tell them who his father was. Never have and never will."

"Actually, I'm not really interested in his father. What I do want to know is who your son is and where he is now."

Eva hummed a few notes, a tune Beatrice couldn't make out. "I named him, my baby boy. I knew he was a boy and I knew I'd have to give him up and they'd most likely call him something else, but before he was born, I used to talk to him, sing to him and tell him stories. I called him Frankie. They all thought I was daft at school, you know. Me and my LPs. The other girls were crying and screaming over 45s of The Beatles and The Hollies and The Stones, but not me. I was an old-fashioned girl in many ways."

"Eva, your son? What name does he use now?"

She burst into loud cackles, pushing Beatrice's annoyance to the limit. She wanted to slap the silly old lush, who was rocking back and forth in amusement.

"You'll never guess what he does for a living! At a caravan park, in Dorset somewhere. When I told him why I'd named him Frank, his face was a picture."

Beatrice was already on her feet. "You called him Frank, after..."

"Ol' Blue Eyes. And now my little Frankie is..."

"A Sinatra impersonator." She walked into the hall and dragged out her mobile, leaving Eva mumbling the words to *New York, New York*.

The church bells struck the hour at exactly the same time as Beatrice's phone vibrated in her hand.

"Nikos! I was just about to call you. I need you to make an arrest. Take Toni Dean in for questioning and I'll gather all the evidence we need to charge him. Nikos? Are you there?"

"*Yes, I'm here. Beatrice, we have a problem.*"

"What is it?"

"*The ship is due to sail, but two people are missing. One is Toni Dean. The other is Oscar Martins.*"

Chapter 27

He smelt him before he saw him. Voulakis, as ever preceded by the smell of onions, entered the bridge, shadowed by Xanthou. Nikos acknowledged neither, concentrating on making notes and listening to Beatrice's voice at the other end of the line. Their third call in the space of an hour.

"*... two key aspects of concern. If they're working together, are they planning a second attempt on the life of Joyce Milligan, or returning to the UK to pursue the surviving Hirondelles? Or have they split to do both? What extra measures have you taken?*"

"Alerted all border controls, doubled hospital security and Forensics are in the process of analysing both their rooms, as you advised."

"*Good. Keep me informed of every development. I'll get a flight back as soon as I can, hopefully tonight. The taxi is approaching the airport now.*"

Nikos revolved his chair to face his colleagues. "Beatrice, one other thing. Chief Inspector Voulakis has taken over as senior investigating officer, so he'll be your key contact. I am currently in an assistant role. He's just arrived, in fact, so perhaps you should speak to him."

He heard her swear with surprising force. "*Why the hell has he stepped in?*"

Nikos summoned all his resources of diplomacy and hoped Beatrice would pick up the subtext. "After a complaint from

Inspector Xanthou of the South Aegean Region, the Police Supervisory Board asked Chief Inspector Voulakis to take charge. The case is still a collaboration between the Cretan Regional Force and Scotland Yard. The Chief Inspector has chosen to retain both myself and Xanthou as assistants. Would you like to talk to him?"

"What I'd like to do is to kick Xanthou's arse. Bloody weasel. Still, at least they didn't give the case to him. Yes, put Voulakis on."

Trust her to get it first time. Nikos grinned, with no attempt to hide it, and handed the phone to Voulakis. He circled the name Toni Dean on the pad in front of him and vacated the seat to put some space between them.

"DI Stubbs, hello." Voulakis settled into the chair and looked at the paper. He beckoned Nikos. "Yes, a few changes in recent hours. And just ten minutes ago, I received a call from the airport police in Athens. They have detained Mr Oscar Martins, attempting to board a flight to London. I'm sending Inspector Stephanakis to interview him now."

Xanthou exhaled a sound of disgust and folded his arms. Neither Nikos nor Voulakis paid any attention.

"Yes, of course you can, if you can get a flight this evening or early tomorrow. I'll inform Stephanakis you'll join him in Athens. Here in Rhodes, Inspector Xanthou will take charge of hospital security and protecting the injured lady..."

Nikos scribbled her name on the pad.

"... Joyce Milligan. The *Empress Louise* must sail in approximately twenty minutes, but forensics teams are searching the cabins. I understand you have information about Toni Dean?"

As demotions go, it could have been worse. You could say a lot about Voulakis, but his management of the situation was both professional and partisan. Nikos was in position to make an arrest, while Xanthou was babysitting an old lady. Which must have been almost as infuriating as sharing his office with a senior Cretan officer with a passion for garlic, onions and olives. Each time fatigue hit Nikos while he waited in Athens Police HQ for Beatrice, he pictured that supercilious face wrinkling in disgust. It boosted his spirits without fail.

For the third time, he tried to focus on the Wikipedia biography of Oscar Martins. A respected professor with several publications to his name, a widow and father, nothing to link him to Dean or to Swallows Hall, and no police record. He tried the opposite route. Toni Dean's website ¬– *The Voice of an Era* – contained photographs, videos, testimonials and reviews but gave no personal information apart from contact details via Sunnyside Caravan Park in Weymouth. The ship's HR records were more useful, confirming Beatrice's findings, and showing Dean's age as fitting the profile of the Swallows Hall child. Yet none of his previous cruise ship contracts had coincided with voyages taken by Martins, so where did they meet? What would make two such men work together, if indeed they had?

A door opened. A uniformed officer, talking to someone out of sight, gestured towards Nikos. Beatrice. Her hair was wilder than usual as she marched across the deserted room, but her ready smile and bright eyes reassured him.

"Have you had any sleep since I last saw you?" he asked, holding out his hand.

She shook it and sat on the edge of the desk. "Enough. You?"

"No, but I can catch up. Depends on how long this takes."

"It won't take long. I'm quite sure Martins is unconnected to this case. We must make certain, of course, and exhaust every avenue of enquiry. Is there any news of Dean?"

"Nothing concrete, but the Wiltshire force sent an email this evening. Doreen Cashmore has received two anonymous phone calls. She found the first message on her answer phone. A male voice saying 'Welcome home'. The second call was more threatening. When she picked up, a man said 'Hello Doreen. You can run but you can't hide'. She's gone to stay with her family for a few days."

"Could they tell where the calls originated? This might be a smokescreen."

"They're working on it. All they know is the caller did not dial an international prefix. Whoever called her is in the UK."

"Hmm. Until we have proof he's followed them, let's work on the assumption he's still here. Now we really should get this interview over with. I'd prefer to observe, if you don't mind. I think it might complicate things if I were in the room."

She stood up but he remained seated and looked up at her. "Have you told me everything I need to know, Beatrice?"

Her eyes flicked downwards and she exhaled.

Tiredness made Nikos take a risk. "Voulakis said I would like working with you. He was right. Not what I expected but definitely an education. I respect your judgement. What I don't understand is why you'd risk being alone with a potential killer. Everyone on board knew who you were and why you were there. Martins engineered situations just to get close to you. Taking him to your room was..."

"Stupid. I agree. I feel more foolish than you know. Perhaps there is one thing I should say. Oscar Martins expressed an interest in me."

"I know. That's what I said."

"No, I meant a different kind of interest. Of the... er... romantic nature."

Nikos kept his expression blank. "He made a pass at you?"

"I suppose you could call it that. He kissed me."

"And what did you do?"

She dragged her gaze to meet his. "I kissed him back."

For the want of any better ideas, Nikos wrote that down. "Right. I see. In that case..."

"Yes. It's better if he doesn't know I'm here. You conduct the interview, I'll observe from behind the glass."

Either Oscar Martins was telling the truth or he maintained one of the best poker faces Nikos had ever encountered. No, he'd never met Toni Dean nor seen his act. No, he had no connections with the Hirondelles and had not dined with them once.

Swallows Hall was not a name he was familiar with. He could offer little evidence of his activities ashore, as he explored the islands alone. Yes, he had left Detective Inspector Stubbs immediately prior to the attack on Joyce Milligan. Surely the *Empress Louise* had CCTV cameras which would prove his assertion that he had returned directly to his own cabin?

The *Empress Louise* had no CCTV, but Nikos knew key card records would confirm if anyone had entered Martins' cabin at that time. Whose hand used the card was another question. Was he playing dumb? The man appeared eager to help and perfectly calm, so perhaps it was time to push him.

"We'll check. My problem is this. I have a list, not a long one, of people I wanted to question further. In one day, two people on that list disappear. No official check out, no request for a refund, nothing. When someone does that in the middle of a murder investigation, it makes me suspicious. So to eliminate you from my list, I need an explanation, Mr Martins."

"Of course. I apologise." He studied his hands for a moment. "Here you are, interviewing me, when far more pressing problems demand your attention. Particularly as I presume your colleague is still in the UK, handling that end of the investigation?"

Nikos said nothing.

"So then, let us be brief and you can get on with your job. I chose to leave the cruise for wholly selfish reasons. Since losing my wife, I tend to steer clear of personal relationships. Cruise ships such as the *Empress Louise* are stuffed to the gills with lonely folk on the prowl. As far as I'm concerned, they're welcome to each other. All I want is some occasional conversation, a change of scenery and plenty of peace and quiet.

"On this occasion, I encountered someone unexpected, in pursuit of something far more intriguing than a replacement spouse. I found myself drawn to her. She wasn't the slightest bit impressed with me or my books, which made me like her all the more. The same evening the unfortunate Milligan lady was assaulted, I made two startling discoveries. Firstly, the object of my affection was in a long-term relationship. Secondly, I'd fallen in love with her. What a silly old fool.

"In the cold light of day, I saw the situation as hopeless. Staying on the ship would only make things difficult for her and painful for me. I took the easy way out, Inspector. Better to leave immediately and do my best to forget her."

Nikos scratched his stubble, wishing there was a way round the unavoidably embarrassing question. "For the record, Mr Martins..."

Martins looked up and past him at the mirrored window. "I think we all know I'm talking about Detective Inspector Beatrice Stubbs."

04.02. Beatrice was awake in her hotel room, staring through the darkness at the ceiling. Once again, Oscar's face flashed into her mind, looking directly at her as if the mirrored glass did not exist. Once again, she felt her colour rise, even as she lay alone in the dark.

Nikos had joined her in the observation room immediately after Oscar's confession and she'd been grateful for the lack of light. They agreed to release him without charge and Beatrice, the unforgivable coward, stayed where she was until a car had taken Oscar to an airport hotel. Hiding was gutless, certainly, but the alternative was too awful to contemplate. The pain in his eyes had been almost unbearable when she was in the next room. If they'd come face to face...

She turned over, towards the column of blue light from the hotel's neon sign seeping through the curtains. The feeling was unbearable precisely because she knew it only too well. She'd made her decision to cut off all contact with Matthew almost a quarter of a century ago but the agony of emptiness that followed was as raw in recollection as it had ever been. The hollow sense of nothing to look forward to, the conviction she could never be happy again, the constant ache of missing him and knowing he was going through the same. No matter how much she told herself she'd done the right thing, it made no difference and she banished all thoughts of alternatives.

And now Oscar was in another hotel room across the island in the same misery, wishing he'd never boarded the *Empress Louise*. She squeezed her eyes shut and forced herself to address the question of her own feelings. The discomfort and embarrassment, the fillip to the ego, the guilt and sadness all mingled together to echo what she'd said to James. *I can no longer bear to be in my own skin.*

Her attraction to Oscar was undeniable and she'd sensed the danger from the start. Yet she spent time with him, enjoyed the attention and even, if she was brutally honest, took some gratification from his attempts to charm her – all the while ignoring her partner of twenty-four years and his plans for their future together. The pattern of behaviour was not new. Immature, evasive and rebelling against... what? She scrunched up her eyes and tried to block out the question James had put. His voice and image took shape in her mind like a hologram.

To what extent are your fears about marrying Matthew related to your fear of becoming Pam?

The problem with truths is once they're inside your head, you cannot block them out. The time she spent with Matthew was perfect. Growing runner beans. Village life and knowing everyone's business. Bickering over breakfast. Cooking together and entertaining the girls. Mushroom-picking and walks in the forest. Sunday afternoons doing the crossword in the conservatory. She relished it all, at weekends. Much more so because she could still be the outsider with the exciting busy job in the city. She could escape.

To what extent are your fears about marrying Matthew related to your fear of becoming Pam?

In a whisper, she answered Hologram James as truthfully as she could.

"Because if that part of me is gone, there's nothing left to chase. All the time he can't have me, he'll keep trying. Once I give in, I've played the final card and I've been netted. Then all I can look forward to is a slow withering of interest until someone more exciting and lively catches his eye.

"My God. I'm actually afraid of myself."

She turned over again and tried to empty her mind by doing a few half-hearted yoga breaths. She had to be up in three hours. Her internal cinema screen replaced James with a close-up of Oscar's eyes. The colour of real ale in the firelight, crinkled up with laughter. Hypnotically intense and magnetic. Flat and deadened behind the glass.

Her mind flitted back to the taxi driver, and his 'Do as you would be done by.' When faced with personal gratification or the honourable thing to do, Oscar had chosen the latter.

Which made him a better person than her.

Chapter 28

The taxi hurtled along route 95 to Sgourou. Maggie nudged Rose and smiled. She was relieved to get a reassuring nod back. Rose had not been keen to spend their last day in Greece on a hospital visit. It had taken all Maggie's persuasive powers to drag her along, citing her own experience in a foreign hospital, thousands of miles from home, frightened and weak and very alone.

Maggie could not explain the sense of responsibility she bore to the Hirondelles, but she had to do something. A kind of atonement. After breakfast, they sought police permission to visit Joyce Milligan. The inspector, dressed more like a Brighton rocker than a detective, granted it easily.

The hospital had the air of a private nursing home and the approach bore out what the officer had said. This little clinic was much easier to keep secure than that sprawling great place in the centre of Rhodes. It had its own driveway, a small car park and none of the attendant chaos that comes with A&E facilities. The security checks at reception were rigorous and Maggie appreciated the inconvenience for Joyce's sake. An orderly escorted them to a private room, which had an officer outside and nurse within.

Perhaps because the safety arrangements had absorbed her attention, Maggie was unprepared for the emotional impact of seeing Joyce. Her face was a nightmarish patchwork of grey-blue bruises and raw pink abrasions, stitched together with ugly black thread. Although she was sitting up in bed, a tube ran into her nostril and a neck brace supported her head. Her wintry blue eyes looked pitifully vulnerable without her glasses. Maggie's throat swelled, preventing speech.

Rose never had that problem. "Joyce, we're so happy to see you!" She stood at the foot of the bed, her tone cheerful. "Looks like you've been in the wars."

A familiar light danced in Joyce's eyes and her voice surprised Maggie with its strength.

"You should see the other fella."

The nurse smiled at their laughter and stood up to leave. Maggie was glad, as her presence and that of the orderly made her self-conscious.

"Not lost your sense of humour, then?" she asked.

"No, just my teeth."

Maggie couldn't swallow her gasp. "He knocked your teeth out?"

"Knocked them over, strictly speaking. They were in a glass by the bed. Fortunately, I always carry my old ones as spares ever since my sister's bulldog tried them on for size."

She flashed them a cheesy grin, provoking more laughter.

Rose parked herself at the end of the bed. "We thought a visit from us might cheer you up. How come it's the other way round?"

"You're very considerate and I'm grateful. Seeing two friendly faces is an absolute tonic. Now, where's the gin?"

Maggie glanced at the door and dropped her voice. "Even if you were allowed, which I doubt, we'd never have smuggled it past security. They're ferocious."

Joyce followed Maggie's sightline. "Spoilsports. No, I can't complain, they are taking very good care of me. I reckon they'll be glad to see me go, though, I must be a terrible nuisance. If the old bellows hold up after today's tests, I get a police escort to the airport and a first class flight home, courtesy of the cruise line. Speaking of which, shouldn't you be en route to Patmos by now?"

Rose explained the most recent developments, remaining factual and neutral about their departure and the cancellation of the cruise. Maggie leant against the windowsill to admire the grounds. It was nice to see a bit of greenery after all the sea and sunshine. Flowers and shrubs alongside brightly coloured benches surrounded a cluster of sun umbrellas over a patio. Maggie could think of worse places to convalesce. Several people in dressing gowns or uniforms strolled the path, a motorcycle courier walked back up the drive and an ancient Volkswagen took three tries to fit into a parking space. The driver finally emerged, a bent old man carrying a string bag of oranges who didn't bother locking the car.

That was when she heard it. The chainsaw rattle of a big bike, tearing through the silent afternoon. The sound distressed her for some reason. She had a feeling she'd heard it before.

After a late lunch back at the hotel, during which Rose chattered on enough for both of them, they retired to their room. Since beginning the cruise, they'd fallen into the habit of having an afternoon nap. In Greece, it seemed rather continental and modern, as opposed to sad and wasteful at home in Edinburgh. But today, Maggie had too much on her mind to sleep. She lay in silence for a few minutes then sat up and looked over at her friend's bed.

"I want to go back, Rose."

Rose, on top of her duvet, her hands folded across her stomach, didn't open her eyes. "Me too. I'm about ready for home. If we'd known Joyce was going back today, we could have booked the same flight. Never mind. We'll be on our way tomorrow."

"That's not what I mean. I want to go back to that day on Santorini. I want to remember everything that happened."

Rose opened her eyes and frowned. "And the point of that would be...?"

"I have a feeling I forgot something. Today, a wee memory

popped up and I want to go over it again. Just to be sure."

With a deep sigh, Rose rolled to face Maggie. "Marguerite Campbell, it'll guarantee more nightmares, I warn you."

"Humour me. We wanted to explore Santorini on our own and we ordered a picnic."

"Very well. Yes, the picnic. We rented that moped and went looking for a spot where no one else could find us."

"Those narrow roads and all the tourist coaches made me nervous."

"Then we found that little lane up the cliff."

"You had your cornflower dress on."

"And you had a sun hat. There was a smell of rosemary."

"I saw a butterfly. I couldn't find the salt."

"We thought we were so clever, avoiding the crowds."

"We argued about the cruise. It was so quiet."

"Yes, the silence. The peace." Rose closed her eyes.

"Then I picked up the camera and saw those two people in an empty car park. I recognised the Hirondelle uniform. The man was a member of staff, I thought. You said I was rubber-necking. He picked her up and threw her and I couldn't understand what I was watching and I pressed the shutter just after he'd gone and I cried and you asked me what's wrong and it wasn't quiet any more because..."

"The motorbike."

"Yes, a big snarly noise..."

"... like a chainsaw."

"You remember!"

"Yes, I do. Because you could hardly speak and I couldn't even hear you when you did."

"The thing is, Rose, it's a special kind of motorcycle. I can almost see it. Handlebars high up, long sort of body and the people who ride them always have beards and sunglasses."

"Choppers. Like in *Easy Rider*. You're spot on. How peculiar we should think of that now. When we gave our statements, I was so busy talking about what we'd seen, I never thought about what we heard. I'm not sure it's important, but we should inform the police anyway. How about we go to the station after our nap?"

"I think we should go now."

Chapter 29

Nikos owed Beatrice a break. She put up a bit of a fight, but the combination of exhaustion and the awkwardness of last night soon prevailed. He insisted she get some rest. He'd slept better than she had, that much was obvious. Her face was shadowed and worn, like an ancient gravestone. He offered the use of his hotel room, which she eventually accepted. It would be another long day and she needed to get some sleep before escorting Joyce Milligan home that evening. Nikos took the Martins report and the details she'd found in Britain into the station.

In his pre-caffeinated state, he opted to avoid Xanthou and instead, in a corner of the police cafeteria, he reported directly to Voulakis. The reaction was not what he expected. Voulakis, jubilant, assured him they would both be home in Heraklion tomorrow. The suspect had been identified and traced to Britain; the Martins lead proved a dead-end and he could not wait to tell Hamilton that Beatrice Stubbs was breaking old romantics' hearts. As soon as Joyce Milligan was off Greek soil, they were home and dry. It was over to the Brits. They should both expect some high-level recognition for a job well done. He hurried off to call a photographer.

Nikos, unconvinced, got another coffee and found an empty space in the open plan office where he could use his laptop. Before recording the events of yesterday, he read the case notes, updated this morning by Xanthou. Something was wrong. Doreen Cashmore's answering machine had recorded another threatening phone call, this time traced to a payphone in a Dorset shopping centre. Three calls. No action. On the ship, three murders and one attempted with no hint of warning. This man used surprise to his advantage, so why advertise his intentions now? The result would be a terrified target, increased security and fewer opportunities for him to strike. It had to be a distraction. Attention on the Cashmore woman left him free to attack any other of the Hirondelles.

He had no choice but to call Xanthou. The response was typically unhelpful. No, he had not requested CCTV footage from the shopping centre in the UK. That would be a job for the British police. For the Hellenic Force, and the Rhodes Region in particular, this case was over. And he had a lunch appointment with his new girlfriend, so if Nikos didn't mind...

What a *malaka*. Nikos ignored the attitude and sent a rapid email to his contact in Wiltshire, asking for advice on getting images of the payphone or caller from the shopping centre security team. He called the hospital and checked Joyce Milligan was fit for travel. He bribed a sergeant into bringing him a falafel salad from the canteen and reread all his notes on Toni Dean. His eyelids were beginning to get heavy when his email pinged. Wiltshire's DS Helyar confirmed that Dorset Police had requested the footage from Brewers' Quay Shopping Centre. Security officers at the centre partially identified the caller at the precise time Doreen Cashmore received her third threat. The individual in question was known to security officers as an occasional nuisance, harassing schoolgirls, smoking joints and drinking alcohol on the premises. His name was Jez Callaghan, he was approximately twenty-five years old and his place of employment was Sunnyside Caravan Park, Weymouth.

Nikos checked Dean's website. The same caravan park. An indistinct image was attached. Baseball cap, angular bones, baggy jeans. Difficult to get too much of an impression of his face, but it was obviously a young man who looked nothing like

Frank Sinatra. He emailed back, with a polite request that Jez Callaghan be brought in for questioning.

When Voulakis and Xanthou returned from their respective lunch meetings, Nikos was on the phone to Beatrice, who was impatient to be involved. He waved his notepad with some urgency and caught the cynicism in Xanthou's sly look. On the other end of the line, Beatrice announced she would come into the station to discuss procedure and hung up. The phone rang again immediately. It was the front desk.

Nikos got to his feet and addressed Voulakis. "There are two witnesses at reception who say they have some information about this case. I'll go. Just need to update you quickly first."

"No, no, you sit down. Xanthou can handle the witnesses. His English is fluent. But of course, he had an excellent teacher!"

He laughed at his own joke, eliciting the first unified response from his inspectors since the case began. Voulakis didn't seem to notice their cold lack of amusement and continued grinning at them both. Xanthou shook his head in disgust and left the room.

Voulakis heaved himself into the chair opposite Nikos, exuding goodwill and the unmistakeable scent of coffee and ouzo. That explained it. His boss's humour, crude at the best of times, reverted to schoolboy when he'd had a drink. He nodded and scratched his belly while listening to Nikos explain his discovery.

"Excellent! You are an exemplar to us all. The fact is, we can now hand this case over. We write up all our findings and hand it over. Successful conclusion for us! We should celebrate!"

"If Toni Dean is not in the UK, there is nothing to celebrate. He could still be here. When Xanthou returns, we need a briefing before the police escort departs for the airport. Everyone must be aware of this threat."

"Nikos, relax. You never stop! It's over and you did a great job. I'm giving you a glowing report. Let the Brits take it from here and we can get back to Crete. I don't know about you, but

I find the food here very bland. We leave at four, pick the old woman up, take some pictures and send her off to the airport. Tomorrow's front page will be all about the heroic joint efforts by the Hellenic Police to keep the dear old thing safe from a nasty lady-killer. Let's just finish the paperwork and we can get a flight home tonight."

Although far from fresh when she arrived at the station, Beatrice looked better than she had that morning. When Nikos returned with a coffee for her, she was sitting bolt upright opposite Voulakis. A worried frown pinched her brows as she listened to the arrangements.

"A single outrider doesn't exactly qualify as a police escort, Inspector."

Xanthou entered the room and spoke before Voulakis could reply. "It's all we can spare. There's a summit at the Palace this week, involving several VIPs. It requires a lot of extra security."

"And don't forget you have Inspector Xanthou himself, who is trained in personal protection. It's not a long journey and we really have no reason to expect any problems," said Voulakis, with a reassuring if slightly patronising smile.

"As you say, it is not a long journey, and if you and Inspector Stephanakis are coming as far as the hospital, could you not come to the airport with us?"

Voulakis raised his shoulders to his ears and shook his head with exaggerated regret.

"Sadly not. We too have a flight to catch this evening, so must return to file our reports and close the case from the Greek side. I'm sure you understand how important the paperwork is." He wandered away in the direction of the coffee machine.

Beatrice followed him and continued talking. Nikos wished her luck, but held out little hope. If his boss could take the lazy route, he would.

Nikos looked at Xanthou. "And the witnesses?"

Xanthou ignored him, checking his emails.

Nikos cleared his throat and spoke louder. "Inspector Xanthou, what did the witnesses want?"

"Nothing. A waste of time. God, I am so looking forward to seeing the back of all you old women."

The one positive thing about the journey to Sgourou was having Beatrice as his sole passenger. Voulakis wanted to ride in the Jeep with Xanthou and examine the security features himself. An arrangement that pleased everyone.

She was quiet at first, looking out of the window. After about ten minutes, she spoke. "I wish it were you taking us to the airport."

"So do I. But so long as Xanthou and the other officer stay with you until you're in the Departure Lounge, I don't foresee any problems."

"No. Although I'd be a lot more relaxed if we knew Dean was definitely in the UK. Yes, you're right, the man would be insane to try anything here. You know, I am heartily sick of flying. When I get back, I am point blank refusing to travel anywhere which involves airports for at least a year. By which time, I hope to be retired."

"Retired? Already?"

"It's early retirement, if I can take it. I've had enough, Nikos. Time to leave it to hungry young talents like yourself. And I wanted to say, I really do think you are a talent. Working with you was a pleasure."

Nikos kept his eyes on the road but couldn't hold back the grin. "Coming from you that means a great deal. For me, it's been a real learning experience."

"Mostly on how to be unprofessional when it comes to suspects, I imagine." She returned her attention to the passing scenery of garages, ceramic factories and furniture stores.

"Shit happens, Beatrice."

She didn't respond, her forehead leaning against the window. The light industrial units petered out, leaving trees and shrubs.

"Listen, I'm not going to judge you. I wouldn't be with my girlfriend if we hadn't bent the rules a little. Do you ever think you'll come back to Greece? I'd like to introduce you to Karen. I think you two would get along." He indicated and pulled into the hospital driveway.

"Thank you. Yes, I think I probably will, one day. But it won't be on a bloody cruise liner. And I would be delighted to meet Karen. If you two ever happen to be in London, give me a call. I'll show you some of the city's best-kept secrets."

"I'll take you up on that. Oh shit, look at this. God help us."

Voulakis, Xanthou, a motorcycle outrider, two doctors and a nurse stood around a seated Joyce Milligan in front of the hospital door, while a photographer rearranged the tableau.

It took half an hour to get a sufficient variety of poses to satisfy Voulakis and do a formal round of thanks and farewells. Nikos ground his teeth. They could have dispensed with this whole PR job, escorted their guests to the airport and been on their way back by now. It was strangely sad to say goodbye to Beatrice, especially with an audience. Thankfully, Joyce complained that she'd received no cheek kisses and raised a laugh to break the moment.

The cases were stowed in the Jeep, Joyce Milligan was stretched out in the back seat, the staff waved on the steps, the motorcycle outrider was in position and the party was finally ready to depart. Voulakis belted himself into the passenger seat and sighed with satisfaction. The Jeep pulled away, the bike behind it, and with one last wave at the medics, Nikos followed them down the drive. An impulse tugged at him to turn left instead of right, but he gave a quick toot of the horn and turned back towards the city, watching them recede in his rear-view mirror.

"Relax, Nikos. They're in radio contact and we can keep up with them every step of the way."

"We could have been with them every step of the way if we'd

skipped the photographs."

"Getting good PR for both regional forces and Scotland Yard cannot be underestimated. Yes, I was on the fussy side with the photographer, but it's important to project the best image of all of us. I wasn't going to let Xanthou, and therefore the South Aegean Region, grab all the limelight."

Nikos knew this was an appeal to unite against a common enemy and wished he had the maturity to resist. He was thinking about how to frame a response when Voulakis started laughing.

"What?"

"You know what he did? This morning, when I said we'd take pictures for the press, Xanthou went out at lunchtime to get his hair cut. The vanity of the man! I was coming back after lunch and saw him come out of Antonis the barber's."

Nikos joined in the laughter. "He told me he was lunching with his new girlfriend."

"Some girlfriend! Antonis is fifty-seven and has a moustache!"

"He's so false. Smiles and charm with Joyce Milligan for the pictures, but did you see the way he shoved her into the Jeep? At least Beatrice is with them. She'll look after her."

"I think he's had enough of old women today. Well, he can go back to preening himself in front of tourists from tomorrow."

"Yes, best place for him. Why has he had enough of old women? This case?"

Voulakis yawned. "I suppose. Not glamorous enough for him. Plus those two ladies came in this afternoon, the original witnesses, and he had to listen to their chatter for over an hour."

"Over an hour? Why?"

"Nothing important. They'd remembered something from the Santorini incident."

"Did he tell you what it was they remembered?"

"A noise, apparently. After seeing that man throw the old lady off a cliff, they heard a motorbike start. They heard it again this morning and recalled the sound. As Xanthou said, it's prob-ably the closest thing to excitement in their lives, so they have to wring out every last drop."

Nikos snapped his head to look at Voulakis.

"A motorbike?"

"So they said. It's just a way of getting involved. That's why they went to visit the Milligan woman. Desperate to be part of the action."

Nikos indicated and pulled over into a concrete merchant's yard. "Wait. They visited Joyce Milligan?"

"Why are we stopping?"

"They heard the same sound of a motorbike? When? Where?"

"Today. At the hospital."

Nikos reversed into a three-point turn and started the siren.

Chapter 30

Joyce sighed as the car turned the bend and they lost sight of the hospital staff.

"Such lovely people. I wonder if I can come back next year, perhaps with fewer injuries."

Beatrice swivelled in her seat. "Even if you turned up bouncing with health, I'm sure they'd be delighted to see you. Are you comfortable?"

"Well, I'd rather be back there, riding pillion with him." She jerked her head at their escort. "I asked him if he was married, but he went all coy."

Xanthou, unsmiling, said, "He doesn't speak English."

Joyce pushed herself round to look out the back and gave the outrider a girlish wave, a ripple of gnarled knuckles. Beatrice chuckled to see him lift a gloved hand in response.

"You see, the language of love is universal." Joyce winced as she returned to her original position.

Beatrice frowned. "Joyce, are you..."

"I'm right as rain, my dear. Don't worry. Might just give the surfing a miss next weekend."

Xanthou indicated and took a quieter road uphill towards the centre of the island. The Jeep climbed to greener areas and Beatrice regretted the onset of dusk. Peaceful roads, forests and views of which they would see very little as the light faded.

"This is a quicker route than going back through the city, I assume?"

Xanthou nodded once, like an extra not paid enough for dialogue.

Beatrice tried again. "The journey takes around twenty minutes, I believe?"

"Depends on traffic."

So that would suffice for small talk. They rode in silence for several minutes, Beatrice inhaling the scent of evening foliage. She looked back at Joyce.

"Warm enough?"

"Snug as a bug in..." The remainder of the rhyme was drowned out by the roar of an overtaking motorcycle, startling Beatrice and causing Xanthou to touch the brakes.

"Idiot!" Xanthou spat.

He was right. Even on such quiet roads, overtaking on a bend was a stupid and unnecessary risk.

"Definitely," Beatrice agreed. The sound of the bike's engine faded into the distance.

"Drivers like that will be dead soon," said Xanthou.

"But sadly they take others with them." She flipped down the sun visor to look in the vanity mirror. "You all right in the back there?"

"Fine, Beatrice. A bit peckish is all."

"We'll have time for a snack at the airport. Our last chance to sample..."

Three things happened at once. Beatrice realised the road behind them was empty, with no sign of their escort. The police radio burst into life, urgent voices speaking Greek, and her mobile rang. Caller display showed Nikos Stephanakis. She hooked a finger in one ear to block out the background noise and answered.

"Beatrice! Stop immediately. Dean may be lying in wait or following. I believe he's still in the area. We're about five minutes away, so stop now and turn around. We'll meet you. Tell the

outrider to keep his position at the rear."

Beatrice looked behind them. "OK, we'll stop right away. But our outrider has disappeared."

Nikos swore. She ended the call and tried to attract Xanthou's attention. He was yelling into the police radio and driving faster than was safe.

"Stop the car, Inspector! We have to turn around!"

"Don't be stupid. This is a few old ladies creating a fuss over nothing. And Stephanakis is one of them. We're going to the airport as planned. And if Dean is following us, turning round delivers the chicken straight into the fox's jaws." He turned the radio volume to a background buzz and drove still faster.

"Inspector, I am senior officer here. You obey my orders. Stop the..."

Xanthou braked sharply, causing Beatrice to drop her mobile. On the road ahead, stark in the glare of the headlights, lay a motorcycle and its rider. The torso was clearly visible while the lower body seemed trapped beneath the chassis. There was no sign of movement. Xanthou switched off the engine, unclipped his seatbelt and withdrew his gun.

"No!" Beatrice caught hold of his jacket. "If this is an ambush..."

Xanthou shook her off. "... then I am armed. If not, I can help. Call an ambulance." He got out of the car, his gun trained on the stricken biker, and approached.

Beatrice scrabbled for her phone and scanned the surrounding woodland. The silence, the forest, the cool evening air stretched her senses to screaming point. Once she'd located her mobile, she twisted to reassure Joyce, who was staring past her at the road ahead.

"Beatrice...?"

"Don't worry, he'll be fine. He's..."

A shot blasted out, ringing round the trees and shocking both women into silence.

Xanthou crumpled and hit the ground.

The body under the bike remained inert, but out of the trees, a figure emerged. Dressed in a black ski mask and a leather jacket unremarkable in its lack of identifying features, the man trained his gun on the Jeep.

"Joyce, get down. As low as you can." Beatrice opened the glove compartment, but found no gun. She dialled Nikos on her mobile with shaking fingers.

"Officer down," she whispered. "Passenger safe. Armed man approaching."

The figure moved towards Xanthou, his focus still on the Jeep. Beatrice glanced to her left and checked the ignition. Xanthou had left the keys there. Faintly she could hear Nikos's voice from the mobile and Joyce's uneven breathing. A brace of sitting ducks. She released her seatbelt. His gun still trained on the car, the man kicked Xanthou's prone body and looked down. There was no response. He snatched up Xanthou's gun, straightened and began to approach the Jeep. His mask hid his features but she caught a flash of white teeth in the headlights as he yelled in her direction, his gun aimed at Beatrice's face.

"Stubbs! Put your hands where I can see them!"

Beatrice dropped the phone into her lap and raised her palms to the level of her head.

Joyce's shaking voice came from the back seat. "Go, Beatrice. Get out now and God bless you."

Beatrice did not move. "I'm not leaving you."

The man paced towards them.

"Go on. He's not interested in you. Get out and go. Please don't ask me to meet my Maker with you on my conscience." Her voice broke.

Beatrice's whole body shook, but she remained where she was. "No. I have a duty of care."

"So did I." She was crying, her words hard to make out. "We thought we were doing the right thing. Please, Beatrice..."

The gunman opened Beatrice's door.

Chapter 31

As the car rounded the corner, Nikos took in the situation in a millisecond. In the headlights, a bike and a body. The outrider. The temptation to ride on past and find Dean arose but Nikos slammed on the brakes, hit the hazard flashers and drew his weapon.

The motionless uniform lay at the edge of the road, his bike on its side about twenty metres farther ahead. Nikos handed his mobile to Voulakis, instructed him keep listening to Beatrice and to call an ambulance. He got out of the car and approached the uniformed man. The headlights illuminating his movements made him a perfect target if anyone was lying in wait. He crouched beside the motorcycle officer, whose name he couldn't recall and holstered his weapon. The helmet was scratched and scuffed. He lifted the visor, holding his breath. No blood, eyes closed, breathing regular, strong pulse.

"Can you hear me? Are you hurt?"

No response.

He squinted at the car and saw Voulakis setting up a POLICE warning sign on the bend. When he looked back down, the motorcyclist's eyes were open.

"Hi, hello? Can you hear me?"

"Where's my bike?"

"Here. It's fine. Do you know what happened?"

He tried to sit up. Nikos put a hand on his shoulder. "Stay

still. Wait for the ambulance crew."

The rider relaxed onto the ground.

"Someone hit me. A biker. He tried to overtake and I signalled to stand back but he did it anyway and hit me with I-don't-know-what. I came off the bike and..."

"What's your name?"

"Tsipras."

"What day is it?"

"Thursday."

"What kind of bike do you ride?"

"Honda Transalp, XL700V."

"You'll be fine, Tspiras."

"Is he hurt?" Voulakis had joined them.

"I can't tell. He needs to be checked by an expert. Let's leave the helmet in place." Nikos rested his hand on the rider's arm. "How are you feeling?"

"Weird. Dizzy. Shit! What happened to the ladies?"

The very question tearing at Nikos. He stood up and faced Voulakis.

"Sir, I'm going after the Jeep. Dean is on two wheels and while I'm in pursuit, I want the same advantages. I'll take Tspiras's bike; you stay with him and keep trying DI Stubbs. Radio and mobile. I'm going to need back-up so move the police vehicle to one side."

He grabbed his mobile and ran for the Honda. It had been a while since his motorcycle cop days, but this kind of bike and Nikos were made for each other. He heaved it upright and swung into the saddle. Seven words pulsed through his mind as he gunned the ignition. Beatrice's voice, professional and calm. "*Officer down. Passenger safe. Armed man approaching*".

Beatrice heard Joyce flinch as the gunman wrenched open the door.

"Get over and drive. Do it quickly and don't make me hurt you."

He shoved her shoulder with his left hand, while the right

continued to aim his gun at her. She clambered over the gear-stick and lifted her legs after her.

"Mr Dean, my driving skills..."

"My name is not Mr Dean. Now fucking move!" He turned the police radio off.

She started the car, put it into first and moved forward, easing around the fallen bike, its dummy rider and the immobile shape that was Inspector Xanthou.

A strong smell of ammonia hit her nostrils. Joyce Milligan's fear had manifested itself. The man swore and opened his window. In the mirror, Beatrice couldn't see Joyce at all and assumed she was still in the foot well.

"Come on, speed it up." A bass, rough, West Country accent through gritted teeth. In only five words, this voice revealed itself as far from the transatlantic syrupy timbre of Toni Dean. If not Dean, who the hell was under the mask?

She accelerated and changed gear. He slid down in his seat and reached for something on the floor. Beatrice's mobile. He tossed it out of the window without taking his eyes from her.

Dusk had departed and night crept over the landscape. The scene was monochrome and sinister in the headlights, trees casting long-fingered threats across the grey tarmac.

"Slow down. Now turn right. Don't indicate! Yes, that track there. Go on."

Sandy and overgrown as it was, the track was no match for a police Jeep. They bounced and lurched away from the main road, branches and brambles scratching at the windows, causing Beatrice to duck more than once. Moonlight made visibility surprisingly clear. Nevertheless, Beatrice switched to full beam, mainly to advertise their own visibility. Her concentration on the terrain concealed frantic activity in her head.

How to get him off guard, how to alert the rest of the force to their location, how to protect Joyce without getting herself hurt in the process, how to convince the gunman she was no threat.

After a few minutes, in which Beatrice grew increasingly

concerned by the total absence of sound or movement from the back seat, the track descended steeply into a small clearing with a stone-built herder's cottage in the centre. It seemed long abandoned, although there were signs of recent activity judging by the amount of tyre tracks in the dust.

She brought the Jeep to a bumpy halt, but didn't switch off the engine.

"Don't stop here. Pull up to the hut."

A memory, or rather the resentment of one, surfaced in Beatrice's half-consciousness. A police driving instructor, who thought he was a Marine drill sergeant, teaching her to drive. *What are you doing?! Put it in first! No, don't accelerate yet, you moron! Hear that? That's the gearbox screaming! What is wrong with you!?* He'd tried to humiliate her into tears. He failed, she passed. Most importantly, she learned more about power games than driving.

She pressed down on the accelerator and clutch simultaneously, then tried shoving the gearstick into first. The graunching clash of metal made her wince.

"For fuck's sake!"

"I'm sorry," she sniffed, breaking her own breaths to sound nervous and emotional. "Driving isn't really..."

"Right. Stop the car here and get her out."

"Mr Dean, can I say something?"

"MY NAME IS NOT FUCKING TONI DEAN! Just shut your mouth. If you keep quiet and do as you're told, I'll leave you out of it. Just get her out of the car. Do not talk to me and DO NOT get in my way!"

Spittle flew from the gap in the ski mask. Beatrice could not see his eyes, which under the circumstances, was a good thing. She opened her door.

Contrary to expectations, Joyce was conscious. She said nothing and her eyes were unreadable in the dark. Her skin was both moist and cool, a smell of urine emanated from her clothes and she doubled over in pain as Beatrice helped her from the car. Yet her grip on Beatrice's hand was as strong as ever. The man watched them from a short distance, his gun as still as a signpost and his Maglite pointed to the entrance. He gestured with his head for them to go inside.

The building resembled a bunker. Squat, square with a flat roof and thick walls, a rough wooden door and deep-set windows without shutters. Outside, a few large rocks circled the remains of a bonfire.

Beatrice shoved open the door into blackness and immediately thought of spiders. She supported Joyce as they stood just inside the doorway. With an impatient exhalation, the man pushed past and lit an old-fashioned kerosene lamp. A weak yellow glow reflected off the whitewashed walls. No spiders, breadcrumbs on the table and the scent of a recent fire. So this was where he'd been hiding. The barrel of the gun directed them to the single bed against the wall. Beatrice and Joyce sat, clutching each other's hands. The man paced to each window, listening and checking, his gun cocked. Finally he turned to look at them. He let the gun fall to his side and seemed to be waiting for them to speak.

The mask induced a disproportionate amount of fear. Beatrice tried to convince herself it was only a stage crooner under there, a man who dyed his hair and bleached his teeth and should have been in Butlins. It didn't work. They waited for him to say whatever it was he needed to say. Whatever it was that had made him kill three elderly women and attempt to murder a fourth. What drove him to shoot one police officer and abduct another. He would need his moment. They always did. Whether to camera, to victims, to YouTube, they needed their fifteen minutes.

Right on cue, he slipped his hand under the neck of the ski mask and eased it off his head. A feeling of vindication and sickness swept over Beatrice.

Nikos was right. Toni Dean. The tan, the teeth, the bleached hair. She clenched Joyce's hand so hard she heard the poor woman whimper. He'd just shown his face to two witnesses. Which implied that after tonight, no one would be left to identify him.

Chapter 32

Each time Nikos took his hand from the throttle, he could hear distant sirens behind him, growing louder. Ambulance? Back-up? He hoped it was both. The road wound upward, the temperature dropped and moonlight through the trees created a cinematic effect. He needed another pair of hands. Not just an officer in support but two more limbs with opposable thumbs to hold his gun while he steered.

On the straight, he drove as fast as he dared. At every corner, he slowed, not only for safety but to avoid announcing his arrival. On an awkward bend, he thought he saw a light flash through the forest but when he looked again, it had disappeared. His inattention to the road, even for a second, was a bad idea. Ahead, stark in the single beam of the headlight, lay two bodies, one under a Harley Davidson Chopper. Nikos braked, dismounted the Honda and readied his gun.

The decoy under the Harley did not concern him. Xanthou, on the other hand, lay on his back with his hands pressed to his chest. His eyes were closed and his lower jaw spasmed, chattering his teeth together.

"Xanthou!"

No response.

Nikos checked his pulse and noted the blood seeping through the clothes beneath his clenched hands. He ran back to the bike to radio Voulakis.

"At the scene. Xanthou has a serious gunshot wound to the chest. This injury is life-threatening so make this the ambulance's priority. The police Jeep is missing, as are its passengers and there is no sign of Toni Dean. They can't have gained too much distance, so I am going in pursuit."

He tore the Mylar blanket from the first-aid kit and rushed back to the shivering detective. The reflective material would keep him both warm and visible.

"Xanthou, listen to me! Medical help is coming." He tucked the blanket around his body and patted his face. "I have to leave now. Dean has taken Joyce Milligan and DI Stubbs. You'll be fine and the ambulance is only a few minutes away. I have to go. Sorry. Just... hang on."

He kicked the Honda into life and drove away, clenching his teeth and wishing his medical training would stop the cold hard facts pounding through his brain: chest-wound, internal blood loss, patient into shock, lungs fill. Cause of death – drowning in own blood.

Nothing you can do but get him to hospital. If you stay and hold his hand, you'll only be there to watch him die. Find Beatrice. Find Joyce. Find Dean.

They must have taken the Jeep but how the hell was he supposed to know where? The Filerimos forest boasted many tracks up and around the monastery.

A small blue glow, like a pilot light, shone from the verge. Nikos drew alongside, donned gloves and picked up the phone. Missed calls: Voulakis, Voulakis, Stephanakis, Stephanakis, Stephanakis. All callers trying to contact Beatrice Stubbs.

Astride the bike, Nikos closed his eyes and concentrated with an intensity he'd never used before. Why hadn't Dean shot them there and then and left them to bleed to death like he had Xanthou? He intended to kill Milligan, Nikos had no doubt. Why the hiatus? Dean had taken them somewhere else for a reason. Torture? Interrogation? Whichever, it couldn't be public and it couldn't be far.

Nikos bagged the phone and stuffed it in his jacket. He was just reaching for the radio when he heard a sound. An ugly crunching of gears, the sort of noise you'd make when driving a strange vehicle. It came from the forest.

The police Honda purred cautiously along the road, Nikos watching for any kind of right turn into the woods big enough to accommodate a Jeep. A siren further down the route grew closer. An ambulance, please God. He crossed himself and offered a prayer for Xanthou's health. Then a break in the trees, tyre tracks and a right turn. Nikos crossed himself again.

Uneven terrain and an uncertain reception made him cautious, clashing with the imperative to roar ahead and prevent whatever Toni Dean had planned. The dusty, stony track ascended to a peak and Nikos knew his headlamp would shine over the ridge like a searchlight. He killed the lights and edged up to the ridge as quietly as the bike would allow. Below, a squat stone cottage sat in a clearing. The Jeep, parked in the shadows, appeared empty. Nikos scanned the area but the only sign of life was the dim glow coming from the cottage. He switched off the police radio and called Voulakis on his mobile. He kept his voice low. Voulakis promised caution and assured him that back-up, mere moments away, would approach with stealth. Nikos pulsed the throttle once and allowed the impetus and gravity to propel him towards the stone building.

Close enough. He left the bike behind the Jeep; accessible for a rapid escape, but sufficiently hidden from the windows. There was no glass in any of them and sounds up here would carry like goat bells. Communications devices on silent, Nikos withdrew his weapon and emerged from the cover of the Jeep.

Inside the cottage, a shadow crossed the window. A weak solitary light barely cast enough illumination to create a reflective square on the ground, yet Nikos focused his whole attention on the dim ochre gap as he crept forward.

"Stubbs, stand up and turn around." Dean stood in front of her, a roll of masking tape in one hand, and his gun in the other. With one last squeeze of Joyce's hand, Beatrice did as she was told. He wrapped the tape around her wrists, yanking painfully on her shoulders to test it was secure. She made no attempt to pull her wrists apart once he'd finished, knowing it would induce panicky feelings of impotence. Instead, she sat beside Joyce and took calm breaths.

"Right. Better safe than sorry. You are a copper, after all. See, you shouldn't even be here. I've got no beef with you. But you can't stop interfering, can you? That's what you're all about. Interfering in other people's lives."

He walked away, facing the window. Joyce laid her hand on Beatrice's arm. A gesture of reassurance, but her trembling set Beatrice off like a mimosa tree. He cleared his throat as if to prepare himself and dragged a chair from the small table. He sat opposite, resting his right hand – the one with the gun in it – on his left. Close up, the Dean sheen was less polished than usual. The contact lenses were missing. His trademark baby blues were a pale grey, reddened and bloodshot as if he'd not slept. His dyed hair lacked its flyaway, freshly shampooed bounce and hung limp across his right ear. The only sign of the showman was a smudge of mascara beneath his eye. So whether on stage or planning an ambush, the man still enhanced his eyelashes. Beatrice began to see how little she understood this person and his motives.

"And you, Joyce Milligan, you'd know all about interfering, wouldn't you? Playing God and ruining lives. Do you know how long I've spent wondering why? Give or take a few months, thirty-eight years. They told me the summer before I started secondary school. 'In case I found out from someone else.' Thirty-eight years wondering why my parents didn't want me. What a waste. I went through every scenario. I'd been kidnapped and sold. They'd been killed in a car accident and I somehow survived. He was famous and handsome and secretly watched me grow up from afar. She died in childbirth and he couldn't cope alone. He'd left her and she'd turned to prostitution. They were desperately poor and wanted the chance of a better life for me, but giving me away broke their hearts and they died of consumption. Yeah, right."

He beat the gun against his palm. Beatrice searched for something to say. Dialogue would buy time.

"Many adopted children..."

"SHUT UP! Shut your trap right now or I'll shut it for you. In fact, fuck it. This is not about many adopted children, it's about me. And it's none of your fucking business."

He jumped to his feet and grabbed the tape, tore a stretch off with his teeth and slapped it violently across Beatrice's mouth, knocking her backwards. The smack reverberated through her head, inducing tears of pain and the taste of blood where she'd bitten her tongue. He pulled her upright by her hair and pressed his face close to hers.

"You never listen. None of you. Can't tell them, 'cos they think they know best. If you can't tell them, you got to show them. One more time, Stubbs, and I will teach you the lesson you fucking well deserve." He brought his tensed fist to her cheek and snarled into her face.

Beatrice tried to stem the panic, breathing through her nostrils, inhaling Dean's sour breath. Beside her, Joyce whimpered, distracting his attention.

"Shut up, Milligan! Or you get the same. Listen, I could have killed you in the car. The only reason you aren't dead yet is because you have to understand what you did. You wrecked my life, and hers. Have you seen her lately? She's a fucking mess. Your fault! Everything I've ever done has turned to shit because I spent my life wondering why I wasn't good enough. It was your fault! Now I'm pushing fifty and I'm still doing the rounds on floating retirement homes. Your fault!"

He walked away, shaking his head. Beatrice watched his heaving back as he tried to get his emotions under control. He spoke, his voice calmer.

"I stopped wondering and decided to find out for myself. A private detective got the info in about ten days. My father wasn't a movie star. My mother wasn't dead. He was 'Unknown' and she was a fifteen-year-old schoolgirl. That was all there was to it. Some silly little slut got up the duff, gave the baby away and forgot all about it."

He turned back to face them, his eyes wide and an unsettling smile on his face. His gun rested in his hand, pointing away from them for now.

"The detective was worth the expense. Her home address was in his report. So I went there, with one thing on my mind. I wanted to wreck her life like she'd wrecked mine. To make her take responsibility. But she wasn't responsible, was she, Joyce?"

Hyperventilating through her nostrils was making Beatrice light-headed. She willed herself to slow her breathing down, inhaling deeply and relaxing into the release. She had to stay conscious. Beside her, Joyce seemed catatonic, hypnotised by Dean. Her body, pressed against Beatrice, no longer shook with fright and she shed no more tears. She seemed patient and resigned to her fate.

"No. Responsibility belongs to The Hirondelles. A fucking bunch of dried-up spinsters took her choices away. And mine too. You conniving hags, with no life of your own, you destroyed us. You might as well have drowned me at birth. But you didn't and I found you and made each of you pay."

He cocked his weapon, aiming at Joyce's forehead. "It's finished now. You are the last."

"I'm not the last."

"You are. The Hall woman is going to live the rest of her life terrified of her own shadow, which is exactly what she deserves. Couple more calls should bring on a heart attack, I reckon. So yes, you are the last."

Joyce spoke, her voice weakened but steady. "You killed two of my friends and then you sang at their memorial service."

A flash of those teeth again. "Yes, I enjoyed that. Nice touch, wasn't it?" He opened his mouth and sang the first line of *My Way*, not taking his eyes off her.

Joyce stared right back.

"Me too. Few regrets. Just the one. I really wish I had."

Dean's expression did not change. "What? Wish you had what?"

"Drowned you at birth."

Waiting for the right moment was a matter of assessment, opportunism, snap judgement and a cool head. The lighting was poor and Nikos found it impossible to judge the layout at such a distance. At one point, Dean came to the window and stared out into the darkness. Nikos could not see the man's gun and without any knowledge of the scene inside, dared not pull his own trigger. Nor did he dare move in case he gave his position away.

Dean retreated and Nikos heard shouting. This was the right moment. In a low ducking run, he reached the window and flattened himself against the wall.

Dean kept up a monologue, of which Nikos heard snatches. 'My father wasn't a movie star,' 'Responsibility belongs to The Hirondelles,' but the content was of less importance than the sound. Each time his voice became less distinct, Nikos knew he'd turned away from the window. He edged closer and moving his torso like an Egyptian dancer, managed to get his eye and gun around the window frame.

Dean had his back to Nikos, whereas Beatrice and Joyce faced in his direction. His blood raced as he saw the tape across Beatrice's face and her hands behind her. Neither woman could see him, their attention held by the man towering over them with a gun dangling from his hand.

Joyce Milligan said something and Nikos detected a change in atmosphere. Dean's voice rang out in song, an eerie sound in the moonlit forest. Nikos watched him step back and aim his gun at Joyce Milligan. He had to take the chance. He aimed for the right shoulder, an attempt to disable rather than kill, and upwards in case the bullet continued its trajectory. He pulled the trigger and for the first time in his life, shot a man in the back.

Dean jerked forwards, the gun slipped out of his grasp and clattered onto the flagstones, and he went down, first onto his knees then onto his left side, and collapsed.

Nikos pressed his hands onto the windowsill and heaved himself up. He climbed over the sill and landed softly on the ground beside Dean. He picked up the handgun and clicked on the safety catch, stuffing it in his belt.

Beatrice's breathing was shallow and her eyes bulged. He holstered his own weapon and went to release her. She shook her head and used her eyes to indicate Dean. He looked over his shoulder. The man was inert and posed no threat. He tore the tape from Beatrice's mouth.

"He's got Xanthou's gun!"

A rush of movement behind Nikos set off an automatic reflex. In one fluid movement, he withdrew his weapon, twisted over his shoulder and without a second's hesitation, pulled the trigger. Dean jolted and slumped back.

Above his own ragged breathing in the shocking aftermath of the gunshot, he heard Joyce Milligan reciting the Lord's Prayer.

Blood trickled like a meandering stream from a bullet hole on the right shoulder of the leather jacket. But the fatal shot was to the neck, an ugly wound now pulsing blood in gouts. In Dean's left hand, a police issue Heckler and Koch. Due to the nature of the injury, Nikos did not attempt to check the carotid pulse, instead taking Dean's gloveless right hand to confirm what he already knew.

Nikos Stephanakis had just killed a man.

Chapter 33

Joyce Milligan's wish to return to the Kalithera Clinic in Sgourou was granted far sooner than she could have imagined. Beatrice doubted the staff had sufficient time to change the sheets. Distressed and emotional, the octogenarian was cleaned up, given a sedative and as much reassurance as possible. Reduced yet visible security remained in place. While Toni Dean would be committing no further acts of revenge, the question of an accomplice had not been resolved.

Beatrice wanted to go to the Andreas Papandreou Hospital to see Xanthou. His condition was critical and her collegiate loyalty compelled her to his side. But she also wanted to remain at the scene to gather evidence with Nikos and the crime scene crew. After all, she had been the only person to witness who, what, when and how. Plus she knew why.

In the end she did neither. Voulakis insisted she go to the clinic with Joyce and get checked by a doctor. He escorted Xanthou to hospital, and Nikos took charge at the scene. The Hirondelles had been informed so as not to prolong the agonies. For the moment, Beatrice was redundant.

After Joyce had finally let go of Beatrice's hand and submitted to sleep with a grudging resentment, Beatrice bit her tongue and underwent a full examination. Her mind was full of Xanthou's waxy pallor, the terror of facing a masked gunman, the shock of watching a person killed in front of her and the constant voice reminding her of all her mistakes. She needed to be with Nikos. Her white angel repeated *Dean's dead. It's over. He can't hurt anyone else.* Her black demon said nothing. He simply shook his head.

At eight o'clock she arrived at the police station to find Nikos alone in the canteen, bent over his laptop. He saw her and stood up to pull out a chair.

"Are you OK? Shouldn't you be at the clinic?" he asked.

"I'm fine. The doctor said so. A bit shaken, obviously, but I had to come here. Any news?"

His shoulders sagged. "No. Critical is the last I heard."

"Why are you in the canteen? I went looking for you in the office."

"Guess how popular I am with the Rhodes officers? While one of their inspectors is fighting for his life, I have to report him for misconduct. He dismissed two important witnesses and ignored key evidence which could have averted the situation. Not only that but disobeyed an order to turn around. The South Aegean Division of the Hellenic Police is going to hold an inquiry. Here, in Rhodes. Voulakis and I will have to testify."

"What happened to the outrider?"

"Dean broadsided him and he crashed into the forest. Concussion and some stitches is all. He'll have to take the stand as well."

Beatrice waited for his eyes to stop roaming. "Regardless of Xanthou's injuries, you wouldn't be doing your job if you didn't accurately report what happened."

"If that stupid bastard dies, he'll be a hero and we'll look like cheap rivals trying to score a point."

"You couldn't have done otherwise. The truth has to come out."

"I know." He formed a visor with his hands and looked down at his keyboard. Beatrice waited. That was one of the main reasons she was here. Sharing their joint experiences and the emotional impact was an essential part of the debrief. It should never be rushed.

He looked at her sideways, his deep brown eyes clouded. "I'm the one who should really be under investigation. I shot a man."

"Was that the first time you've had to kill someone in the line of duty?"

His jaw clenched and he nodded once.

"Don't worry. I'm not going to say anything as trite as 'It gets easier'. It doesn't, at least not for me. I've been put in that situation twice, where you're forced to choose your own life over someone else's. I chose mine and those two people's deaths, or rather lives-that-might-have-been, still haunt me. The fact is, you shot someone who would have shot you, or me, or Joyce instead."

"I didn't know that at the time."

"You did. I told you he was armed."

"I didn't see the gun. I couldn't see his left hand. The light was bad, he wore a black glove and I just reacted to the movement. He could have been unarmed and asking for help."

Beatrice observed the muscles work in Nikos's jaw. "In an extremely pressured situation, you made a judgement call. It was the right one. Beating yourself up over whether it might have been wrong is pointless and a waste of energy. So stop it."

The silent, empty, darkened canteen seemed to echo her words. The laptop screen illuminated Nikos's eyes.

"Is it that easy?"

"No. I told you. It doesn't get easier. You have to fight it every day. Ask yourself what would have happened if you hadn't shot Dean when you did. Right now, I'd be on the phone to Karen, breaking the news of how a second's indecision led to the premature end of your career. Of your life."

He said nothing and Beatrice let the image play out in his mind. Eventually he looked at her again, resignation ageing his smooth features.

"You're right. Thank you. As first cases go, I could have had an easier one."

"But would you have learned as much? About yourself, I mean."

"Maybe not but at least I'd be able to get some sleep. This week..."

The display lit up on his phone. He answered and Beatrice watched his face for clues as the conversation, monosyllabic and in Greek, told her nothing. He didn't talk for long and placed the phone back on the table. His jaw muscles began pulsing again.

"That was Voulakis, at the hospital. Xanthou died twenty minutes ago."

Chapter 34

Admin Assistant Melanie squealed when Beatrice walked into the office at New Scotland Yard on Friday afternoon.

"You been in Greece!" she said, in the same tone one would use when congratulating a person on a promotion or pregnancy.

"Yes, I have. Why..."

"It's on my shortlist!"

Beatrice took a second to re-enter the alternative world of Melanie. "Ah, the honeymoon destination shortlist."

"No, Beatrice! You're getting scatty, you are. This is for the Hen Weekend. Honeymoon's been sorted for ages. Luxury Caribbean cruise for three weeks."

"Oh yes, cruise ships. I've heard they're lovely."

"Holiday of a lifetime. So, dish the dirt on Greece, then. Food, people, toilets, air-conditioning, door handles, quality of entertainment and safety levels for single women?"

"Melanie, let's have a coffee one of these days and I'll fill you in on... did you just say door handles?"

"Too right. Couldn't get on with them in Milan. Me and my sister got stuck in the restaurant bathroom for half an hour 'cos we couldn't figure out how the door handle worked."

"I see. The thing is, I need to talk to Hamilton. Is he in his office?"

"Yeah. In a right antsy mood an' all. Best of luck."

For the first time, Hamilton's scowl actually lifted when she entered the room. Rather than their usual arrangement – she opposite as if in the headmaster's office – he stood up and gestured to the visitor corner. With a certain discomfort, she sat in the leather armchair while he opened a cabinet.

"You're not driving, are you, Stubbs?" he asked.

Door handles, driving... she was beginning to feel as if someone had changed the code and forgotten to tell her.

"No sir. I don't, if I can help it."

"Good. It's Friday evening, almost, so I think a small toast to your achievement might be in order. I presume you drink whisky?"

"Yes, sir." Her unease grew. Hamilton in 'a right antsy mood' was offering her a drink and using expansive terms such as 'achievement'? Something was wrong.

He handed her a crystal glass and raised his own. "A job well done. Serial killer apprehended, case closed and satisfied collaborators. Your good health!"

"Good health," she replied and took a sip. The taste was strong, peaty, smoky and warm. It made her think of wild coasts and heretics.

Hamilton eased himself into the chair opposite and crossed his legs. "Chief Inspector Voulakis is very pleased. The loss of the South Aegean Inspector was a damn shame, but as far as I understand, that was largely his own fault. Operation closed and most satisfactory. Apparently you and the Stephanakis chap made a jolly good team. Might be able to offer him something here at a later stage."

Beatrice tried a quick smile. Hamilton's brow creased.

"What is it, Stubbs? Come on, spit it out."

"I agree, sir, the case was brought to a conclusion of sorts and I'm pleased the remaining ladies are safe. Inspector Stephanakis made a superlative colleague. I'd very much like to work with him again. It's just that witnessing two fatal shootings tends to spoil the mood for celebration somewhat."

"Hmm. Full picture, Stubbs. On the instructions of Inspector

Nikos Stephanakis, Wiltshire police arrested one Jeremy Callaghan, identified as the anonymous caller. Also known as Jez. Didn't take much for him to buckle. Seems he and Dean, real name Keith Avis, have worked at the same caravan park for the past five years. This Callaghan character gave DS Helyar some illuminating information."

"How do you mean, sir?"

"Avis was a dangerous mixture. Towering ego. Possibly a case of over-identification with his act. Believed he should be pulling crowds in Vegas. Not only that, but a bully, a blackmailer and an extreme right winger. Member of more than one questionable organisation. Usual paranoia about immigrants and homosexuals bringing the country to its knees, and strong views on the role of women."

Beatrice thought about that. "Who was he blackmailing?"

"Several entertainers at the caravan park and Callaghan himself. Provided them all with recreational drugs then threatened to expose them. Gained confidences only to use the information."

"Nice man."

Hamilton flicked his finger against his glass, creating a dull echo. "According to Callaghan, he'd given up on Britain and planned to emigrate to America. He was refused a visa, which he blamed on an incomplete birth certificate."

"Was that the real reason he was refused?"

"Hardly likely. His affiliations already marked him out as undesirable. Fuelled some sort of fire, nevertheless. Very angry man looking for someone to blame."

"His birth parents."

"His birth mother. In his mind, it was all her fault. As I said, odd ideas about women. So he sought her out, with every intention of 'ruining her life'. Callaghan said he was no more specific than that. Whatever happened when Keith Avis aka Toni Dean met Eva Webber we'll never know, but we can safely assume she told him about Swallows Hall, the names of the teachers and the summer of 1965. All he told Callaghan afterwards was that he'd changed his plans."

Beatrice pondered the golden liquid in her glass. "Thank you for the bigger picture, sir. It helps, a bit. Would you share that information with the Hellenic Police? I'd like Inspector Stephanakis to know we appreciate his investigative rigour."

"Fair enough. Tell me, what did you think of Voulakis?"

She chose her words carefully. "He seems a little less precise than I'm used to, but he made me most welcome. I liked him. I had no idea you had been friends so long."

"Indeed. We go back a long way. I introduced him to the woman who is now his wife."

"So he said."

Hamilton inhaled the aroma of his Scotch. "What else did he tell you?"

"That you and he 'awarded' the first ASBOs ever issued."

He gave a short snort of laughter. "True. We did. Probably even used the word 'award' in those days. Now, look here, Stubbs. You and I need to have a chat about your future. I'm chairing a meeting with you, Rangarajan and his DS for this coming Monday to discuss the logistics of handing over Operation Horseshoe."

"No, sir." She placed her drink on the low table, making sure to use a coaster. "Firstly, I won't be here on Monday. I am taking a week off in lieu and will return the following Monday after I have discussed and decided my future plans with my partner. Secondly, if the result of those conversations means early retirement, I am absolutely within my rights to be taken seriously by my senior officer. Loose cannon or not. Until I know what I want for my own future, I will make no plans or commitments to any projects I may not be able to fulfil."

She lifted her chin to Hamilton, daring him to argue. He sat back and swirled his drink around his glass, studying her.

"Don't waste it, Stubbs. That's a sixteen-year-old Lagavulin. A week in lieu is acceptable. We'll schedule a bilateral meeting for the following Monday and take it from there. On a personal note, I hope you'll postpone retirement. You are an extraordinary detective inspector and an asset to my team. A loose cannon and a bloody nuisance without a doubt, but someone I would prefer to keep."

She sipped at her whisky to hide her smile. "Thank you, sir."

Back home in Boot Street, she paused outside Adrian's flat. Sounds of *La Cage aux Folles* drifted into the hall, so she decided against disturbing him and stuffed a note under his door. Upstairs in her own place, she threw a laundry load into the machine, repacked her case for a week in Devon and checked her messages. A voicemail from Rose Mason, announcing their safe return to Edinburgh and inviting Beatrice to join them on a weekend jaunt to Wiltshire for a 'survivors' reunion'. Beatrice smiled at the sardonic inverted commas. She was copied in, along with Chief Inspector Voulakis on an email from Hamilton. The main recipient was Nikos Stephanakis and the content conveyed warm gratitude how influential his work had been.

Satisfied, Beatrice had a shower, brushed her teeth and although it was only ten past nine, crawled into bed. She set the alarm on her phone and finally made the call she'd been planning all day.

"*Beatrice?*"

"Hello, Matthew. I'm back."

"*Hurrah! And the case?*"

"The case is closed. Semi-satisfactorily. I'll tell you the sordid details when I see you. Listen, I've told Hamilton I'm taking a week off to think about my future. May I come to Devon? I thought we might talk this over together."

"*Of course. Nothing would make me happier. You sound very... chipper.*"

"I am. You asked me to think about what I want. And I did."

"*Ah. Good. So do you know what you want, do you think?*"

"I do."

Acknowledgements

With thanks to:

Triskele Books – Gillian Hamer, Liza Perrat, JD Smith, Catriona Troth, Barbara Scott Emmett, JW Hicks and Perry Iles for editorial advice, support and teamwork; Florian Bielmann and Janet Marsh for admonishments; Jessica Bell for language guidance; Nicole Horler and Stephanie Sorgo for monikers; James Lane and JD Smith for design genius; Stella Antoniou for her culinary expertise; Dr Neal for his medical nous; Antony Sorgo for technical advice and the secret policeman's tireless patience with my questions.

Any errors are entirely my own.

Also by JJ Marsh

Behind Closed Doors

"Beatrice Stubbs is a fascinating character, and a welcome addition to crime literature, in a literary and thought-provoking novel. I heartily recommend this as an exciting and intelligent read for fans of crime fiction." – Sarah Richardson, of Judging Covers

"Behind Closed Doors crackles with human interest, intrigue and atmosphere... author JJ Marsh does more than justice to the intelligent heroine who leads this exciting and absorbing chase." – Libris Reviews

"Hooked from the start and couldn't put this down. Superb, accomplished and intelligent writing. Ingenious plotting paying as much attention to detail as the killer must. Beatrice and her team are well-drawn, all individuals, involving and credible." – Book Reviews Plus

Raw Material

"I loved JJ Marsh's debut novel Behind Closed Doors, but her second, Raw Material, is even better... the final chapters are heart-stoppingly moving and exciting." Chris Curran, Amazon reviewer.

"Some rather realistic human exchanges reveal honest personal struggles concerning life's bigger questions; the abstruse clues resonate with the covert detective in me; and the suspense is enough to cause me to miss my stop." – Vince Rockston, author

Tread Softly

"The novel oozes atmosphere and JJ Marsh captures the sights, sounds and richness of Spain in all its glory. I literally salivated as I read the descriptions of food and wine. JJ Marsh is an extremely talented author and this is a wonderful novel." – Sheila Bugler, author of *Hunting Shadows*

"There are moments of farce and irony, there are scenes of friendship, tenderness and total exasperation - and underlying it all a story of corruption, brutality, manipulation and oppression with all the elements you'd expect to find in a good thriller, including a truly chilling villain. Highly recommended". – Lorna Fergusson, *FictionFire*

Human Rites

"Enthralling! The menace of Du Maurier meets the darkness and intrigue of Nordic Noir. Keep the lights on and your wits about you." – Anne Stormont, author of *Displacement*

"Human Rites has got it all: organised crime, Beatrice Stubbs, nuns, Stollen, wine, Adrian and Expressionist art, with the added delights of a German Christmas, gay men's choirs and a farty Husky. She's back and she's brilliant!" – The Crime Addict

Thank you for reading
a Triskele Book

If you loved this book and you'd like to help other readers find Triskele Books, please write a short review on the website where you bought the book. Your help in spreading the word is much appreciated and reviews make a huge difference to helping new readers find good books.

Why not try books by other Triskele authors?
Receive a complimentary ebook when you sign up
to our free newsletter at

www.triskelebooks.co.uk/signup

If you are a writer and would like more information on writing and publishing, visit http://www.triskelebooks.blogspot.com and http://www.wordswithjam.co.uk, which are packed with author and industry professional interviews, links to articles on writing, reading, libraries, the publishing industry and indie-publishing.

Connect with us:
Email admin@triskelebooks.co.uk
Twitter @triskelebooks
Facebook www.facebook.com/triskelebooks